R... ...Blithe

"Hornblower-style sea adventures ... fantasy in this novel of a young man fresh out of the academy and taking his first assignment as a midshipwizard on a dragonship. . . . The mix of sea adventure and fantasy is entertaining, a fun adventure, and a promising start to a new series."   —*Locus*

"Fascinating seafaring technology, and the battle scenes do not shy away from the harsh reality of warfare. . . . Shape-shifters, naval lore, and elemental magic describe this action-packed blend of Hornblower and Harry Potter."   —*VOYA*

"Horatio Hornblower meets Harry Potter in a tale of magical martial warfare on the high seas."   —Mel Odom,
Alex Award–winning author of *The Rover*

"Recommended wherever nautomaniacs peruse the fantasy shelves."   —*Booklist*

Also by James M. Ward

Midshipwizard Halcyon Blithe

Dragonfrigate Wizard Halcyon Blithe

✾ ✾ ✾

James M. Ward

A TOM DOHERTY ASSOCIATES BOOK
NEW YORK

This is a work of fiction. All of the characters, organizations, and events portrayed in this novel are either products of the author's imagination or are used fictitiously.

DRAGONFRIGATE WIZARD HALCYON BLITHE

Copyright © 2006 by James M. Ward

A Tor Book
Published by Tom Doherty Associates, LLC
175 Fifth Avenue
New York, NY 10010

www.tor.com

Tor® is a registered trademark of Tom Doherty Associates, LLC.

ISBN-13: 978-0-7653-5111-1
ISBN-10: 0-7653-5111-0

First Edition: December 2006
First Mass Market Edition: December 2007

Printed in the United States of America

0 9 8 7 6 5 4 3 2 1

I would like to dedicate this book to my loving wife, Janean. She's proven herself the best of companions in our thirty-five years of marriage.

Acknowledgments

Like all the other authors in the known universe, I had many others who helped me get this book together. In my mind, first among those is my good friend and editor, Brian Thomsen. The hardworking people of Tor need thanking and I hope we work together on many projects in the future. Certainly my own two proofreaders, Mike Gray and Craig Brain, need a great deal of credit for reading the material and telling me what needed changing.

Dragonfrigate Wizard Halcyon Blithe

PROLOGUE

Dispatch to the Admiralty

Airday, the eleventh in the Month of Queen Ledia

I, Captain Olden, write this dispatch before entering battle off the coast of Drusan, not ten nautical miles from the enemy city of Ordune. Under my command, the dragonship *Sanguine* left the Arcanian capital of Ilumin twenty-six days ago under full sails, with fair weather at our backs.

As per orders, I joined the blockade of Ordune under Fleet Commander Tempest. We became one of sixty total ships of the line sailing picket duty in and around the port of Ordune. The port is filled with enemy ships and I'm proud to add my ship's naval might to those ready to give their lives to prevent supplies from flowing out of the port and to other parts of the enemy empire.

During the course of the trip, I held a court-martial of Midshipwizard Halcyon Blithe for the charge of using high magic against the dictates of the Navy Articles. He was judged guilty; please let the record show I pardoned him for extraordinary services done for the ship. In the course of his duty on board ship, I learned that Midshipwizard Blithe is not only a rope speaker but a dragon speaker as well. I have promoted him to midshipwizard third class, as dragon speakers in the navy are on the fast track for promotion and Blithe's further actions aboard ship make this promotion a good idea.

Elan Swordson I have promoted to midshipwizard first class for duties rendered in the capture of enemy vessels while we were on our way to the duty station.

First Officer Dire Wily revealed himself as a Maleen shapechanger. Please note—steps must be taken to prevent other shapechangers from taking Arcanian ships to the bottom of the sea.

Commander Griffon's new blast-tube shells performed admirably and I highly recommend that they become the standard ammunition for all blast-tubes on the king's warships. We were able to demast the first-rater from two miles away with a skillfully laid pair of broadsides. Closing, we rushed to attack the fleeing frigates and took the *Migol* first-rater and one of the frigates in prize.

I'm recommending Major Aberdeen for promotion for his action against the *Migol*.

Lieutenant Solvalson commands the first-rater prize ship and his orders instruct him to sail that ship back to a friendly port. He has fifty marines, ten able seamen, twenty junior seamen, Midshipwizard Surehand, and Midshipwizard Murdock to watch over the remaining Maleen crew.

In the action, the *Sanguine* has forty-four crewmen with assorted wounds and twenty-eight dead from the battle. The dragon itself stayed true to its training. None of the shots struck the body or neck of the beast.

The third frigate, named the *Defiant*, escaped.

We continued our voyage for three more days and joined the fleet blockading Ordune.

At the time of this writing, signal flags from the command ship of the fleet would have us close with the enemy as they try to break out of their port and our blockade. My orders from Commander Tempest are that I'm to take my ship to the end of the enemy line and engage them there. I will place this dispatch on the first prize ship going back to Ilumin. At the writing of this dispatch, we are approaching the enemy line of engagement and face a first-rater, a fifth-rater, and a mortar ketch.

In conclusion, the admiralty should consider some test to make sure shapechangers aren't replacing crewmen and destroying ships in times of danger.

Tannin oil should be placed on all ships of the line to be used to thwart enemy spells of protection.

May the gods watch over our king and protect this dragonship from harm.

Captain Olden,
Captain of His Majesty's Dragonship *Sanguine*

I

✤ ✤ ✤

Encounter the Enemy

"Fire!"

BOOM!

Fifty-two blast-tubes, on three different decks, unleashed their hellish shot at the enemy in the distance. The deafening noise filled the dragonship in a wave rocking the hull on the back of the sea-dragon first-rater. A wall of round shot arced forth, reaching out for the enemy first-rater at the end of the line.

The *Durand*'s own broadside missed the *Sanguine* by a wide margin, churning up the sea in plumes of water as tall as the *Sanguine's* one-hundred-and-fifty-foot masts.

The living sea dragon that was the warship *Sanguine* roared a challenge to the enemy in the distance, surprised to hear no roar back. Every time it fought the distant creatures floating on the sea, amazement filled its tiny brain. Enemies' growl and roar not go BOOM.

The sea dragon didn't understand the nature of the shell on its back, but it liked the small pets that scurried around the shell and fed it wonderful treats like hay and lettuce. As in all battles, the dragon knew there would be good eating for it in the near future.

Elan Swordson, a midshipwizard first class, stood at the edge of the quarterdeck on the back of that dragon, able to see over the smoke. He noted the successful hits on the *Durand*. Smiling, he looked back to see the officers on the quarterdeck all working toward maneuvering the ship. He didn't like not controlling a blast-tube, and he especially didn't like to see Halcyon Blithe on a tube in the middle of the tube deck. "I'll go down and make sure the salt chests have full jars," he suggested to the second officer.

She nodded and he went off to the tube-deck.

The wall of smoke from the tubes of the *Sanguine* obscured any chance of seeing what their shots might have struck. Hundreds of men worked at reloading their tubes as the dragonship ignored the prevailing winds and tacked quickly to port, allowing the other side of the ship to bear its deadly blast-tubes on the not-so-distant enemy.

For one member of the *Sanguine's* crew, all the noise and smoke and the dragon roaring its challenge presented no distraction to what he was doing. Through the confusion of the battle, Halcyon Blithe, midshipwizard third class, commanded a blast-tube crew facing off against the Maleen first-rater *Durand*. His six-foot lanky frame bent intently over the blast-tube, waiting for the enemy to appear in the firing port. There was an intense red glow in his eyes, part of his demon heritage that those respecting him never asked about. Like many other spellcasters on the ship, he had a long white war braid down his back. It marked him a wizard of power, and he used that magic to heat up the blast spike about to be driven into the touchhole of his deadly weapon. He was a good-looking man of sixteen years, but today his handsome face was twisted in a snarl of hate and fury. He was fighting one of the Maleen ships on a special written list he constantly carried in a pouch next to his heart.

"Stand by!" Halcyon shouted to the blast-tube crew of the Deadly Dori. Every ship of the line had crew who named their blast-tubes. The Deadly Dori blast-tube fired a thirty-pound sphere of iron up to one mile from the ship.

Over the blast-tube, Halcyon faced the *Durand* in the distance, and this battle for him was very personal. Halcyon began muttering to himself. "You and three others shot my father's ship to the waterline."

At the same time, he made sure his crew did everything perfectly. "My father struck his colors and you fired at him anyway. I'm here to bring the revenge of my family down on your heads!"

As they all worked, no one could hear what he was mumbling. Blithe didn't care. The enemy in front of him helped to kill his father. Halcyon was fighting for more than king and country. He was fighting for his father.

Ashe Fallow, the master chief petty officer in charge of keeping the flow of blast-gel moving from belowdecks to the many blast-tubes on the blast deck, noted Halcyon's look and grew a mite worried. Few things missed the steely eyes of the chief. A thin man at a little less than six feet tall, he seemed shorter as he was constantly slouching, displaying a relaxed style even in the heat of deadly battle. Bald at fifty, he was a lifetime navy man and liked it that way. The chief decided to hover near the Deadly Dori, just to keep an eye on the young Lankshire officer. *Officers always need help*, he wryly thought.

"Damn your eyes, Fallow, can't you see that salt chest is empty!" Swordson shouted at the chief. "I don't want your men lagging behind the shots being fired."

A salt chest stood behind each of the blast-tubes during battle. It held a large supply of salt with jars of blasting gel placed in the chest. The packed salt kept hot sparks from igniting the jars. The packing also kept crashing materials from breaking the jars in the heat of battle.

"I have three gel monkeys working on this section of the deck, bringing the blasting gel from the orlop deck to these blast-tube carriages. They can't move any faster than they are now." Fallow's words fell on deaf ears. The midshipwizard was watching what Blithe was doing.

"Steady on!" Denna Darkwater commanded her squad at the center of the upper blast-tube deck. Darkwater loved a good melee. She was just under six feet tall, and her troll heritage showed from the long blue hair now in a war braid down her back to her dark greenish flesh, which resisted sword strokes and pike strikes like the best armor. In spite of her monstrous heritage, she was a lovely woman with muscles of steel. There were thirty-two small ivory skulls woven into her braid—one for every enemy officer she'd killed in hand-to-hand combat.

She too was surprised at the look of hate on Midshipwizard Blithe's face. In the short time she'd come to know Halcyon, she'd learned to like and respect him. She would gladly watch the young midshipwizard's back.

He was an officer, but she liked him nevertheless.

Normally, tubes fired in a solid wall of shot. Halcyon's tube waited not for the prow of the enemy ship to come into line with the blast-tube, but for the center of the ship. He wanted the maximum chance for his shot to hit. He'd also decided to use all the long-range loads of gel in his tube. He didn't just want to hit the enemy; he wanted to pummel them to kindling.

Swab sticks and prybars hit the deck as six men jammed their hands over their muffled ears. Each of the crew had a scarf tied around his head. Under the scarf, each forced sailcloth into and around his ears.

Filled with deadly intent, Halcyon watched his blast-tube bear on the *Durand*, the enemy first-rater, not a thousand yards away. The enemy showed pockmarks in its port section from the *Sanguine*'s previous blasts.

BOOM!

The rest of the port tube crew fired their blast-tubes the instant the long barrels bore on the prow of the enemy ship in the distance. A wave of sound blew everyone back and a wall of smoke filled their vision. Showing no nervousness at all, Halcyon held his fire as the ship rolled up the next wave and down to the bottom on the ocean's roll.

"Fire, you idiot! What's wrong with you?" Swordson shouted.

Feeling the young midshipwizard's murderous intent, the dragon roared its hate at the *Durand* and turned itself just right to allow Halcyon's tube to come in line with the middle of the enemy first-rater.

The dragon was able to see what Halcyon was seeing. It had grown more and more in tune with the midshipwizard's mind over the last week.

There was no tension or doubt in Blithe in the deadly moments of this battle. His entire focus centered on the *Durand*. The Maleen warship was an enemy that took part in the destruction of his father's warship in the battle off Porlun, a little more than a year ago. Halcyon knew every enemy ship that took part in that action. He'd vowed to be part of their destruction and this was his first chance to accomplish that promise made a year ago. He tried hard to contain his rage, but his face told a different story and his grim disposition caused his blast-tube crew to rush their duties.

Through the blast port, he waited until the movements of the enemy ship allowed the shot to have a chance to strike the center of the enemy's deck. The dragonship swayed down into the bottom of the ocean's roll. Halcyon held a steel spike above the touchhole of the blast-tube. Ramming that spike into the jar of blasting gel was usually enough to set off the explosion of the tube. The heated spikes guaranteed the successful blasting of the tube. On ships with magically able crew, those who could use magic were in charge of heating up the spike with their magical energies instead of heating the spike in a small brazier kept between each pair of blast-tubes for spike-heating purposes. Heating the spike with his magical ability, Blithe jammed it into the touchhole, and stood aside. He took great satisfaction in using his magic as the cause of the destruction he sent the *Durand*'s way.

BOOM!

The smoke of the blast blew back onto the deck with blinding effect. The stiff morning breeze forced the choking smoke in everyone's faces. They blinked back the sting of the smoke. Halcyon Blithe's orders had them quickly pick up their equipment to reload the tube.

On the quarterdeck, Second Officer and blast-tube Master Andool Griffon looked down on her tube deck to see why one of her tubes fired so late. The second volley sparsely struck the prow of the enemy in the distance and she was well pleased with its effect even if only half of the shots reached the hull of the *Durand*. She noted the late shot landed amidships, smashing through a blast-tube port. She'd be talking to that midshipwizard.

"Captain," she shouted over the noise of the quarterdeck crew readying their double blast-tubes. "The starboard side is again ready to fire, if you please."

"Hard to port!" came his order.

The two great wheels, crewed by four able seamen, spun the great ship's prow to obey the order. Huge twists of rope deep in the ship forced the fins of the sea dragon to turn the ship. They weren't dependent on the wind to tack, giving the *Sanguine* a deadly advantage in battle as the swimming action of the sea dragon propelled the ship in tighter turns than a wind-powered ship could make.

Swordson left in disgust at Halcyon's luck. If the midshipwizard had missed, Swordson could have done something, but the fool's shot was perfect.

"Swab the tube!" Halcyon shouted.

"Swab the tube!" all of the crew members shouted back in response.

The dragonship lurched as it tacked a third time, moving even quicker this time as it tacked with the wind.

The huge cloth-wrapped stick splashed into a bucket of seawater, and then rammed into the hot barrel of Deadly Dori. Twisted three times, it went deeper and deeper into the barrel with frantic haste. A white painted band on the swab shaft told the tube crewman when he'd pushed in far enough. It came free with a sucking sound, barely cooling the barrel enough to load in another jar of the blast-gel.

Tacking the dragonship, the *Sanguine* belched forth another broadside from the starboard side. The blinding smoke didn't stop any crew from their loading duties.

"Blue gel and bar shot!" Halcyon ordered. Blithe knew the crew would get the blast-gel and load the tube shells without his command. Bar shot wasn't usual at this range, but Halcyon anticipated the battle action of both the *Sanguine* and the *Durand*.

Bar shot blasted out, destroying rigging and masts. The tube master always gave strict orders to aim at the hull to kill as many of the enemy as possible. Using bar shot was contrary to the running orders of the ship, not that anyone was going to question the blazing-red-eyed leader of their tube crew.

Halcyon, knowing the skill of his captain, planned on their ship being closer than medium range as the *Durand* tried to gather way and come in to battle the *Sanguine*.

In the distance, the *Durand* gave its own broadside. The deadly spheres hit the water a hundred yards off the prow of the ship as it tacked. Some of the shots skipped on the water, missing the dragon by a narrow margin. The dragon ducked its head under the water as its training had taught it. A single tube shot could kill it at this distance. It wouldn't raise its head until the ship grappled the *Durand*.

"Fire as you bear!" Griffon shouted to her blast-tube crews.

Starboard tubes began firing in ones and twos as the dragonship turned. Marine drummers beat out the fire-as-you-bear command for all the decks to hear. There was no mistaking the special beat of the drums, allowing everyone to know they could fire their tubes when each tube leader thought it wise.

"On the downroll, men!" Griffon shouted as some of the shots fired in haste while the ship was on the wave's uproll. The Arcanian navy fired its shot on the downroll to strike the hulls of the enemy. The Maleen fleets fired on the uproll, trying to destroy the masts and sails of the enemy. Griffon was duty bound to kill men, not sails, and spars.

Halcyon was trying his best to kill a ship.

On the opposite side from the swabber, crewman Deluari shoved in a blue jar of blast-gel and a wad of sailcloth into the warm mouth of a blast-tube. Slower motions were used for this process, as breaking the two-foot-long jar could cause it to explode. As the jar seated itself, wadding slammed above it as two sailors used a special loader to shove the specially shaped bar shot into the barrel. Some of the tubes had crewmen who could easily lift a shot and load it in without a loader. The oldest sailor on Halcyon's crew was fifteen and none of them had any size to them. Halcyon himself was sixteen and big for his age, but he wasn't about to allow anyone else to aim this particular blast-tube at the *Durand*.

Every shot was going to be his responsibility.

"Pull!" Halcyon commanded, and the four pulleys with their inch-thick hemp ropes forced the blast-tube back out the tube port. While the tube crew pulled, Halcyon twirled the height gear to move the tube slightly lower on its heavy wheeled carriage.

Halcyon levered the tube lower, because the enemy ship was closer now as the *Sanguine* once again tacked to allow the port side to bear against the *Durand*. Taking the gear down its screwed shaft a fourth of its length, Halcyon looked through the tube port to see if the enemy was in sight yet.

Loud whining sounds erupted above their heads as the enemy shot flew overhead. Holes appeared in the *Sanguine*'s sails. A loud crack warned of a hit as deadly spheres connected to lengths of chain ripped up the *Sanguine*'s rigging. A topgallant spar broke in the middle, fell with its load of rope, and crashed into the hammocks above the heads on the forecastle crew. Halcyon looked above his head to see row upon row of hammocks, all tied in tight rolls and acting as nets to catch the sails, rigging, and masts if they fell from tube shot. He didn't allow himself to be concerned. All that mattered were the shots he directed against the *Durand*.

An explosion burst above water off the port bow and splashed a huge ring of shrapnel in a wide circle into the waves.

Halcyon saw the mortar ketch in the distance, as well as the two frigates tacking to fire off their tubes against the bow of the *Sanguine*.

"That last blast was a mortar from the ketch over there," Ashe noted, talking out loud behind Halcyon. "Those mortars are nasty things. The hot shards heat up from the explosion and do terrible burn damage to any target. A real man-killer that thing is, lucky for us they're rotten aimers and we're fast on our tacks. Doesn't bother a Lankshire man, of course; good shot that last one, by the way."

Not three hundred yards away, the *Durand* fired its third salvo. Its wall of flame and death struck too high and the topgallant staysail and its rigging were the only victims. The marines on the blast-tube deck cheered the lousy aim of their enemy and waved their helmets in derision.

BOOM!

BOOM!

Tubes all along the port side of the *Sanguine* went off as their muzzles bore on the enemy. It was the excellent training of Andool Griffon causing all the tubes to fire on the downroll of the ship. Their shells smashed into the hull of the *Durand*, peppering it along the length of the ship.

Halcyon noted the starboard broadside had successfully ripped away the mizzenmast. The *Durand*'s sails and rigging tangled into the sails of the mainmast.

"Stand by!" he shouted once again. Equipment hit the deck as his crew held their ears. The loud noises of the tubes all around him were dull thuds to his ears. He waited, looking out of the tube firing port. Again, he wanted his shot to strike the middle of the ship. Almost all the tubes on the port side had already fired; Halcyon didn't care about them.

The smoke from the other shots had blown clear when Halcyon touched his spike to the hole of Deadly Dori. He used his magical energies to heat the spike. Ramming it in, he stepped aside as the tube carriage rocked back from the blast.

BOOM!

"Sponge the tube," Halcyon roared out to his crew over the noise of others loading their tubes.

All of his crew members shouted, "Sponge the tube!"

A huge cheer rose up from the other crew members of the *Sanguine* on the port side of the ship. Halcyon didn't care; he was loading his tube again to strike against the hated *Durand*. Others along the port side saw his bar shot blast strike the base of the mainmast and watched that mast crash down on the deck.

"Blue gel and double shot, move your asses, damn your eyes!" the midshipwizard ordered his crew to faster action. For some reason, they were looking around to see what the others were cheering at.

"Blithe, look what you did," Denna Darkwater shouted.

Halcyon turned to see her pointing off the port side.

The *Durand*, clearly crippled, showed its mizzenmast and mainmast smashed down on the deck tangling up all the upper tube-deck crews.

Someone was raising a white flag on the fore topmast staysail. Another lowered the ships colors, a sure sign they had given up the fight.

Men were slapping him on the back.

All Halcyon could do was think, *Did I do that?*

"Back at it, you men!" he screamed. "No one said stop firing!"

Normally the *Sanguine* would close with the first-rater, board her, and capture her. Captain Olden had something else entirely in mind as he turned the dragonship and raced toward the nearest frigate.

The fifth-rater had been blasting broadsides at the *Sanguine*, but most of its shots had gone wide. The much smaller warship closed with the *Sanguine*, obviously thinking the larger vessel was going to melee with the *Durand*.

A wall of metal from the port-side batteries raked the stern of the frigate and blew off its rudder.

Lieutenant Commander Giantson was up at the prow of the dragonship. He shouted down to the enemy frigate, "You are ordered to lower your sail. Do not scuttle on pain of death to you all. Do not lower your boats; do not use magic of any type. If you disobey these orders we will open fire with canister shot."

The frigate got the point and struck its Maleen flag.

Once again, the *Sanguine* had a surprise. The captain ordered the *Sanguine*'s jolly boat filled with marines and sailors. While still under the tubes of the *Sanguine*, marines rowing the ship's jolly boat boarded the frigate to take it prize. The *Sanguine* never stopped as a mortar ketch and a frigate presented themselves for battle.

In record time, the Deadly Dori stood ready to fire again, but Halcyon wasn't going to fire it off.

Lieutenant Jordan tapped the midshipwizard on the shoulder. Halcyon hadn't dealt much with this lieutenant, but he knew about him. A broad-shouldered man, he had a patch over one eye, gotten from a melee off the coast of Arcania. Almost six feet tall, he was good with a blade and considered an excellent navigator. His white hair spoke of his magical ability. "Blithe," Jordan said loudly to compensate for the muffled ears. "I've been ordered to take marines and crew in the longboat. The *Sanguine* is going to fire over the heads of the ketch and we're going to take it as prize. You're coming with me."

There was no thought of doing anything but follow his orders. For one heartbeat, he looked in the direction of the *Durand*. It wasn't going anywhere with only its foresail. He was sure the enemy hoped the *Sanguine* would leave to chase other ships and allow it to escape. Halcyon smiled, knowing the nature of his captain. There would be no escaping the Arcanian fleet today.

For a moment, he stood there confused. All he wanted to do was strike at the *Durand*. The expectant look from Jordan moved the midshipwizard to action.

He hustled to the stern and took the rope ladder down to the towed longboat. It was already half filled with crew.

The prow of the *Sanguine* fired its bow chasers over the top of the ketch. Five hundred yards away its captain could see what would happen if his vessel tried to escape. The ketch struck its colors, signaling the *Sanguine* not to fire again.

Once again, Commander Giantson roared forth a command as the *Sanguine* sailed past. "You are ordered to lower your sail. Do not scuttle on pain of death to you all. Do not lower your boats; do not use magic of any type. If you disobey these orders, we will open fire with canister shot."

In the longboat, the men were pulling hard toward the ketch, not more than seventy-five yards away. Lieutenant Jordan steered the small craft through the choppy waves.

"Men, we've been ordered to board the ketch and sail it as quickly as possible for Ilumin port. We'll have to keep a watchful eye over the enemy crew. If we're careful we shouldn't have any problems." Jordan held up a waxed package. "I've got dispatches from the captain and if anything happens to me, make sure these get to the admiralty."

A very unsure Halcyon Blithe sat shivering in his position in the longboat. Sailors worked on either side of him, rowing the boat toward the ketch. Halcyon had no idea what to expect in this boarding action. He'd heard of such actions hundreds of times from his six brothers and six uncles, but this was a first for him. He dearly wanted no one to think him a fool in this action. He checked his equipment and shifted his saber in and out of its sheath.

He looked out to see what was left of the hated *Durand*. The first-rater was a ruin. It still had a foremast, but the other two masts were down. Crew chopped frantically trying to axe away rigging and masts. Blithe was sure the *Sanguine* would be upon it long before the wreckage cleared of the upper blast-tube deck. He was glad he'd been part of the action to ruin one of the ships that attacked his father. His only regret was that his shot couldn't be the one to sink her.

"The prize money will be good for that one."

Turning, Blithe saw Ashe Fallow and Denna Darkwater sitting together two benches behind him. "What are you two doing here?" Halcyon asked.

"Sure and can't a simple petty officer use the skills the gods gave him to help sail a prize ship back to Ilumin?" Fallow said, not really expecting an answer.

"There's big, bad enemy to fight on that ketch," Denna said, grinning as she held her blast-pike up like a battle standard. "I thought I would ride along just to make sure you don't get into trouble, sir."

"Quiet in the ranks there," Lieutenant Jordan ordered. "Row away, my hearties; put your backs into it. We need to get to that ketch while the tubes of the *Sanguine* still bear on her. The enemy crew is afraid of the *Sanguine*'s blast-tubes, not this little boat."

II

Mortar Ketch Prize

HIS MAJESTY'S ARTICLES OF WAR: ARTICLE XXII

Any irreverent and unbecoming behavior during religious services shall be punished as a general or summary court-martial may direct.

As the longboat came to hailing distance the ketch crew were manning the three rail tubes at the stern of the ship. Those tubes, commonly filled with grapeshot, had the deadly potential to kill everyone on the longboat if any one of those weapons fired their way.

"Maleen ketches are all war vessels," Ashe told Denna. "Such vessels battle large groups of enemy troops. The mortars they use are perfect for attacking troops on the coast or battering down coastal fortifications, but they aren't worth a damn in attacking ships of the line. Under the *Sanguine*'s tubes, they should stay silent."

Halcyon ignored the ketch and looked at the battered *Durand* in the distance, his fists clenched. He'd really wanted to be in on the kill of that ship.

The ocean waves slapped against the side of the longboat as the marines rowed briskly toward the ketch.

"Clear away from those tubes or the dragonship will sink you!" Lieutenant Jordan roared out to those he could see at the stern of the ketch.

As if Captain Olden was sensing his lieutenant's need, the double blast-tubes of the *Sanguine*'s starboard side fired over the sails of the ketch. The blast showed the *Sanguine* was more than able to put a broadside into the ketch. Everyone knew what would happen from such a wall of steel.

Halcyon noted the ketch's name, the *Salamander*.

The crew of the longboat sat tense. Any of those three tubes could kill all of them in one blast of grapeshot. The question of whether the personnel of the ketch believed they were in danger from the *Sanguine* or not was yet to be answered.

"Any who aren't assembled at the prow of the ship right now will be killed!"

The lieutenant's words drove most of the enemy crew away from those deadly tubes, and all but one man of the three tube crews left their stations and ran for the prow. There were no troops in the sticks of the mizzen or mainmast. The main sails showed themselves furled tight, but the jibs still allowed the ketch to move at a brisk pace.

Suddenly a twang of a crossbow wire sang out. The ketch's crewman aiming the third tube at the longboat died with a bolt in his eye.

"Sometimes they just need a little push to help them along," Ashe said as he lowered his crossbow.

"You pushed that one right into his grave," Denna replied.

"Quiet in the ranks, I want you all to get on that ship and get amongst their crew," Jordan ordered. "I don't want them thinking about fighting back. Captain Olden has given us one chance and we aren't going to waste it."

Turning back to look at the longboat's crew, Halcyon noted for the first time that there were other crossbows ready to fire at anyone coming to use those stern blast-tubes. His eyes fell on Elan Swordson, looking nervous at the back of the boat. Halcyon hoped to be second-in-command, but that thought was dashed with the presence of First Class Swordson.

The *Salamander* rode low in the water and there were ratlines ready for climbing. The longboat came alongside the ketch and marines quickly climbed up the side of the ship.

Halcyon waited his turn to climb.

"Seaman Jokal, man the helm and head us as close to east as the wind allows. We'll get the sails unfurled as soon as may be," Jordan, the new captain, ordered.

"Aye, aye, sir!" Jokal replied.

Marines with crossbows led the way to the prow where the *Salamander*'s crew cringed.

"Is this all of you?" Captain Jordan asked as he stepped on the ship.

Halcyon could see there were no Maleen marines among the crew. Halcyon shouted in Maleen, "Is there anyone below-decks? Tell us or it will go hard for you."

One of the ketch's crew stood up to say something and the others knocked him senseless.

In seconds, the marines from the *Sanguine* were among the crew, splitting them apart and establishing order.

Jordan looked at Blithe, Swordson, Fallow, and Darkwater. "Acting Lieutenant Swordson, take Fallow and Corporal Darkwater and five of the marines and go belowdecks. Mr. Blithe, you check out the captain's cabin. I'll sort things out here."

"Aye, aye, Captain," they all said at once.

The stern of the ship had a small raised quarterdeck, and inset into that rise was the door usually leading to a short set of stairs and the captain's cabin.

Halcyon rushed the door and found it locked. He wasn't about to call back to the marines and Jordan for help to open the door.

The thick oak door felt braced from behind. Filled with energy and enthusiasm, Halcyon reached out and opened his clinched fist, releasing all the magical energy he could in a massive elemental burst of lightning. The door handle exploded inward, leaving a foot hole in the portal. The timber behind the door burst out as well.

Halcyon reached into the hole and threw back the door. He paused in a moment of indecision. *Should I rush down the stairs or take them one slow step at a time?* he thought. He heard a splash of something hitting the water and that urged him quickly forward. Hurtling down the stairs, he saw a man throwing a weighted sack out a stern window.

"Stop what you are doing, now!" Halcyon shouted in Maleen to the richly dressed man. He'd never advertised the fact that he could speak Maleen. His family had a long tradition of learning the language of the enemy they faced. At fourteen, Halcyon was taught the tongue of their enemy and he could speak it fluently now.

A strange, sweet smell struck Halcyon's senses as he entered the chamber. He looked all around and could see only the one enemy working in the cabin.

The foe facing Halcyon stood tall, his head almost brushing

the seven-foot-high ceiling of the cabin. His uniform was that of a captain, and his chest showed many medals of valor and service. He sported a thin, waxed mustache and his eyebrows were thick and white, at odds with his long dark hair.

He turned, looking disdainfully at Halcyon, a sneer of disgust on his face. His right hand shoved a sack out the window. There were seven other weighted sacks on the captain's navigation table in the middle of the cabin.

Blithe wondered how many more of them had already gone into the ocean's depths.

The man ignored Halcyon and reached for another sack.

In an unsteady motion, Halcyon drew his saber and advanced on the man, the point of his saber inches away from the enemy captain's hand as he reached out for the sack.

"Sir," Halcyon growled with deadly intent, "my name is Midshipwizard Halcyon Blithe." Filled with tension, his voice broke and he squeaked out his last name. He tried to steady himself, but he didn't want the enemy captain to grab another of those sacks, no matter what might happen to him from trying to stop the captain. "By my good right arm and this saber, you will stop your actions. Give up immediately or feel my steel."

For the first time, the ketch captain looked into the stern eyes of the young man before him. "I am Lord Albon Dreg, captain of this ketch," he said in perfect Arcanian. "Allow me to draw my sword so that we can settle this like true men," the captain offered.

"Step away from the table and I am at your service, sir," Blithe said, bowing, but keeping his sword tip between himself and his enemy. Halcyon's eyes stayed locked on his opponent's face. He took a step backward. Honor was important to Halcyon. It was his feeling that respect should be given to all men until they proved they didn't deserve his respect. This Dreg made a noble request and Halcyon felt honor-bound to allow him to draw his weapon.

Lord Dreg drew his long saber and motioned his enemy forward. In heartbeats, the blades tested each other.

In Halcyon's mind, this duel should be easy. All he had to do was delay long enough for marines to come into the cabin and the fight would be over. The midshipwizard never thought of killing the man. If he was really a Maleen noble, there was a possibility that information even more valuable than the capture of the ship could be gotten from the man.

Dreg made the first lunge, using his longer reach. His action showed he hoped to pierce his foe's heart in one long death stroke.

Halcyon was ready for the lunge and backed up out of range. Slashing his weapon down, the midshipwizard tried to disarm his foe.

Weapons clanged, but the captain's grip was sure. He parried the attack and rushed closer to Halcyon. "Your Maleen is excellent. You speak as a royal might. It's unusual to hear such language from a pig of an Arcanian." He meant the insult to distract his enemy and it did.

His slash connected with the midshipwizard's helm. The blade rang off the metal. Halcyon parried the blade away from his face and shoulder, making his own attack.

Dreg's response moved Halcyon's weapon away from his heart, but the razor-sharp blade cut into the man's shoulder as he backed out of range.

"First blood to you, rascal," the captain groaned, retreating to the back of the cabin. "Normally, that would be the end of our little encounter, but I still have a few surprises."

Halcyon allowed his foe to retreat. He knew he had time.

Others would be hearing the sounds of the duel and come in to help. Breathing fast, he had to ask, "Will you surrender, sir? Others will be here in heartbeats."

"Oh, I really need to dump those sacks into the ocean before your pitiful friends come to stop me. Once you're dead, that shouldn't be a problem." As the Maleen foe made half lunges, his other hand made gestures in the air and the appendage started glowing with magical force.

The amazed Blithe had come into the cabin noting the dark hair of his enemy. To the midshipwizard, this meant he wouldn't be facing a spellcaster. Blithe had never seen someone without white hair who could cast spells. Not having the slightest idea what the spell might be, but fearing the worst, he acted without thought. Reaching down, he dropped his saber and lifted up one end of the captain's chart table, upending it toward his foe ten feet away. His arm and leg muscles bunched from the strain, but fear of the spell being prepared lent great strength to his effort.

The massive table arched up, spilling the many bags on top, and the great weight crashed down on the surprised captain.

"Is this a private party or can anyone play?" Ashe asked from the doorway.

"I don't think large, heavy tables are on the approved admiralty weapons list," Denna, the marine, quipped as she checked out the edges of the cabin much more carefully than Halcyon's first glance had done.

Breathing hard, Halcyon first noted that his enemy was clearly out of the fight. All he could see was one limp hand under the spilled table, but he was fairly sure he wouldn't be dueling with his foe more that day.

He turned to see Ashe and Denna, their weapons at the ready.

Excited more than he'd ever been before, Halcyon spoke in a rush of words. "I dueled with the captain. I caught him throwing sacks out the window. I stopped him before he could throw all of them. We should check them for important papers."

"Maybe we should see if the man is still alive first," Ashe wondered.

"I think it's devilishly clever of you to throw a hundred-weight table at your foe. I don't think I've read about this battle tactic in the standard combat books. Remind me to stay behind you in our next battle, who knows what might be flying through the air." Denna smiled as she teased the midshipwizard.

Halcyon's tone was distracted. "I made him stop grabbing bags. Then he wanted to fight. At swordpoints, suddenly he starts casting a spell. He has black hair, how can he use spells? Don't any of these Maleen know about proper rules or order? Everyone knows you don't use magic spells in a duel to the death, don't they?"

Ashe and Denna stood by Halcyon as all three of them looked down at the table and the body underneath.

"Calm down, remember you're a Lankshire man," Ashe advised. He motioned to Denna to go to the other side of the table, and with great effort, they lifted it off the unconscious Maleen captain.

Grunting, Denna observed as she helped move the table, "This thing weighs a ton. You must have been unusually surprised." The big marine's tone showed the respect she felt, realizing the midshipwizard was much stronger that he looked.

"Well, you would be too," Halcyon replied, still sounding distracted. "We were fighting all proper-like and then the man tries to use a spell on me. Not thinking, I dumped the table on him. I supposed that wasn't very sporting of me."

"Let that be a lesson to you," Ashe said, with a grim smile on his face. He reached down and lifted the dark mass of hair from the head of the unconscious Maleen captain. "See, it's a wig, there's blond hair underneath. The man hid his magical nature. He hoped to do some magical mischief later. He's still alive, shall I finish him off?"

"No, Captain Jordan might want information out of him. I saw Jordan brought some manacles of Iben with him just in case we found spell casters. Denna, be good enough to put them on our unconscious captain here and bring him up to the prow of the ship with the rest of the crew. Did you find anything else in the hold?" Halcyon asked, seeming calmer now.

"Lots and lots of mortar shells and blast-gel, but no more enemies," Ashe answered.

"What was our tabled captain doing down here?" Denna asked as she flipped him over and tied his hands behind his back.

"We better get those manacles on him before he wakes," Halcyon ordered Denna. "I know I could do any number of dangerous magical things, even with my hands tied behind my back. This one seems to know a lot of tricks."

"Well," Denna teased again, "he didn't know the trick of ducking a table twice his size, thrown at him by a surprised midshipwizard; imagine that."

Sheathing his saber, Blithe absentmindedly picked up one of the sacks and went to notify the captain of what he'd found.

Denna threw the unconscious captain over her shoulder like a bag of potatoes. The three of them went out of the cabin and joined Jordan and the rest of the marines and crew of the ketch at the bow of the ship.

One of the marines was throwing a bucket of water on the crew member who was knocked senseless as he tried to speak.

Denna threw the body down on the deck. The Maleen captain's head hit the boards with a bone-crunching knock. "I'll get the manacles from the longboat."

As the sailor on the deck sputtered awake, Captain Jordan and Acting Lieutenant Swordson looked down on the captain's body.

"What do we have here?" Elan asked.

"He claims to be Lord Albon Dreg, captain of this ketch," Halcyon answered. "I found him throwing weighted sacks out the window of his cabin." Halcyon threw the sack down on the deck. An eight-pound round shot rolled out of the sack as well as several dispatch cases and sparkling diamonds.

Everyone's eyes grew big at the wealth spilled out on the deck.

"Shove that back in the sack and take it below, Blithe," Jordan ordered. "I'll deal with all of that later."

"Let me up, let me speak," the ketch sailor sputtered. He rose to his feet and took off his cap. "Begging your pardon, Captain, my name is Alvin Collier; I was the mortar master of this ketch. They captured me seven years ago off the Arcanian ship *Crimson*. It was me making sure none of these mortars landed a shot on your dragonship over there, with your pardon, sir. I'm still loyal to the Arcanian king, I am."

Alvin was twisting his cap, looking nervous.

"Capital, Master Collier." Jordan was fairly beaming with this news. "It's always good to return a useful man back to service in the king's navy. Your knowledge of the enemy's ports and movement will be of great value to the admiralty. Help us sort out this crew, how many of them can we use?"

"Right, Captain, I can help with this, I can," Alvin said, standing straighter and smiling. "The crew here is a rough lot and only half of them are Maleen. We were training them to be sailors, we were. Most of them Maleens come from the mountains and don't know nothin' about the sea and its ways. The only bad'un in the bunch is the captain, begging your pardon, sir. He's been on board for only two months, but we've all been flogged at least once. He's a crafty, evil one, he is. Many lords and captains came to talk to him in his cabin in those months. I think he was part of dark doings, if you ask me, Captain, but I don't know what it was."

"Don't trust this man, sir," Elan sputtered. "Clearly a commoner, if he's worked with the enemy for seven years, he must be damaged goods."

Alvin looked hurt at Swordson's attack of his character.

Looking up, Jordan and the rest of the marines looked west. The battle still raged in the two long lines. The *Sanguine* was in the thick of things fighting the next enemy first-rater past the *Durand*. The *Durand* was flying a white flag of surrender. It would now wait for a prize crew. They weren't even chopping at the rigging on the deck anymore. One of the Arcanian frigates was positioning itself to take it over.

Many more Maleen ships than Arcanian ships were ablaze or sinking.

"Halcyon, get up into the mainmast tops. I want you to record the battle action until we're over the horizon. We could be the first ones back to Ilumin and I want to make as complete a report as I can as to the course of the battle," Captain Jordan ordered.

"Aye, aye, sir," Blithe replied.

"Elan, you set us a course for Ilumin and get this deck cleared away." The captain went down into the cabin Halcyon just vacated.

Halcyon grabbed up some parchment, quills, and ink from the navigation table on the quarterdeck. He dumped out a dispatch case, stuffed the things in it, and used the carrying strap to throw the case over his shoulder. He climbed the ratlines up to the top and tied a safety line from the mast around his waist. The air was crisp and clean up there and a mild breeze brought the smells of blast-gel to his nose.

The battle spread out in front of him, to the west and north extending not quite to the horizon. He didn't know the names of the ships on either side, but it was easy to count the types of ships fighting and surrounding the battle.

The midshipwizard started counting blast-tubes all along the line. He dutifully wrote down the ratings of the ships.

Hours later, as the ketch got farther away from the battle, the distance made watching much harder.

"Bring up a far looker," Halcyon hollered down to the deck.

There were still a great many of the captured crew and the *Sanguine*'s marines at the prow of the ship. Some of them had split off and worked at unfurling the mizzen sails.

"What's the battle looking like?" Ashe Fallow asked as he climbed to the top and handed over the ketch's scope.

"We're hitting lots more than they are, but there is a damned sight more of them than us in the battle. What's it like on deck?" Halcyon asked.

"Our stuffy Mr. Swordson is doing a good job," Ashe replied. "He's making it clear to the crew that they can sign into the Arcanian navy or they can remain prisoners in chains all the way to Ilumin. The damn fool captain of this shell has woken up and started demanding his rights. Its clear Swordson doesn't know how to react to the high-and-mighty lord. They're going to be sore tests to each other, mark my words."

"You, Denna, and I will just have to watch over that one and make sure nothing bad happens," Halcyon replied as he opened the scope and started watching the battle five miles to the west.

"I like the sound of that." Ashe smiled.

A huge explosion sounded in the distance.

"What was that?" Fallow said, straining to see the distant battle.

"A first-rater of theirs just vanished. Fire must have gotten to their orlop deck. A Maleen frigate behind them has caught fire from the blast. It's striking its colors; hopefully it will get help to put out the fires on its decks and sails."

"The winds are going to shift soon, giving them an advantage, but I think the fight is all out of them," Ashe observed.

"Admiral Tempest in his warship the *Challenge* has had four of his five Arcanian flags shot away. His mainmast went down before we caught the ketch. He's blasting it out with two Maleen first-raters right now and they've taken a great deal more damage than he's showing," Halcyon said, giving the telescope to Ashe as he wrote down his observations.

"The wind's shifting, it's going to help us on our way. I see we're at least two miles ahead of the frigate the *Sanguine* captured," Ashe observed. "Admiral Tempest has another great victory."

Halcyon wrote as fast and he could.

III

❊ ❊ ❊

Ordering the Ketch Shipshape

HIS MAJESTY'S ARTICLES OF WAR: ARTICLE XXIII

If any person belonging to any public vessel of Arcania commits the crime of murder without the territorial jurisdiction thereof, he may be tried by court-martial and punished with death.

The tips of the few masts of the battle seventeen miles away slipped over the horizon as the ketch moved with the wind. The continuing blast-tube eruptions sounded like thunder in the distance.

"I think we're done watching the battle," Chief Petty Officer Ashe Fallow observed as he could only see plumes of smoke on the western horizon.

A stiff breeze chilled them both while they sat lashed to the mast. They had been sitting on the tops observing the battle for several hours.

"I have to agree, Chief," Midshipwizard Third Class Blithe replied. "I've made all the notes I can on the struggle. I think it's going to be a great victory for Arcania, but only time will tell. I know I've heard old *Sanguine* roaring his battle challenge, even this far away. I hope he fares well. I have a strong sense that old dragon is still in the thick of things. Let's report to Captain Jordan."

"Before we do that, let me speak about something with you, man-to-man," Ashe said.

Halcyon gave him his full attention. Although Ashe ranked lower than Midshipwizard Blithe did, Ashe had helped Halcyon in dangerous times before, and the midshipwizard wasn't about to take the chief's words lightly.

"Meaning no disrespect, you haven't seen much of life yet," the chief said, staring right into Halcyon's eyes. "You might like to view the men found on this ship as normal crewmen. Don't do that. You can trust every one of the *Sanguine*'s men, even Swordson, who doesn't like you at all, but don't give that same trust to any of the crew of the *Salamander*. Even the ones from Arcania, just keep a weather eye out, do you get my drift, Midshipwizard?"

"I know exactly what you mean, Chief. I'll watch your back, you watch out for mine," Halcyon said, a bit embarrassed, knowing Fallow had been able to see the self-doubt growing inside Halcyon. This ship felt odd to the midshipwizard and he couldn't figure out why. He'd been on ketches many times before, but everything seemed out of place on this one. That odd feeling was causing Halcyon to question everything he did. "If ever you think I should know other things, please tell me, with my thanks, Mr. Fallow. I know I still have a lot to learn. I'll keep at my books and let the sea and shipboard life do the rest."

"I'm not the type to hold my tongue," Ashe joked.

As they climbed down the ratlines, men were climbing up. The crew working on the rigging was a mix of *Sanguine* crew and the ketch's sailors.

"Looks like the captain trusts some of the enemy crew to help spread the sheets," Ashe grunted as he moved deftly down the rigging.

"Is using the enemy crew unusual when a ship is taken?" Halcyon asked.

"It all depends on how many of the crew are from the enemy's homeland," Ashe replied. "I've seen Maleen warships crewed almost entirely by Toman and Drusan sailors. The sailors from Maleen are a different sort altogether. We'll make them sleep on deck, so we don't get stabbed in our hammocks belowdecks."

They hit the planks at the same time. The pair could see Captain Jordan now at the prow of the ship with most of the marines. Swordson was on the quarterdeck taking sun sightings and keeping the ship in the wind as much as possible. However, why the new brevet lieutenant was taking a sighting when the ship was heading due east, Halcyon couldn't figure out.

Moving up to the prow, Halcyon looked to the north and the sea, noticing the waves and the lack of foam on their crests. The sea told him he was facing force-three winds. A loud crack boomed overhead, signaling the mainsail filling with wind.

"Sir," Ashe and Halcyon saluted and said at the same time.

Captain Jordan saluted back.

Halcyon spoke up first. "We observed the battle for as long as possible. It looks to be a victory for Arcania with many more of the Maleen captured and sunk than our ships. I'll have a written report for you by the end of the day."

"That's what I saw too, Captain," Ashe said, agreeing with the brief report.

"I'll look forward to the report. Halcyon, I can use your translation skills here, now that I know you speak Maleen." Captain Jordan motioned Blithe to sit beside him. "Chief Fallow, I want you and two marines you pick to go through all of the sea chests below. I don't want any lethal surprises in the middle of the night. Also, make sure all hand weapons and blasting gel go under lock and key with a marine guard. Have I made myself clear?" the captain asked.

"Perfectly, sir." Ashe saluted and hurried away, taking two marines with him.

"Halcyon, we've only got twenty-two of the Maleen left to deal with. We'll have marines watch them day and night, but I want to get their marks on these Articles. The other crew members are from recently beaten countries and I think they are looking forward to serving Arcania. Repeat in their language what I say to this lot, understood?" Jordan asked.

"Yes, Captain, that won't be a problem," Halcyon replied as he looked out at the men. He tried to sound more confident than he actually felt.

Angry eyes looked back at him. All of the Maleen crewmen appeared sullen and still full of fight. They were big men with beards and grim faces. They sat sullenly on the deck. *Sanguine* marine guards surrounded them, weapons at the ready.

Former Captain Dreg followed the conversation from his position off to the side. Manacled to one of the mortars, he clearly didn't like to sit with the rest of the Maleens. The former captain glared at Jordan and Blithe. "None of my Maleen brothers will sign your stinking paper," he shouted at them in Maleen, much more for the benefit of his men than to convince the midshipwizard and the captain.

Captain Jordan ignored the raging Lord Dreg. "Midshipwizard, just repeat to them what I say."

"Yes, sir," Halcyon replied.

"All of the rest of the crew have signed this pledge," the captain told the Maleen sailors while holding up the paper with the marks and signatures of the others on it.

Halcyon repeated this information in the language of the Maleen.

"The king of Arcania wishes to treat all people fairly and with wisdom. If you sign this paper you are giving your pledge that you won't try to harm the crew or this ship in any way while we sail to Ilumin," Jordan continued.

Halcyon had no trouble translating those ideas.

"If you give your word and sign this pledge you are free to move around the ship and you can even gain passage back to the mainland when we reach port. If you don't sign, you will remain on deck, under guard, and end up in a prison barge until your country decides to trade captured Arcanians for you. I should tell you, your country hasn't offered to do that in the twenty years we have been at war." Jordan stood up and tossed the pledge down on the table for emphasis.

When Halcyon translated this, the faces of the men turned grimmer.

"Lies, lies, all lies," Lord Dreg raged at his men. "If you sign that paper you will be doomed when we invade their pitiful little island country."

Captain Jordan ignored Albon, again. His voice rose in volume, filled with deadly seriousness. "I urge you to come up now and sign this paper, but if you sign know this: If you're caught trying to harm this ship, I will hang you by the highest yardarm. Make no mistake about that. If you don't sign, you're in chains for the rest of the voyage."

As Halcyon translated, he pointed up to the main topgallant. From the look on their faces as all of them looked up to the yardarm, none of the men were in doubt as to what would happen to them if caught in sabotage.

They all got up and signed the document with their marks. As they wrote on the paper, it became evident that none of them could read or write, but each had a way to make his personal mark on the pledge document. X's and small images of flowers, animals, and whales stood for the men's word that they would obey orders.

None of them looked at their glaring former captain as they signed.

When the last Maleen sailor made his mark, Captain Jordan spoke up again. "Get them working, Corporal Darkwater. There's nothing like work to take their minds off of doing wrong. I want you to make a head count of these twenty-two at all the even bells, two, four, six, and so on; all day long and all night long. Include Lord Dreg in that list. We will know where these twenty-three are at all times."

"Aye, aye, Captain," replied Corporal Darkwater. Her marines split the group up into four work details and started them on various shipboard projects. There was always something to do on a ship.

"Fine." Lord Albon continued to glare at Jordan and Blithe. "I'll give you my parole as an officer and gentleman. Release me from these insufferable chains. The magic of them is making my head throb."

Captain Jordan moved toward Lord Albon as if to agree to his request.

Halcyon spoke up, remembering Ashe's words. "If I may suggest, Captain, we shouldn't take the manacles off Lord Dreg."

"If an officer and gentleman gives his parole we are obliged to free him, sir," the surprised captain said to Halcyon. "That's also why we don't make the officers of a captured ship sign the

Articles. They are giving their word as gentlemen that they won't act up on their ship, captured in battle."

"Sir, he hid his magical power under a black wig when I first met him. I don't think it wise that you trust him," Halcyon said, not liking to disagree with his captain.

"This young pup knows nothing about me," Albon raged. "I swear to you that I will do nothing to stop the voyage of this ship. Please, as one captain to another, let me free of these terrible manacles."

Lord Albon raised his manacled hands and gave Captain Jordan a pitiful look.

"I feel your pain, sir," Captain Jordan said, stepping back. "You may be free of this deck and I will unlock your shackles. We will keep on the manacles that curtail your magical power. The voyage is a short one, only five days at full sail and favorable winds. Mr. Blithe, order this man's foot manacles undone, but as you suggest keep the manacles of Iben on."

Lord Albon lowered his hands and appeared a beaten man.

"Halcyon, you are the third-ranking Arcanian naval officer of the ship. I want you to work with Mr. Swordson, clear the decks, and get full sail on the sticks. I ordered the men up into the mainmast, but I want those three jibs up as well," Captain Jordan ordered. "I'll be in the captain's cabin looking over those sacks our Maleen captain was so interested in throwing out the window. Do you understand my orders?"

"Aye, aye, sir," said Midshipwizard Blithe, coming to attention and saluting. He walked immediately to the small quarter-deck of the ketch. There he saw seaman Jokal at the wheel with Swordson standing beside him.

"Lieutenant, the captain has ordered us to get as much sail on the sticks as possible and to clear the decks."

Elan Swordson was a large, heavyset man of eighteen. He

never smiled and rarely gave a kind or supporting word to the men. "Orders understood, Midshipwizard? Bide a moment if you please and make the notation on the chalkboard as the details get called out. Jokal, determine course and speed if you please," Elan ordered.

"Course and speed!" Seaman Jokal shouted out. He stood at the wheel. Other sailors of the former crew of the ketch came down from the mizzensail. From the ship's chest by the wheel, they took out the knotted line and sand timer.

One of the sailors looked at the compass on top of the sea chest. "Due east, sir!" he shouted out.

Halcyon made notations on the chalkboard, for the direction. He waited for the shouts to adjust the speed of the ship. He noted the wheel's sand timer made it just near four bells of the afternoon. "Permission to get the cook fires started, Lieutenant?"

"Yes, that should have been ordered before, why didn't you think of that sooner, Blithe?" Swordson said, making it seem like it was a mistake on Halcyon's part that the cook fires weren't making the afternoon meal. "Work with the tube crews to get those artillery pieces squared away. Get the men fed as soon as you can." Elan showed a disdainful twist of his head as he said this last.

Halcyon ignored the expression and went down to the tube-deck. "Seaman Carstars, Seaman Ducay, front and center! Corporal Darkwater, to me if you please!" he ordered.

"Twelve knots, sir!" came the shout from the line tallymen.

"Stow your tackle," Elan ordered as he noted the speed of the ship on the mast board.

The men and Denna Darkwater came to attention in front of Halcyon.

"Seaman Carstars, go belowdecks with two seamen from the *Sanguine* and start the cook fires. I've heard the sound of steers below. We'll have fresh beef for dinner if you please."

"Aye, aye, sir," Carstars said, all smiles. Fresh beef for sailors was a real treat, as they never got the choice bits of beef from a slaughtered steer on a first-rater.

"Also, Seaman Carstars, I want a measure of grog in everyone's belly before the hour is out. The corporal will send down two marines to make sure only a measure is given to each sailor. Don't stint and if you think those Maleen shouldn't get their fair share, belay that thought. We'll treat everyone the same on this ship until they prove we need to hang them." Halcyon thought about the orders he just gave, trying to determine if they were enough. He looked to Denna Darkwater to make sure she understood.

She nodded her head, knowing what orders to give.

"Seaman Ducay, you will take two of the Maleen work crews and get all three jibs up. Take three of the *Sanguine*'s seaman to help. I want them singing a chantey while they work. Teach them 'Goodbye, Fare-ye-well,'" Halcyon ordered.

"Aye, aye, Mr. Blithe," Ducay answered. He left and began shouting orders.

"Corporal Darkwater, I want your marines firing any loaded blast-tubes and then corking them up so that they are weather-ready. Please send a marine down to inform the captain of what we are doing. That marine should then stand guard at the captain's door," Halcyon ordered.

"Aye, aye, Mr. Blithe." Denna saluted.

"Also, if you please, I would like you to set up a guard rotation for your marines. They need to watch the Maleen abovedecks during the night and have posts above and belowdecks during the day," Halcyon said as his mind filled with many other things needing doing.

The efficient Ducay was already getting his crews singing

and hauling up the jibs. The song brought a smile to Halcyon.
For a moment, he stopped to listen to the chantey.

Our anchor we'll weigh,
And our sails we will set.
Goodbye, fare-ye-well,
Goodbye, fare-ye-well.
The friends we are leaving,
We leave with regret,
Hurrah, my boys, we're homeward bound.

We're homeward bound,
Oh joyful sound!
Goodbye, fare-ye-well,
Goodbye, fare-ye-well.
Come rally the capstan,
And run quick around.
Hurrah, my boys, we're homeward bound.

We're homeward bound
We'd have you know
Goodbye, fare-ye-well,
Goodbye, fare-ye-well.
And over the water
To Arcania we must go,
Hurrah, my boys, we're homeward bound.

Heave with a will,
And heave long and strong,
Goodbye, fare-ye-well,
Goodbye, fare-ye-well.

Sing a good chorus
For 'tis a good song.
Hurrah, my boys, we're homeward bound.

Hurrah! that good run
Brought the anchor aweigh,
Goodbye, fare-ye-well,
Goodbye, fare-ye-well.
She's up to the hawse,
Sing before we belay.
Hurrah, my boys, we're homeward bound.

"We're homeward bound,"
You've heard us say,
Goodbye, fare-ye-well,
Goodbye, fare-ye-well.
Hook on the cat fall then,
And rut her away.
Hurrah, my boys, we're homeward bound.

"Corporal, when you have a minute, fetch Mortar Master Collier. You and I and a few of your marines will get some training in how to fire a mortar. Just get me when you're ready," Halcyon ordered.

"Aye, aye, Midshipwizard," Denna Darkwater said with a smile. She rushed off to take care of his orders.

Chief Ashe Fallow came up as the first of the rail tubes were firing.

BOOM!

"Mr. Blithe, we've secured all the weapons, and the marines

are guarding the blast-gel," Ashe said, coming to attention.

"At ease, Chief. Was there anything unusual among their things?" Halcyon asked.

"Meager stuff, clothes all worn thin, hammocks dirty, and with the purser's slop chests filled with clothes and new hammocks. It's a shame how they treat their men, sir," Ashe said with a questioning tone in his voice.

"Well, open those slop chests. We're going to have to have hammocks of our own. Let's give the men new slops to wear. With good food in their belly's and new things on their backs, maybe they will think twice about life in the Arcanian navy," Halcyon ordered with a smile.

"Just the thought, Midshipwizard Blithe, just the thought, if you don't mind my saying so," Ashe said. He left to follow Blithe's orders.

As the men got their grog abovedecks, Halcyon walked the tube deck. He could smell the beef rising up from the cookstove. His stomach gurgled in hunger as the four bells rang out on the quarterdeck. It was the traditional time for grog and a meal. The midshipwizard was inwardly pleased with himself at being able to issue the men grog on time, even if the afternoon meal was going to be a bit late.

Captain Jordan came on the tube-deck.

"Captain on the tube-deck!" the marine guard shouted out.

Halcyon turned and saluted his captain.

Jordan saluted back. Each man was very aware of his former lowly status on the *Sanguine*. Each was also pleased and proud to be the leaders of the ketch, even if it was for only five or six days.

"Marine, give my compliments to the cook," Jordan ordered. "Tell him Mr. Blithe, Mr. Swordson, and I will be eating on the quarterdeck and to set up a table immediately."

"Aye, aye, Captain." The marine saluted and left.

Halcyon followed his captain to the quarterdeck, where Swordson saluted.

"Mr. Blithe, Mr. Swordson, you both have done a good job getting the ship squared away from what I can see," Jordan told Halcyon.

"Thank you, sir, the crew and I did our best," Halcyon replied.

"The crew is a rabble, of course, but you will get them in shape, sir," Swordson said, complementing Jordan.

A small table and benches were brought up to the quarterdeck. It was unusual for officers to eat there, but these were unusual times.

Jordan was looking at the prow of the ship and Lord Dreg, who was looking off into the distance. "After looking through the papers and the sacs it appears to me that our Lord Albon Dreg is someone of power and influence among the Maleen."

"Really, Captain, I don't suppose many lords serve as mere captains on ketches in any navy," Swordson remarked.

"There was an unusual number of jewels and jewelry in those sacks. It also appears from the papers that the Maleen are going to try and enlist the aid of the Dwarven Empire. I don't need to tell you the danger such an alliance poses to Dominal and Arcania," Jordan remarked.

"The country of Dominal has a large dwarven population; you don't think they would turn on their fellow countrymen, do you, Captain?" Halcyon asked.

"The ways of dwarves are strange indeed. I don't know how they would react if the Dwarven Empire, an empire far to the south of Dominal, decided to become allies with the Maleen. I do know that the only thing stopping the nation of Dominal from falling to the invading Maleen is the skill of their dwarven fighting regiments."

"I don't know much about dwarves, do you, sir?" Swordson asked.

"No one does, Mr. Swordson. They're quick to anger and stout fighters; the sea isn't their element, as they sink like stones in the water. I've put those papers with Captain Olden's packet. You make sure if anything happens to me that they get to the Arcanian admiralty, understood?"

"Yes, sir, at all costs," Elan replied.

They ate their meal in silence. Each wanted to give the fine slivers of fresh beef in the wine sauce their full attention. The decks soon became full of crewmen and marines eating and making pleasurable noises at the beef.

There was a cry of anguish from the prow of the ship.

"Something seems to have disturbed Lord Albon. I say now, how did this wine sauce happen, it's simply amazing?" Jordan asked.

Chief Fallow, having finished his meal, stood at the helm so that Seaman Jorkal could eat. "I believe the cook found an unusually large larder of wine used for our Lord Dreg's table. He shortened the supply by a case of fine Sorbol red. I'd wager it's the first time any of the crew have tasted anything that fine. It's the same red wine you're drinking, sir."

Halcyon knew Chief Fallow liked wine and knew a great deal about all types of wine. The midshipwizard suspected the smile on Ashe's face was more a result of shortening the supply of an officer's wine rather than the pleasure of its good taste.

Finishing his excellent meal, Halcyon said to his captain, "With your permission, sir, I will take Mr. Fallow, Corporal Darkwater, and some of her marines with Mortar Master Collier and get a lesson on firing the ketch's mortars."

"An excellent thought, Mr. Blithe. You go ahead, but give a

shout when you fire the bloody things, understood?" the captain asked.

"Understood, sir," Halcyon replied.

Seaman Macarty replaced Chief Petty Officer Fallow at the helm. They found Corporal Darkwater with Alvin Collier belowdecks at the blast-gel hold. As they moved to the mortars on the forecastle, she ordered up four of her marines to learn how to fire the mortars.

Mortar Master Collier took a heavy coat with long sleeves and a pair of heavy gloves out of the caisson of the number-one mortar.

"Yes, I know the coat is blazing hot when battle comes to these waters," Collier said as he put on the coat and saw the questioning stares from the others. "You'll see in a moment why it's necessary. Mortar team one, front and center! Shell team to the prow!"

Men who had been on other details peeled off and came to their stations by the mortar.

"Corporal Darkwater, you'll want to send your marines with the shell team. They bring up the blast-gel and the shells from the stern hold. Let me go over what you need to know of my four beauties here.

"Go and get gel and one shell, boys," Collier ordered.

The men went racing belowdecks.

"The hollow shells have a fuse. It's a hollow pipe made from orange-tree wood. It's filled with an inflammable mixture. Every tube master makes his own fuses of the exact same length," Collier told the group.

"If they are the same length, how does the shell burst right when firing at targets of different ranges?" Halcyon asked.

"Good question, Midshipwizard," Collier replied. "Because

of the angle of fire from these mortars, the time they spend in the air is always the same no matter what the range. The firing angles span a minimum of forty-five degrees to sixty degrees. Ah, here is the very stuff we need. The fuse is supposed to allow the bomb to explode just before it impacts the target."

The men brought up one shell and a cone-shaped blast-gel jar.

Collier took up the cone-shaped jar and continued his lecture. "Each of these mortars has a truncated cone chamber at its bottom to explode in a shaped blast designed to light the fuse of the shell and send it arching into the air."

He carefully placed the blast-gel in mortar two.

They all saw why he needed his long sleeves.

"Even firing the mortar once makes the tube blazing hot. The long sleeves of the bombardier's jacket and his heavy gloves keep his arms and hands from burning. We usually fire no more than three blasts per hour from each of the mortars. We could fire them slightly faster, but there is a danger of the mortar itself exploding. The shells for these mortars weigh one hundred and ten pounds each. The solid metal ones weigh two hundred pounds. The mortar itself weighs four thousand eight hundred and fifty pounds. It fires up to a maximum range of two thousand nine hundred yards.

"Aiming is the fun part," Collier said, all smiles. "Mortar men, your levers please."

Two of the crew took large levers of iron and placed them one to a side on the mortar. Collier took out a large angled compass device and placed it at the top of the mortar. The entire weapon was on a swivel platform.

Halcyon noticed the platform had a level of solid stone covered in thick timbers and then the caisson for the metal mortar. Two of the men could swivel the entire weapon three hundred and sixty degrees, allowing the weapon to fire in any direction.

Naturally, it couldn't fire behind and into the masts, but there was nothing stopping the tube from ejecting its deadly shell to the starboard or port of the ship, as well as off the prow.

Collier explained, "The bombardier uses his compass to aim and correctly angle the weapon for the shot. When the weapon fires, there's a great deal of incandescent gel falling down on the platform. The remaining tube man brooms the area to remove the risk of fire. Now, if you will permit me, I'll fire tubes one and two, showing you the orders for the entire process."

They all moved back to let the men work.

Halcyon shouted "Fire in the hole!" to let the entire ship know the mortars were going to blast.

"Front!" Collier ordered. His men arranged themselves two to each side of the mortar while Collier himself stood on the platform. They all put on rags around their heads and ears to muffle the sound of the blast.

"Lock the levers!" Collier ordered, and two of the men angled the entire platform to fire off the port side and placed metal bars in the moving gears so that the mortar wouldn't move from its proper facing.

"Load the gel!" Collier pantomimed loading in the jar of gel as the mortar crew shouted out the same command.

"Loading placement!" Collier ordered and the men shouted out the command. The mortar was angled to accept the shot. It already had a shell loaded, allowing this step to be skipped.

"Pound in the stocks!" Collier ordered. The men shouted, and Collier pounded in a fifth stock even though it wasn't needed, just to show them all what would happen.

"Aim the mortar!" With this order, Collier and the men all got busy as the crew used levers to angle the heavy mortar and Collier scanned the empty sea with his compass on top of the mortar's mouth.

Collier took up a hot spike from the small firepot alongside the mortar. "Preparing to fire!" he shouted, and all of his crew shouted back, "Preparing to fire!"

All of the watchers placed their hands over their ears.

"Fire!"

KABOOM!

"Broom!" Collier ordered.

Halcyon had heard blast-tubes fire before, but these mortars were much louder. He looked in the distance. At least two thousands yards away and maybe a bit more, the shell exploded. A huge ring of fragments struck the water. They all imagined the damage such an explosion could do to even a first-rater.

There were a great many sparks glowing on the platform. Some of them must have been from the wooden wedges that had also blown apart in the explosion.

"I made sure none of our shells hit your precious dragonship during that last battle. It's a damn sight more difficult to hit a moving target than a fortress wall, and our high-and-mighty Lord Dreg never knew I was faking it," Collier said with a smile.

"And for that, we are very grateful," Halcyon remarked. "Let's get on with the firing of the second mortar, shall we? It's getting dark and the task were best done quickly."

"Midshipwizard Blithe, please put on the coat of a bombardier and fire the second one yourself," Collier suggested with a smile.

Halcyon loved the idea. He went over to the caisson and took out its heavy coat and gloves. First, he took the beeswax he always had in his pocket, warmed it with his hands, and plugged his ears.

"What's that?" Collier asked.

"It's beeswax," Halcyon answered. "I find it works better than stuffing cloth in my ears. It deadens the force of the blast and for some unknown reason I think I can hear better through it. It's an old trick my father taught me."

"Well, I never. I've been in the navy for ten years and never heard of it," Collier said. "I'll have to get me some at the port."

Donning the coat and gloves, Halcyon climbed up on the mortar platform.

Remembering the orders Collier gave, he shouted, "Front!"

Letter-perfect, he remembered all the commands as he went through the firing drill. He even wedged in the four stocks, allowing the wind space to surround the shell in the mortar.

He sighted the weapon off the starboard side and fired it.

KABOOM!

Halcyon remembered to shout "Broom!" after the weapon fired.

Darkness quickly set in, with Halcyon thinking he would ask Collier to teach him how to use the aiming compass in the morning.

On the quarterdeck, a scowling Elan watched Blithe put through his paces. He started making plans to work that midshipwizard. The man was far too keen on his duties and needed to be brought down a peg or two. *I'll teach the fool to beat me in a scuffle*, Swordson thought, remembering his fight with Blithe on the *Sanguine*.

IV

✢ ✢ ✢

Demon Ship

HIS MAJESTY'S ARTICLES OF WAR: ARTICLE XXIV

Such punishment as a court-martial may be inflicted on any person in the navy who is guilty of profane swearing, falsehood, drunkenness, gambling, fraud, theft, or any other scandalous conduct tending to the destruction of good morals.

Seven bells of the morning rang out on the quarterdeck; the mackerel sky foreshadowed a breezy day. The seventh clang signaled everyone was to be finished with the morning meal, and with the ringing of the ship's bell, Halcyon and Collier finished working with the angled compass of the mortar.

"You've come an amazing way, Mr. Blithe," Collier complimented the midshipwizard. "With the skills you've picked up here you can now aim and fire any mortar in military service."

"Thank you, Master Collier, for the lesson," Halcyon

replied, enjoying the mental effort it took to learn the use of the aiming compass.

The midshipwizard looked out to the sea and noted the force-two winds still heading west as seen by the conditions of the waves and sea foam. The cloud formations high above told him they would be getting stronger winds during the day. He hadn't slept much that night. His nerves were all atingle and he didn't know why.

The ketch was making great time. *We have the chance of seeing the Arcania coastline a day early if the wind keeps up,* Halcyon thought.

"Object on the horizon," came a shout from the tops on the mainmast.

Halcyon had the time, so he took a far looker and climbed the mainmast rigging. One hundred feet above the deck, he reached the tops.

Seaman Macnay looked to the east. "I can't make it out, sir," he told the midshipwizard. "It doesn't have any sails, but it isn't big enough to be an island. We're heading right for it."

Halcyon raised his glass.

Seventeen miles in the distance, he saw death sailing their way.

"Macnay, hit the deck and sound battle stations," Halcyon ordered.

There was no doubt in his mind that they were in deadly peril as the midshipwizard watched the demon ship come closer.

Stories of such ships revealed that no Arcanian warship had ever captured a demon ship in combat. They were terrifying metal things with no sails. There was a large wheel of paddles at the back turning the hellish warship, allowing it to ignore the wind. The admiralty wanted to know just how that paddle-wheel was powered, but in the two centuries of encountering the things, a demon ship had never been entered by a human, dwarf, or elf.

"Get off the sticks!" he ordered to the topmen on the sails. There would be no luffing of the sails in this battle. *All the speed we can muster is needed from the full sails that are up,* Halcyon thought.

The midshipwizard hurried down the rigging and rushed to the quarterdeck. Captain Jordan was in the middle of strapping on his sword.

Lord Albon Dreg stood by the helm holding out his manacles of Iben to have them released. No one moved to accommodate him.

"Captain," Halcyon came to attention and saluted. "There's a demon ship on the eastern horizon. It's pushing fast out of the east, straight toward us."

"Demon ship." Captain Jordan's face turned ashen. "Put the wind out of our quarter, sail due south, Seaman Jokal."

"Aye, aye, Captain, the wind on our quarter, south it is," Jokal shouted back.

Swordson went to the railing of the quarterdeck. "Mr. Collier, set your mortars to fire off the starboard side, you may fire when the enemy is in range."

"Aye, aye," Collier shouted out.

Both of them knew the demon ship would be hours away, but the crew hearing they were allowed to fire would cause them to shed some of their nervousness.

The *Salamander* leaned in the wind, but the force-two winds weren't pushing the ketch hard. Looking at the chalkboard, Halcyon saw they were only going seven knots with the wind full on their backs.

"Captain, I need you to order the helm lashed down to keep us heading south. We need to clear this quarterdeck. When their doom-tubes start firing at us, we all need to be on the main deck. I can cover the crew there with my own spells," Halcyon said. His family training was kicking in, powerful demon spells were coming to mind, and dispelling any doubt he might have had as to what he could and couldn't do in the coming conflict.

"What are you babbling about, man?" The white face of the captain spoke volumes about his fear. "Those are demons coming to take us. They'll capture the ship and possess all our bodies. Their doom-tubes will turn the deck crew to dust. We can't give our maneuvering advantage away to the enemy!"

"Captain, my family has been fighting demons for generations. I have some protective spells that will hold off their magics," Halcyon said, as he took a firm grip on the arms of the captain to steady him.

A little of the crazed look left Jordan's face. He stared back at Halcyon. His one good eye looked a little less wild. There was almost a resigned aspect in the tone of his voice. "Let's give your magic a try, Mr. Blithe. Swordson and I will go amongst the crew and ready them for battle. Jokal, lash down the helm."

"Lord Dreg, leave this quarterdeck," Halcyon ordered. There were men all along the sides of the quarterdeck loading the rail tubes. "Tube men, leave your tubes and take up weapons on the main tube deck, now!"

Jokal lashed the helm so that the ship headed south as long as the wind stayed at its present course.

Halcyon waited at the top of the stairs of the quarterdeck as the men cleared the deck. He drew his sword and felt the energy of the special rubies in the hilt of the weapon. The runes along the side of the blade glowed bloodred, sensing the demons in the distance. Halcyon's sword, like all Blithe household weapons, held incantations and runes effective against demons. All of the weapons the Blithe family ordered for themselves held demon runes in the blades and along the pommels, and special arcane blood rubies held special magics designed to aid in the casting of spells against demons.

This foe filled him with a deadly calm. For six long years, he'd been trained to fight demons. He was taught rituals to combat their magic. He sliced his left hand with his sword to begin the most important of those rituals. Having no magic until half a year ago, he had never cast the demon protection spells he knew, but that didn't make him hesitate for a heartbeat.

To hesitate against demons, Halcyon knew, was death.

Unknown to Halcyon, others saw his eyes come alight with a red glow. With the first uttering of his guttural demon magics, the muscles on his arms and legs bulked up in unnatural knots. The white hair on his head burst its war braid and started flying around his head, displaying a terrifying life of its own.

"He's turning into a demon!" screamed Swordson in alarm, drawing his weapon.

The first drop of Halcyon's life's blood splashed against the top of the quarterdeck stair. A plume of red smoke rose up from the stair and arched out over the heads of the crew. The stink of brimstone and fresh blood flowed out from the smoke. Halcyon slowly walked down the stairs, uttering his spell in a tongue no one could understand. Each word barked out, hurting the crew's ears just to hear the sound of them.

"Rush him, he'll kill us all!" another shouted.

Others started running as far as possible away from the midshipwizard.

"Steady on now!" Ashe Fallow shouted in his best parade-ground voice. "Mr. Blithe looks fierce, but he's one of ours, don't you know. Mr. Swordson, consider the men, sir, and calm down a bit if you please." Fallow's tone of voice made that an order and not a suggestion.

"Marines, center line, you will cut down any coward not doing their duty!" Corporal Darkwater shouted. Her words were like a bucket of cold water on the crew. Not a soul raised his weapon toward Halcyon.

The fifteen marines from the *Sanguine* spread themselves out in a line along the center of the ship. Seven of them held heavy crossbows and eight of them held the Arcanian blast-pike. They looked fierce and just their presence calmed down the nervous crew.

"It's an hour, maybe more before they'll get close enough for the crossbows and rail tubes," Darkwater whispered to Fallow, not wanting the two nervous commanding officers standing nearby to hear.

"You and I know that, but calming down these crewmen is more important than anything else. If fifteen strong men standing firm in the face of death doesn't stiffen their spines, let them jump overboard," Ashe said, twirling his own blast-pike in a nervous motion he would never admit to.

As Halcyon walked the starboard and port sides of the ketch, his dripping blood caused plumes of red smoke to cover the deck and sides of the ship. The unnatural sound of his voice made crewmen move to the other side of the ship as he approached. Only the quarterdeck at the stern of the ketch failed to be covered by his spell's bloodred cloud of haze.

The mortar crews started to shift away, but Mortar Master Collier wasn't having any of that. "Hold your positions, ya swabs, or those demons are the least of your troubles!" The tone of his voice held the four mortar crews in their proper places. "Bombardiers, sight your weapons!" All of the men on the weapons got to work angling the mortars for maximum range while their bombardiers used their sighting compasses to gauge the range of the enemy and properly position their mortars.

There was an unnatural stiffness in Halcyon's body, clearly brought on by the casting of this demon spell. His sleeves and pant legs ripped as his body expanded with the effects of his magic. The transformation was alarming even to his friends. He wasn't the lanky young man they all knew. His face became filled with sharp angles and his eyebrows grew longer and thicker. Something was happening to his jaw to make it larger and squarer. His frame became massive and he looked able to lift any weight.

Captain Jordan, not caring what Blithe looked like, got in his face. "Why didn't you cover the quarterdeck in your spell?"

"I don't have the blood force to cover that area," Halcyon replied in a deeper, distracted voice, speaking his words much slower than normal. "Get the eight solid shot up by the mortars."

Jordan sputtered, not liking to take orders from the midship-wizard. "Why should we do that?"

Ashe had been following the conversation, fearing in Halcyon's changed state that he might say or do something he would regret later. Fallow didn't wait for the order to come from the captain. He cuffed several of the sailors cowering at the railing. "You men get the eight solid shells from the hold, now! Seaman Macnay, go with them and make sure they don't get lost. We'll need blast-gel as well."

"Aye, aye, Chief," Macnay replied.

Captain Jordan stared in a daze at Fallow. There was a questioning look on his face. It took a moment for him to realize that Fallow was just doing what he should have ordered. "I better start acting like a captain," he muttered to himself. "Seaman Porter, take a far looker to the prow and report on the demons and the look of their craft. Mortar Master, use your compass, and shout out the range of the enemy! Water the deck! Raise the boarding nets. Get the hammocks strung. Get the sand spread, what's wrong with all of you!"

Nets came from the hold. Strung up along both sides of the ship, they'd temporarily hold up boarders. Often they caught and held parts of the masts blown off in the battle.

The stench of the red haze covering most of the ship grew stronger as Halcyon finished circling the deck. It was a strange smoke, but the spell still allowed them to see through the haze. The large drops of blood placed all around the deck continuously erupted in plumes of the demon haze that constantly replenished what the wind took away.

The sharp words of the captain kicked the crew into action. Their fear of the known danger of demons was temporarily put aside for work they knew how to do.

Buckets rose and fell from the ocean, their contents splashing over the decking and lower sails so that sparks from the mortars or hot shot from the enemy wouldn't start a shipboard fire. None of the water touched the blood spatters, as magic pushed the water away.

Barrels of sand came up from below and handfuls were thrown everywhere about the deck. Some of the men started going up to the quarterdeck with the sand.

Halcyon turned on them, his eyes blazing red. In deep guttural tones he screamed, "No one goes up there!"

The crewmen leapt off the stairs as if the steps were on fire. None of that crew dared to look Halcyon in his face. "Sorry, sir. Your pardon, sir," they said to the decking.

The midshipwizard had been uttering strange words since he started the red haze spell. He'd clearly finished with that spell and now he stood looking up at the large mainsail. His left hand was held over the flat blade of his saber. Dripping blood continued to flow from his hand, but not a drop fell off the glowing weapon and he wasn't even looking at where the blood flowed.

"Captain, you must take these off me," Dreg pleaded with Jordan. "I can be of service to the ship and crew. Do you think I want to die at their talons?" Albon held his hands out to be free of the manacles that prevented him from using magic.

Jordan looked him in the eyes and still didn't like what he saw. He threw the manacle key to Denna Darkwater. "Corporal, go in the captain's cabin and bring out Lord Dreg's sword and give it to him."

"Nine miles to starboard," Collier estimated from his mortar position.

"When they grapple us, give him the key to those manacles," Jordan finished.

Clearly, from the look on his face, that wasn't the order Dreg wanted to hear. He stiffly went over by the door to his cabin to wait for the sword.

"Aye, aye, Captain." Denna went below to get the weapon.

Halcyon's aspect was terrifying everyone on the ship. Demon magics changed him, but that didn't stop people from wondering which side he was on.

"It appears to be all metal," Porter shouted out. "There are two decks and there isn't a creature visible on the decks. A dark green plume of smoke is rising from the stern of the ship and that paddlewheel is turning faster. They are changing course to come directly toward us. There are six large tube ports on the port side and four tube chasers in the prow!"

Chief Fallow wouldn't admit it, but he was feeling a hot fear in the pit of his gut. Twelve years ago, he'd been in a fleet tasked with fighting just one of the demon metal ships. They'd won the fight at the cost of four of their ships. Eventually the foe had been battered and sunk, but the hellish nature of the fight had scarred Fallow's mind.

He also didn't like the changes happening to young Blithe.

As the young midshipwizard worked his demon spells, he kept changing physically, growing larger and more demonlike. Ashe sent up a quick prayer to the luck goddess that his Lankshire officer would change back after they won this fight.

Halcyon waved his bloodied sword into the air and a huge icon of blood wrote itself on the mainsail. It was as if a giant quill with blood for ink made the twenty-foot-tall bloodred icon glowing with mystical power on the sail.

"The giant wheel of the demon ship has stopped," Porter shouted out in glee minutes later.

"Eight miles and it's not gaining any more," Collier shouted.

"By the gods, what is that thing Halcyon has painted on our sail?" Ashe asked to no one in particular.

All smiles, Denna came up to him and said, "He's taunting them. That mark is the same in troll runes as it is in demon script. He's telling them to go to the nine hells. They now know there's a demon master on this ship. His mark and the large size of it are making them think twice about attacking. Our midshipwizard is playing a big bluff. He should be a marine."

"You four come with me." Ashe purposely picked four Maleen crew and they went into the hold.

"Who is the ship's carpenter?" Captain Jordan shouted to the crew.

A man stood up from his cowering position at the railing and turned toward Jordan.

"Take men, get your sharpening wheel up on deck, and start

sharpening all the blades. I want every weapon razor-sharp in the hour or I'll know the reason why." Jordan's order caused the men to rush belowdecks.

In minutes the large sharpening and grinding wheel was spinning and men lined up to get their daggers and cutlasses sharpened. Even Lord Dreg was at the front of the line getting his sword edge kissed by the stone.

"Seaman Carstars, Seaman Tourloon!" Jordan shouted for two of the dependable men he knew from the *Sanguine*.

"Aye, sir!" They both came up to him.

"Carstars, get those cook fires blazing again. Tourloon, go down into the captain's cabin and take the silver forks and knives you'll find there and give them to Carstars to melt in his cookpots. As you get pans of melted silver, bring them up on deck and have the crew's weapons dipped in them. I don't know if it will do anything, but it might help some against their hides. Understood?"

"Aye, aye, Captain." They both smiled at the thought of the good idea.

Crew had brought up the eight solid shot for the mortars. They took the two-hundred-pound spheres and racked them in the caissons of the four mortars. They would be the next shots fired after the loaded shells targeted the demon ship.

"Collier!" Jordan shouted even though he was only ten feet from the man. "I want you to get the two biggest Maleen crewmen and position them at the prow of the *Salamander*. Place four blast-gel jars at their feet. If that demon ship comes close enough to board, they are to hurl those jars at the ship. Understood?"

"Aye, aye, Captain," Collier shouted back.

Fallow and the Maleen crewmen brought up several small casks of wine from the hold with tankards hanging from the casks. Seeing this, Jordan went to bark at them, and then he realized what Fallow was up to and moved to check the netting.

"It's coming at us again," Porter shouted, worry filling his voice.

"Nine miles out and gaining," Collier barked.

"You men start handing out a tankard to each and every man-jack aboard." Not cowed at all, Ashe Fallow opened a bottle of Arcanian red wine and poured a large portion into a tankard as he approached Halcyon. "Drink this, don't argue. This good red will replace some of the blood you've lost," Ashe said in a stern voice. He'd seen spellcasters changed from their spells before. *I don't much like what I'm seeing in young Blithe*, he thought.

The red haze covering the ketch also covered Halcyon in an even thicker smoke. His long white hair looked bloodred and wildly twisted and pulled at his skull in stark contrast to the slow movements of Halcyon's body and the slow nature of his voice. He looked at Fallow as if he was startled at the man's words. The midshipwizard sheathed his bloody sword and took the tankard offered him. His other hand was covered in an unnatural glove of wet blood. The stench of brimstone came off his body in waves.

Without thinking about it, Fallow stood downwind of the officer.

"Is there anything I can do, sir?" Ashe asked.

Halcyon stared at Fallow intently. He drank the tankard empty and absentmindedly dropped it on the deck. In an emotionless deep voice, he said, "I might need some of your blood. Stay close."

Ashe tipped up the bottle and finished it, not commenting on the thought of giving his own blood to a wizard wet behind the ears who might not know what he was doing with forces he might not be able to control.

The midshipwizard started uttering a new spell and his bloody hand heated up in a fierce glow. Waves of heat came from that hand, hotter than an armorer forge. He walked up to the solid shells arranged by the mortars. Ashe followed as ordered, but wondered just how much blood the officer would be taking from him.

"The tube ports are opening," Porter shouted.

"Seven miles out," Collier barked again.

There was no doubt the pace of the demon warship had picked up.

Halcyon stared at the first of a pair of solid shot on the caisson of the first mortar. He began chanting, and with every word he spoke, a strange bloodred icon appeared on the side of the shell.

Slowly he pushed his white-hot, bloodied hand onto the shell. The steel color of the ammunition turned red from the place he touched until the entire sphere was pulsing red. As he lifted up his hand, there was a deep palm mark melted into the surface of the sphere.

There was a look of terror on the faces of the tube crew. They'd never seen anything like the spellcasting of this young midshipwizard. Sailors were a superstitious lot to a man. Arcanians were used to crewing with wizards, but the old crew of the ketch didn't know what to think.

Collier shook them all out of their fear with his words. "Well done, Mr. Blithe. I know what you've done will help kill those hellish bastards!"

"Lieutenant Swordson, what are you doing with your saber?" a worried Fallow asked, looking at the glowing green weapon.

"Blithe's family isn't the only one with demon-killing skills," Elan nervously answered. "If I'm killed, be sure to pick up this weapon and stick it in Blithe. It will take all the fight out of that demon spawn."

"That demon spawn is all that's between us living or dying to my way of thinking. If you die, I'll take care that something happens to your sword. Mark my word on that." Ashe positioned himself between Swordson and Blithe, and he intended to stay that way for the course of the battle. *Lankshire men have to watch each other's backs*, he thought.

The men around the mortars ripped their eyes away from what the Arcanian was doing to listen to their mortar master. He at least was a known element and if he was enthusiastic about what was happening, they knew to like it as well.

Halcyon ignored Collier. He moved from solid shell to solid shell. His demon magics turned the steel shell red and his palm made a deep indentation in each one of the shells. When he was done, he was visibly weaker, sagging from the effort, but all the shells were treated and ready to fire.

Ashe waved for Denna to force another tankard of wine into Halcyon's good hand.

"It's raised the no-quarter signal," Porter shouted back to the crew.

No quarter meant the ship wouldn't be taking prisoners and this would be a battle to the death.

"Three miles out and closing fast," Collier shouted as he sighted across the compass on top of the number-one mortar.

"We've got to strike our colors," Dreg shouted, standing toe-to-toe with Jordan. "If we don't give up and your fool of a midshipwizard does something with his spells, the demons are going to hurt us worse."

Denna Darkwater came up behind the Maleen lord. She would take her next action at the order of the captain, but she was ready for whatever he wanted to do.

Captain Jordan sneered at Dreg. "This is now an Arcanian ship. We don't give up in the face of danger. There will be no striking of our colors. Lord Albon, find somewhere on the deck to make your stand and act like a man."

The amazed Albon moved his mouth but no words came out.

Jordan ignored him and moved to get a line of melted silver along the blood groove of his blade. He was one of the last to get this done. "Seaman Carstars, get Collier's permission and pour some of that melted silver on each of the loaded mortar rounds. It can't hurt and might help."

"Aye, aye, Captain," said Carstairs, rushing off to talk with Collier.

"They're firing!" Seaman Porter shouted.

Most of the crew ducked; the fifteen marines and most of the Arcanian seaman stood tall and watched the attack.

Screams came to the deck of the *Salamander* in waves. Two miles away the shots of the demon artillery erupted in black smoke. The smoke continued to trail the shot the entire two miles. Huge skulls flew at the ketch, screaming a dread intended to paralyze the enemy hearing it. The skulls magically increased in size as they approached and struck the red mist surrounding the ketch. Three of the skull shells turned to white dust. The fourth hovered over the quarterdeck of the ketch. The skull seemed to scream and dart its hollow stare all over the quarterdeck, to no effect. The skull and black smoke dropped into the ocean on the port side of the ship without making a splash.

On the *Salamander* only Ashe noticed Halcyon as the demon weapons struck the haze. Three of the four blasts hit the haze and turned to white dust. At the same time Halcyon staggered and three welts appears on his face as his eye blackened and turned ugly.

"Fire in the hole!" Collier shouted, and it served to act as a signal to the other three bombardiers.

KABOOM!

KABOOM!

KABOOM!

KABOOM!

The four mortars belched their destructive spheres.

Halcyon could tell all four fuses were lit and burning, as his magically enhanced senses tracked the shells flying through the air. He knew there were fifty demons on board the enemy vessel closing fast. One of the demons was vastly more powerful than the rest. It knew of Halcyon's presence as well.

"Front!" Collier commanded in the first command of the loading process. His commands hustled the men into loading the magicked shells into the mortars even before they saw the affects of the first shots.

At the same time as two of the mortar shells exploded over the demon ship, it fired again, this time a little over a mile away. The other two shells exploded far short of their target.

Thousands of white-hot fragments struck the metal sides of the paddlewheeler to no effect. The demons stayed inside their ship and sailed it ever closer.

Dread filled the faces of the *Salamander*'s crew. If their most powerful weapons couldn't hurt the demon ship, what chance did they have?

A raging Lord Albon hobbled up the steps of the quarter-deck, screaming, "We must give up! We must surrender!" His sword was out and it was clear he intended to cut the lashings on the helm.

Captain Jordan rushed the stairs, striking like lightning. He grabbed Dreg from behind before the fool could cut the lashings.

Four more shots from the bow chasers raised out of the demon ship. Three more of the skulls turned to white dust, their demon-powered screams doing nothing. The shot striking the quarterdeck covered Jordan and Dreg in the deadly magic of the demons. Their bodies turned to dust, as did the skull doing the damage.

In a heartbeat, Elan Swordson became the captain of the ketch.

Halcyon, taking the magical punishment of the shells into his body, fell to the deck. His face displayed terrible bruises as if it had taken the force of the demon shells like fist blows as they struck the enchanted shield he made. Ashe caught his body and gently laid him on the deck. Halcyon's features were now demon ugly and all pushed in from the effects of the demon doom-tubes, the terrible bruises filled his face and head. The boy was barely conscious and barely recognizable as the friend Ashe knew.

"Get those mortars firing!" Ashe screamed.

Less than a mile away, a middle-ranging shot for the mortars, the weapons fired their magicked shells.

The loaders didn't want to touch the demon shells Halcyon made. That didn't stop them from using the hooks and levers to load the mortars.

As the wooden stocks were wedged into the mortar, they burned as they touched the sides of the demon-enchanted shells.

Moving as fast as they ever did, the mortars were loaded and fired in record time.

"Load the seconds, you swabs, or we're all dead!" Collier screamed.

Three huge plumes of water erupted around the demon ship as mortar shells struck the water. The last shot went through the metal roof at the back of the demon ship with a huge crash.

A broadside of the demon-tubes shot out at the ketch, but the successful strike of the mortar changed the course of the ship. Only one of the screaming demon shots struck the red haze.

Halcyon screamed in terrible pain and his other eye puffed up as if a huge fist had just struck him a blow.

Four more mortar shots ranged out at the demon ship. This time, two of the weighty shells met their marks and went through the upper deck.

Hulled, the demon ship sank like a stone. There were no survivors bobbing to the surface.

The cheers of the ketch's crew were deafening. They'd done the impossible. Ashe held the almost unconscious midshipwizard up, to see the enemy sink away. The last thing Halcyon saw was the upraised weapon of Swordson, ready to strike at him. He closed his eyes, not caring if he lived or died.

V

❧ ❧ ❧

Another Board of Inquiry

HIS MAJESTY'S ARTICLES OF WAR: ARTICLE XXV

Such punishment as a court-martial may adjudge may be inflicted on any person in the navy who is guilty of sending or accepting a challenge to fight a duel or acts as a second in a duel.

Halcyon woke with a start in total darkness. Raising his arms, he heard the clanking of heavy chains.

"Not again! By the gods that made me, can't I sail on one ship without being thrown in irons?" he asked the darkness.

The darkness failed to answer back.

Trying to sit up was difficult, as there were clearly more than one set of chains on him. He silently vowed to himself that he would soon do something about the manacles attached to his arms and legs. The twice-blasted manacles of Iben were on his wrists, preventing him from using any magic.

Sitting up, he was able to slip half of the cuffs off his arms as if they had been put on a much larger man. None of the ones on his ankles stayed on and he just shook them off.

He heard a muffled shout somewhere in the dark. "The prisoner's awake!"

Minutes later, Chief Fallow opened the hatch, and light blinded Halcyon for a moment. "Spell stunning they call it, I'm told," Fallow said. "When a wizard uses more energy than he should, he falls into a deep sleep until his body can recover. Our good Mr. Swordson thought you might be a demon and ordered you put in chains no matter how much we all argued against that. I made sure you didn't get stabbed for your efforts. It would appear our new captain would bear a little watching where you're concerned."

"It would appear I made a mistake when I beat the tar out of him on the *Sanguine*. Do I have to stay in here until we land?" Halcyon complained.

"No, we'll get you cleaned up and those manacles off your wrists. I'm just here to determine if you're a demon and should be killed or not." Fallow's smile was far too large to suit Halcyon. "I volunteered for the duty at the risk of my life. I might even get a commendation for it. Are you a demon?"

"If demons are starving, and if demons need to use the head, and if demons have to suffer foolish wet-behind-the-ears captains, then . . ." Halcyon stopped for a second and thought about who might be listening behind the door. "Master Chief Fallow, I am not a demon. May I be freed, please?"

"Why, of course, Mr. Blithe. Reach out your hands and I'll free you of those final manacles. I figured you would be shrinking back to your original form. That's why all those other manacles fell off your feet and hands. Food is on the way as I suspected what your answer would be. You are now second-in-command of the *Salamander*. If anything would happen to our good captain, you would be in command. I, for one, hope he doesn't trip in the night and fall overboard."

The chief's tone wasn't as clear as his words.

Food and water came in and Halcyon was left alone to change, clean himself up, and eat. Finishing his meal, Halcyon removed the bandage he now kept at all times over the demon mark on his thigh. There was a constant ache coming from that area. The demon mark showed up ugly and red on his skin. He hated the fact that the mark appeared in the form of a demon head with horns. There was nothing to do about it, but he would have to talk to his brothers to see if they had such a mark. Rewrapping the bandage, he took a few moments to think about Midshipwizard Merand and her kind advice the day she spotted that mark.

"Navy crews were a superstitious lot," Merand had told him, "and when they find out there is a chance their officer could turn into a demon in the heat of battle it made them terrified of said officer."

There's only a slight chance I'll turn into a demon, Halcyon thought. *Even then, it only has a small chance of happening in the Month of Demons. There's nothing I can do to stop it anyway, or so those in the know say about such things.*

The meal filled him with energy. He got up and started getting on the clothes set out for his use while he slept. He winced often as he tried to use his left hand to get dressed. The hidden demon mark was the least of his worries right now. He didn't want to see what the cut looked like under the bandage. It started bleeding and soaked the wrapping as he finished getting dressed.

The battle and the demon magic he used seemed a distant

blur in his memory as he thought about those events. The demon-inspired spells he used, he suddenly realized, would be easier for him to cast if he ever needed them again. Using his magic senses he could tell the demon spells he'd learned as a child would take far less of his magical strength to cast now and he had no idea why. The incantations almost glowed in his mind's eye. He shuddered at that thought. His gut told him using such spells brought him closer to transforming into the demon thing he hated most.

A fresh shirt and work pants lay out for him, but he couldn't find his jacket anywhere. Getting dressed, he belted on his sword and went on deck.

The marine on the other side of the door came to attention when Halcyon opened it. "Lieutenant Blithe on deck!" the trooper shouted.

Lieutenant, that had a different sound to it, Halcyon thought.

Sand from the battle still crunched under Halcyon's feet as he came onto the blast-tube deck. The fresh salt air revived him and put a spring in his step.

As he climbed the stairs to the quarterdeck, Seaman Jokal saluted, "Thank ye for saving us, sir."

Halcyon thrilled at those kind words. He saw Captain Swordson scowling.

"I'm reporting for duty, Captain," Halcyon said, saluting.

"And it's about time." Swordson saluted back. "I've been doing double shifts for two days. Are you well enough to command while I sleep?" This last was said in a tone that begged Halcyon to say no.

"Ready and able, sir," Halcyon replied in a steely tone.

"Fine, I'll be below. Call me immediately if anything happens," Swordson ordered.

As Swordson closed the door on his cabin, Fallow and Dark-water saluted Halcyon. They had big smiles on their faces. He saluted them back.

"Brevet Lieutenant Blithe, good to see you up and around," Chief Fallow remarked, there was an about-time tone to his voice.

"For a time it would seem our good Captain Swordson would have had you kept in irons until we returned to Ilumin. Our written reports forced his hand when he read them and discovered we had copies we would be turning in as well," Denna said. "We lost Captain Jordan and the Maleen Dreg in the action, but the rest of the crew is in good spirits and happy to be alive thanks to you, sir. The demon ship sank with all hands, not that we stayed around for survivors."

"I noticed the sand is still on the blast-tube deck, why is that, Chief?" Halcyon asked as he noted the ketch's course and speed on the chalkboard.

"We wanted to wait until you were up and able to give permission to clear it away. We didn't know what with your spells if it was safe or proper to remove it. With your permission, I'll get a detail on the sand and also order up a man to redo that soaked bandage on your hand," Ashe replied.

"Clear it away," Halcyon ordered. "When are we expected to reach Ilumin?" Halcyon still felt a great unease. Part of it was having Elan Swordson as his captain and knowing the man hated him.

"At this course and speed we should see Ilumin tomorrow morning," Chief Fallow answered back.

"Corporal, please bring up the chief's and your reports. I'll want to read them before I prepare mine." Halcyon planned on filling his time with the tasks he knew needed doing. He hoped to ignore his uncertainty at command with hard work.

"They are right here in the map chart cupboard, Mr. Blithe, let me get them for you," Denna answered.

Halcyon couldn't get over being the only lieutenant of his own ship. He walked back and forth on the quarterdeck reading reports. He talked to both Chief Fallow and Corporal Darkwater about the praise they put in their reports about his actions. Their written words made him embarrassed. Both of them refused to change a word of their reports.

Later that day, scanning the sails and rigging lines, he noticed the dimly glowing blue color on the halyard of the flying jib. To his rope-speaker senses, it stood out clearly. He could tell that a strong shift in the wind would cause that line to snap.

"Take down the flying jib and replace its lines!" Halcyon shouted the order and men climbed the lines and did his bidding.

Topman Macnay had clearly been working with the crew as the work detail started chanting up a halyard tune.

From Gold Town we're bound away,
Heave away (Heave away!) Santy Ano.
Around from Alm to Et Bay,
We're bound for Ilumin Town.

So heave her up and away we'll go,
Heave away (Heave away!) Santy Ano.
Heave her up and away we'll go,
We're bound for Ilumin Town.

Salamander's fast with a bully crew,
Heave away (Heave away!) Santy Ano.

An up-north warship with a bright captain, too.
We're bound for Ilumin Town.

So heave her up and away we'll go,
Heave away (Heave away!) Santy Ano.
Heave her up and away we'll go,
We're bound for Ilumin Town.

Back in the days of the last great king,
Heave away (Heave away!) Santy Ano.
Those were the days of the good old times,
Way out in Ilumin Town.

So heave her up and away we'll go,
Heave away (Heave away!) Santy Ano.
Heave her up and away we'll go,
We're bound for Ilumin Town.

When I leave ship I'll settle down
Heave away (Heave away!) Santy Ano.
I'll marry a girl named Sally Brown
Way out in Ilumin Town.

So heave her up and away we'll go,
Heave away (Heave away!) Santy Ano.
Heave her up and away we'll go,
We're bound for Ilumin Town.

We've been bold enough, so I've been told,
Heave away (Heave away!) Santy Ano.
Gold in plenty to pay us so I've been told
Way out in Ilumin Town.

So heave her up and away we'll go,
Heave away (Heave away!) Santy Ano.
Heave her up and away we'll go,
We're bound for Ilumin Town.

The day was perfect for sailing. The winds were fresh to the west. The white clouds stayed high in the sky.

Halcyon had to write his own report on the action of the ketch to add to the dispatches from the *Sanguine*. He didn't know how the admiralty would respond to his use of demon spells. The only consolation was the fact that through the years others must have battled demons with spells like the ones his family had taught him since he was an infant. He couldn't remember any of his brothers or uncles talking about such battles, but such combats must have happened.

He shook his head, not believing his luck at even temporarily being second-in-command on a warship, even if he would return to being a third-class midshipwizard when they docked. Halcyon couldn't help but be pleased with how this would look on his record.

The day proceeded calmly and the ship handled well in the brisk winds.

At sunset Halcyon and Chief Fallow stood on the prow looking out to the east.

"Our captain stirs," Ashe remarked, seeing Swordson open his door.

The marine guard shouted, "Captain on deck!"

Halcyon went to the quarterdeck and the waiting captain. "Sir, the ship is cleared and steady on the course you set. During the night watch, I changed out a rotted halyard line. My report on the battle with the demon ship is with Chief Fallow and Corporal Darkwater's reports."

"Excellent, Mr. Blithe. That rope-speaking ability you have serves the ship in good stead. Before turning in, please check the cordage below for rot. You're dismissed," Elan said with a sharp tone.

"Aye, aye, sir," Halcyon said, saluting and going below.

Behind his back, Swordson narrowed his eyes at the leaving brevet lieutenant. Elan didn't like any of that man's abilities. His report wouldn't be as glowing as the other two on Blithe's actions.

Blithe checked all of the cordage in the hold and found it all sound. He found his place in the hammocks and thought he would never get to sleep as he worried about what Swordson would say in his report about the action against the demon ship. In ten heartbeats, his hammock swayed with the ship and he was sound asleep.

"Battle stations!" came the shout from the quarterdeck. The words floated down into the hold.

Halcyon woke with a start. He didn't bother getting on his boots. He rushed out of the hold, belting on his saber. Hours ago, he'd entered the hold in darkness, and now the sun was bright in the east; clearly, he'd gotten out on deck in the better part of the early morning.

"Mr. Collier, don't load the tubes, just yet," Swordson ordered from the quarterdeck.

"Gateway Fortress on the horizon!" came the shout from the mainmast tops. The crewman pointed to the east.

"Two frigates to the south, we can't make out their colors, sir," Chief Fallow reported.

Halcyon wondered if his Lankshire chief had slept a wink that night. He felt guilty at sleeping through two watches.

"Center line your marines, Corporal. These may be Arcanian warships one would expect so close to Ilumin, but it's better to be safe than sorry. Good of you to join us, Blithe." Swordson's tone was enough of a censure.

"Aye, aye, Captain," Darkwater replied. She began shouting orders to her men. Most of them were up and about, ready for action anyway.

Halcyon looked at the pair of frigates coming up on them from the south.

"Raise the colors, Carstars. Show them we are a prize crew. I see their Arcanian colors so we've nothing to worry about," Halcyon ordered.

"I'll make that determination, Mr. Blithe," Swordson barked.

Halcyon noticed he didn't countermand Hal's orders.

The colored flags going up the mainsail were a series of special flags; each signaled a word in a set of codes changed every six months. The set of nine small pinions going up declared the *Salamander* a prize ship taken by the Arcanian navy. No one could make a flag signal message without the proper codebooks.

One of the frigates, the *Red Dragon*, sailed close. An officer with a speaking tube shouted from the prow. "Lower sails and heave to for boarding, *Salamander*."

"Furl the mizzen and mainsails," Swordson shouted out.

In just a few moments, the frigate's longboat came alongside.

The ketch's ratline ladder lowered to allow the officer access to the deck.

Up came a lieutenant from the *Red Dragon*.

Seaman Carstars piped him aboard.

Halcyon waited with Swordson for him on the quarterdeck with Chief Fallow and Corporal Darkwater.

A surprised look came on the lieutenant's face when he saw how young Swordson and Halcyon appeared.

"Lieutenant Halsy, at your service, sir." The young lieutenant saluted.

"Captain Swordson, late of the *Sanguine*, our Captain Jordan was killed in action on the way here. I assumed command of the ship, being the highest-ranking officer," Swordson said with pride. "Please feel free to inspect anywhere you wish to make yourself comfortable. When you're finished, come join me for a glass of wine to see you off. Mr. Blithe, attend the lieutenant and answer any of his questions."

"Thank you, sir. I will be at your service, allowing you to go on your way after a brief check of things," the lieutenant replied.

"Aye, aye," Halcyon replied, standing too and following the lieutenant down the quarterdeck ladder.

Halcyon took him down to the hold. "Are you forced to search every prize that comes close to Ilumin?"

"Standard procedure calls for a check of every hold and every cabin," Halsy remarked. "You've never seen an enemy ship filled with blast-gel crash into a naval fortress wall. It's a sight no one wants to see twice. Have you seen any action in the taking of this prize?"

"We've news for the admiralty on a huge action off of Ordune. The enemy had a much larger fleet and tried to break free of the blockade. We fought at dawn and gave them a real thrashing. I suspect we are the first of several prize ships coming from that battle."

"Amazing news, Lieutenant," Halsy said. "I'll get off so that you can deliver those dispatches."

They went back up to the quarterdeck and Halsy was all smiles as Swordson handed him a glass of good Ilumin red.

"You captain an excellent craft, I envy you," Halsy remarked. "You know to sail into Ilumin bay from the north entrance past Gateway Fortress, don't you?"

"I'm sure someone would have told me," Swordson said, looking at Chief Fallow. "I thank you for the word of advice. Good day to you, sir." Swordson saluted and watched the lieutenant rush off the deck.

After Halsy was off the ketch, Swordson was fuming mad. "Imagine the cheek of the man. Telling me how to sail into my own port. I'll show him how to sail."

The sails were set, and within the hour they could see the light tower atop Gateway Fortress. The fortress stood on a man-made prominence at the mouth of the harbor. Huge chains with links ten feet wide were attached to the fortress and sagged under the water all the way to the fortresses on both ends of the harbor. When enemy ships came, the chains rose to prevent enemy ships from entering the harbor, and even several direct blast-tube shots wouldn't be enough to burst the links.

"Prepare the seven-tube salute!" Ashe ordered.

"How do you know it shouldn't be the twenty-one-tube salute?" Swordson asked.

"I looked to see if the admiral was on his flagship in the harbor. You can't miss that flagship. The *Dealer* is the biggest ship in the fleet, made with a layer of thick copper between good Arcanian oak sheaths. It's the only two-hundred-tube ship in the fleet. It must be on maneuvers out of the bay with most of its support ships. As we cross the chain, order the salute, sir," Ashe advised.

The city was amazing, laid out in a blaze of many colors. The north side of Ilumin Bay was filled with shipyards where new ships left skids every month and war-battered ships were patched and sent once more into battle. From that quarter, the smell of fresh-cut wood overshadowed even the odor of the bay.

The east end of the bay appeared dominated by the huge bloodred granite admiralty building rising up on a hill on Queen's Street. The building was almost a mile long and three stories tall; the people in the chambers of that building controlled all the fleets of Arcania as well as being in charge of the stocking and crewing of those ships. Arcania was an island nation and this was one of the most important buildings in the empire. Atop its roof was a tower with a set of four signal flags flying under the Arcanian eagle banner. It's said the eagle of Arcania had flown over the city and that building for over five hundred years.

"Fire the salute!" Swordson ordered.

Seven of the rail tubes ignited, one at a time. The ketch announced itself and honored the home fleet.

Halcyon read the flags on the admiralty tower without a codebook. They said, *Commanders bring dispatches immediately.*

"Mr. Blithe to the quarterdeck," Swordson ordered.

Halcyon came up and saluted.

"Mr. Blithe, I want you to take these dispatches to the admiralty while I take care of setting the ketch to rights. You'll have to wait, maybe days, while the admiralty takes its own sweet time in dealing with you. I've seen it happen dozens of times myself and I don't want to put myself through that. I'll await any orders on the ketch. Do you understand your orders, sir?"

"Perfectly, sir, I'll carry them out immediately," Halcyon said, saluting again. Blithe went back to the prow of the ketch to watch them enter the harbor.

In a few minutes, Chief Ashe came up to him.

"Jokal's steering for Prepon Fortress, Lieutenant. That's where all the prize ships are docked. The corporal and I will take care of the easy paperwork on the ketch just to make sure Swordson doesn't do anything stupid. That will leave you free to take a coach to the admiralty," Ashe told Halcyon.

"I've never been in the admiralty, but my family has talked about it. Have you been there?" Halcyon asked.

"My kind doesn't set foot in that place and when we do, it's never good news for the ranker doing the walking. Let me give you another bit of advice," Ashe said. "When you come in the front door you'll meet some type of door officer. It doesn't matter who it is, they're all alike. Normally, you would tell him you're a lieutenant with dispatches from the fleet of Ordune. If you do it that way you'll be left to stand on your heels for hours if not days."

"Well then what should I do?" Halcyon asked.

"Use your heritage. Tell the door flunky you are Lord Blithe wanting to see the lord of the navy. Your family name means more than your brevet lieutenant's rank. They get captains and fleet admirals in there all the time. Lords hardly ever come calling and when they do, it usually means bad news for the admiralty," Ashe said with a wink. "Give it a try and see what happens."

"I will, Chief Fallow, I will," Halcyon said.

"Plan on sleeping there overnight," Ashe advised. "I'd be amazed if they let you back on this ship. I know they will want you nearby to talk about the dispatches. Don't worry about us. We'll be crewed in the Seamen's Quarter. If you need us, send a runner there. They'll know where to find Chief Petty Officer Ashe Fallow or Marine Corporal Denna Darkwater."

For the next few minutes, the two of them watched the city

as the ketch sailed effortlessly to the prize ship docks.

"Macnay, cant the spars. A ship's captain died defending this ship," Fallow ordered.

"Aye, aye, Chief," Macnay replied, and went into the rigging to carry out that order.

Normally, the spars were set at perfect ninety-degree angles from the masts. Tradition dictated that whenever a captain died on his ship, at the first port of call the ship's masts were angled as much as possible to show the ship mourned the loss of its captain.

Halcyon remembered last year when all of his father's surviving fleet docked and canted their spars in honor to the death of his father.

As the ship came to the dock, Halcyon was over the side and on the dock while the ship was still moving. The dispatches and the report he wrote were in the dispatch case he carried in a bag over his shoulder and he single-mindedly focused on getting to the admiralty. Prepon Fortress, used to dealing with officers, had a coach ready for him and it rode hard down Prepon Way for several miles and then on to Queen's Street.

The admiralty building loomed huge in Halcyon's vision as he got out of the coach, tipped the coachman, and walked up to the giant double doors. The bloodred granite of the building's fashioning was a grim reminder of the importance of the defense of Arcania. As he neared, the doors opened and four stewards, lieutenants, motioned him forward. Each was a wizard armed with a blast-pike.

Halcyon looked down a wide hall of white marble. Huge murals hung on the walls. Most of them showed scenes of battles at sea. He could see many doors on either side of the corridor and another double set of doors at the end of the corridor at least a hundred yards away. More than a hundred people, officers mostly, moved from the corridor into chambers in a constant flow of the king's navy business.

The entire scene was a bit overwhelming for a young man from a very rural county of the empire. *Full speed ahead*, he thought, not knowing what else to do.

Just inside the hall sat a huge desk piled high with work. A marine captain looked up from his notes with a questioning expression on his face.

"I'm Lord Blithe of Lankshire. I need to see the lord of the admiralty," Halcyon said.

The man stood up. Halcyon's title clearly meant something to the man. "Lord Blithe, I'm Captain Allen Dundee, please wait in the Nobles Chamber, Lieutenant Gryphon will take you there. I will personally take your card to the lord of the admiralty," said the captain behind his desk. He reached out a small silver tray, waiting for Halcyon's card.

A suddenly embarrassed Halcyon knew how this worked. He even had a set of cards on the *Sanguine* in his sea chest. Such cards were made of the finest paper using gold leaf to name the lord and his county of origin. Those cards were a bit far away in Halcyon's case. "I must apologize. I've recently seen action off the coast of Drusan at the naval battle of Ordune. All of my cards are on the first-rater dragonwarship *Sanguine*. You will have to accept my word as to my title and lands."

The captain looked as if he didn't believe Halcyon. "Well, this is highly irregular, but I will see what the lord wants to do. You'll be called on shortly. Lieutenant Gryphon, take the lord to the Nobles Chamber."

Gryphon walked away, expecting Lord Halcyon to follow.

"Captain Dundee, my uncle, John Blithe, naval master of the exchequer, has an office somewhere here. Please send a message that his nephew is here for a short time. Ask him if he has a moment to see me, if you would?" Halcyon asked innocently.

It was as if a blast-tube exploded near the four minor officers. They all stood straighter and a new look of respect came to their faces.

Dundee bowed low. "The message will be sent, Lord Blithe. Now if you would, please attend Lieutenant Gryphon."

Passing several doors down the huge corridor, the lieutenant threw open an oak door covered in scenes of sailing ships. It opened on a huge room with crystal lanterns on the ceiling and paintings covering every wall. There were many tables in the room. The floor was of red marble. The large padded chairs looked extremely comfortable. Over a hundred could have sat in this room. There was no one around at present.

"Can I bring you refreshments, Lord Blithe?" the lieutenant asked.

"No, but I would like to know if my uncle can see me," Halcyon replied.

"That's being looked into. I will bring word when we know."

"Thank you, Lieutenant Gryphon," Halcyon said, becoming lost in the grandeur of the chamber. Halcyon loved art. In their castle home, they had ten tapestries with woven scenes and five paintings of former relatives. Just one of the huge paintings in the Nobles Chamber was larger than all the tapestries and pictures put together in Halcyon's castle, and there were at least twenty of those giant-sized paintings just on one wall.

The lieutenant closed the door behind him.

Halcyon had no idea how long he waited in the Nobles Chamber. He hadn't even gotten through looking at the first wall's worth of paintings when the door to the corridor flew open.

"Hal! I can't tell you how happy I am to see you, boy!" Uncle John said, rushing into the room with his arms wide open.

The Blithes were a hugging family. A military family, they all knew how short life was. Everyone got used to giving and receiving quick hugs from a relative the instant they saw them. Halcyon hadn't seen his politically powerful uncle since his father's funeral last year.

John Blithe was the second-oldest of seven brothers and served thirty years as a captain and fleet admiral before the king made him the naval master of the exchequer. At a little under six feet tall, he was a broad-shouldered man with a short limp. His big blue eyes were constantly in motion as he quickly walked up to his nephew and threw his arms around him. He was fiercely hugging Halcyon when he said, "I didn't expect you back for a year or more, boy. Is everything all right?"

"More than all right, Uncle John. I have these dispatches from a glorious victory off the coast of Drusan. My orders had me sail a prize ship back to Ilumin, we battled along the way, and our captain was killed. I had to become the lieutenant. Me, can you imagine a midshipwizard green out of the academy being second-in-command of a mortar ketch?" Halcyon said this all in one breath, gasping for air as his uncle hugged him even tighter with that news.

"Put the boy down, John," a very reserved voice spoke from the door. "We need all the midshipwizards we can get right now."

They turned to see Lord Carl Bassler, the supreme lord of the admiralty, watching them from the door.

Both of them saluted their commanding officer.

"None of that, it's a rare time when Blithes get together. I don't want to get in the way of a family gathering. I do want to read the dispatches he's bringing. Hand them to me please, Midshipwizard. You'll stay in the officers' quarters tonight and probably for the next week as we go over these reports you've brought. Report here tomorrow morning at nine bells and we will go over this information. You two go back to your hugging and whatever it is Blithes do when they get together." Smiling, the second-most-powerful man in the Arcanian Empire left and closed the door behind him, dispatches in his hand.

Halcyon and his uncle looked at themselves and started to laugh. They sat and talked of old times and more pleasant days until late into the day.

The admiralty's officers' quarters were large chambers filled with bunks. Halcyon at sixteen wasn't given a choice of beds. With his rank still at lieutenant, he was assigned a much nicer space than a midshipwizard would have been given. He and his uncle had dinner and talked about the course of the war. He slept that night better than he had in a long time. The next morning, after a light breakfast of bully beef, a lieutenant came looking for him.

"Today, Midshipwizard Blithe, you will face an admiralty board of inquiry. They will go over matters in the dispatches you brought and ask you questions under oath. Follow me," the serious lieutenant said, not waiting for Halcyon to say anything.

"So much for being a lieutenant," Halcyon said to himself.

A long walk took them to one of the countless chambers in the admiralty. Halcyon got quite turned around and didn't know how to get back to his quarters or even find the front door from where he was now.

He walked into a roomy chamber, packed with people, mostly military men. Three admirals sat at the judges' table positioned in the back of the chamber. When Halcyon walked in, he was escorted to a dock and stood all alone in front of the three very stern-faced men.

The middle judge tapped a ship's bell on the table three times with a large dagger and the room grew silent.

Halcyon noted the handle of the dagger was pointed toward him when the blade was put down. He'd just recently learned that this meant he wasn't currently in trouble. That thought didn't stop his nervous stomach from gurgling loudly.

"I am Admiral Black, Admiral Dupont sits on my right, and Admiral Alexander sits on my left. Midshipwizard Third Class Halcyon Blithe, you stand before your judges in a board of inquiry. In that dock you are under oath to tell the truth under pain of imprisonment if you should be caught in a lie."

The nervous midshipwizard watched the court clerk scribbling as fast as he could, every word the admiral said.

"You were assigned to the *Sanguine* as your first duty assignment. Is that correct?" Admiral Black asked.

"Yes, Admiral," Halcyon answered. The midshipwizard looked around the court and saw only stern-faced men. The seriousness of his situation wasn't lost on the young officer.

"Captain Olden reports in his dispatch that you used high magic on the heart of the dragon. He held a court-martial on the matter, judged you guilty, and pardoned you. Is that correct?"

"Yes, Admiral Black," Halcyon said, suddenly feeling very nervous.

"Midshipwizard," Admiral Dupont angrily interrupted Admiral Black. "Your foolish action could have destroyed a warship badly needed by the empire. It was a rash act and if I had been the captain you would have hung the next day."

The admiral didn't ask a question, so Halcyon said nothing. Halcyon's face drained of blood. He knew the admiral was right. The Navy Articles were clear on the subject of using high magic on board ship for any reason.

A calm Admiral Alexander said, "He's been pardoned, Tom,

that's not why we are here today. Let Lawrence continue."

"Ahem," Admiral Black continued. "You used high magic to stop the dragon's heart from blowing up. A saboteur cursed you, and in becoming cured, it was revealed that you are a dragon speaker as well as a rope speaker. Is all of this correct?"

"Yes, Admiral," Halcyon replied, trying to say as little as possible.

"If I may?" Admiral Alexander asked. "In the battle of Ordune you were part of a fleet facing superior numbers of enemies in open battle. Is that correct?"

"Yes, Admiral." Halcyon had no idea where this questioning was going, but he was vastly relieved to hear the admiral's words and the fact that they didn't care about his use of high magic.

"During the course of the battle, you were ordered to take the prize ketch *Salamander*, under the orders of your Captain Olden. Lieutenant Jordan reported that you were of help because you knew the language of the Maleen. Is this correct?" Alexander asked.

"Yes, Admiral." Halcyon tried to keep calm. All three admirals were scowling now as if they were eating something that tasted bad.

As Halcyon looked around the room, he saw no sympathetic faces. He looked upon a large group of naval veterans. Scars, eye patches, and sun-darkened skin returned his looks without smiles. Halcyon had no doubt he could be in trouble again. All he could hope for was that they wouldn't punish him for his use of demon spells against that deadly ship.

"Your report and the reports of Chief Fallow and Marine Corporal Darkwater speak of a battle with a demon ship. The captain of the ketch, an Elan Swordson, reports that you turned into a demon in the course of the battle. The statements from all of you are amazing. You must now tell the court how a lad of sixteen who just came into his magic eight months ago could have used the spells and even known the demon spells used to destroy that demon ship?"

"Clearly he isn't a demon now," Admiral Black noted for the record.

No one was smiling. There was a clear accusation in the question that Halcyon was irregular or did something wrong. As Halcyon marshaled his thoughts, he wondered if they thought he was a spy or traitor or maybe even a demon spawn. His gut wrenched at that idea. He loved his country more than his life. How was he going to convince them of this?

"If I may," a voice spoke up from the back of the crowded chamber.

"Let the record show that Lord of the Exchequer John Blithe is asking the court for its time. Lord Blithe, come forward and say what you will." Admiral Black waved Halcyon's uncle forward.

Uncle John came to stand before Halcyon in his dock. Somehow, Halcyon could sense that everything would be all right now that his uncle was speaking for him.

"I would remind the court that Blithes have been nobly serving in the royal navies of Arcania for over seven generations." John Blithe moved back and forth in front of the three judges and sternly looked at each and every one of them. "Many generations before that, my family foolishly consorted with demons and as a result there is a demonic heritage running through the family line. We aren't proud of that fact, but who among us can control their heritage?"

The crowd gasped at this statement. Such heritage filled Arcanians with fear. Demons were heartless monsters known for their evil power. Could those consorting with demons be any less evil in their natures?

Lord Blithe continued. "Down through the centuries my family has diligently worked to fight the evil done by demonkind. We've spent a great deal of our wealth on equipment to help others and us in that fight. When Halcyon was born the seventh son of a seventh son, the family realized that in Halcyon we had a magnificent fighter of evil. At a very young age, he began his training in the ways of demonkind. When he was twelve, we were disheartened to see that he didn't come into his magic, but his training never stopped. Great expense brought us the best in demon-fighting spells. Despite the fact that he couldn't cast them, he was trained in their use. At sixteen, Halcyon came into his magical heritage. This allowed him to enter the naval academy for midshipwizards. You see before you a young man able to fight the worst of demons on their own territory. On the subject of his ability to speak Maleen, we Blithes have been in the thick of battle for generations. We've learned a trick or two as a family and one of them is know your enemy. All the Blithes can speak Maleen and our children are taught that language at an early age. Don't think wrong of him because he has talents you all might not have. There are no secret agendas following the boy. He's an honest navy man sworn to protect Arcania. That's all I have to say."

Uncle John turned to Halcyon, shook his hand. His uncle sat down in front of him, a protective shield against all the navy might want to throw at the Blithes.

Admiral Black rose. "We thank you, Lord Blithe, for that explanation. Your words clear up several mysteries we had about Midshipwizard Blithe."

The three admirals talked quietly together for several minutes. Finally, Admiral Black stood up.

"I believe this court has heard enough testimony. On a strong suggestion from Captain Olden's report, we've decided to act. Mr. Blithe, please leave the dock and come before us."

Halcyon had no idea what was going to happen next, but the order was easy to follow.

He came to the front of the table and Admiral Black came around.

"With the power invested by the king of Arcania into my hands, I promote you, Halcyon Blithe, to Midshipwizard First Class."

Smiles of approval erupted from the courtroom.

Halcyon stood there, thunderstruck. Of all the endings to this court, he didn't expect this one.

Admiral Black went on, "Midshipwizard Blithe, we'll need your talents on the quarterdeck as soon as possible. Study hard for your lieutenant's tests so that I can be pinning captain's stars on your shoulders in a year or two."

He turned Halcyon around to face the court and he received a rousing applause started by his uncle and joined in by everyone in the room.

VI

A Kingly Moment

HIS MAJESTY'S ARTICLES OF WAR: ARTICLE XXVI

Such punishment as a court-martial may adjudge may be inflicted on any person in the navy who is guilty through negligence or carelessness in obeying orders or culpably inefficient in the performance of duty.

"Augh," Halcyon groaned with a splitting headache.

The midshipwizard slowly got up from his cot wondering how the entire admiralty building could be shaking so much from side to side; then memories of last night hit him hard. His uncle insisted they celebrate Halcyon's promotion and took him to several taverns filled with eager ship's officers all wanting to buy him a tankard of ale. Navy traditions held that great luck would come to any officer who bought a newly promoted midshipman or midshipwizard a drink.

As Halcyon rubbed the sleep out of his eyes, he was fairly sure most of the Arcanian navy stood extremely lucky today.

The sun blazed down on him through the high windows of his room. He couldn't remember a time when the sun was so bright. He used the washstand to clear the gum from his eyelids, but that didn't help the throbbing behind his eyes.

Uncle John told him he would be serving on a new dragon-frigate. He was looking forward to the duty. Stationed on a new ship, with his original sea chest across the sea, he would have to purchase an entire sea chest of things. He had his magical military equipment, as he was wearing it when he left the *Sanguine* for the *Salamander*, but his jackets, shirts, and other things needed for normal shipboard life were all still on the *Sanguine*, not to be seen for who knows how long. Uncle John had given him more than enough gold to buy whatever he needed.

Leaving the officers' quarters, he bumped into his friend Dart Surehand.

"Dart, what are you doing here? Look at you, they've made you a First Class Midshipwizard," Halcyon said in surprise.

"Halcyon, well done on your promotion. When I got back to Ilumin on the *Migol*, my father and his brother, the king, didn't want me on a warship again. I put a stop to that type of thinking; I'm going out on the *Migol* when it's refitted. I had to promise to take an Ilumin post after this tour of duty, but I should see some action on the ship you and I captured."

Dart Surehand was a large sixteen-year-old with massive muscles and a charming, royal way about him. He didn't want his highborn heritage getting in the way of his naval service, but his father and his uncle, the king, had other ideas. They held thoughts about his fate that Dart constantly battled. Dart had been unusually kind to Halcyon when they met and served on the dragonship *Sanguine*. Halcyon saw Dart leave for Ilumin in a prize ship just a few months ago.

"I have to get a new sea chest for my next assignment. I was just going out now to shop for the things I need," Halcyon said, glad to see his friend again.

"Sink me, Hal; you're going to have to buy a bit more than uniforms this morning. I'm bringing you this." Dart handed the midshipwizard a stiff white envelope with the king's royal seal in wax on the back. Someone had carefully written "Lord Halcyon Blithe" on the front of the card in golden ink. "When I saw that they were dragging you to the ball tonight, I got permission to bring over the invitation myself. Sink me if they aren't godawful affairs, but it will be good to partner with a shipmate tonight at least."

Halcyon turned the envelope over and over in his hands, still a little groggy from the night before. There were ribbons flowing from the huge wax seal on the back. His name appeared in gold ink on the front. He opened it up, hating to rip the expensive paper. The letter inside was just as stunning. Written in more gold ink, it read,

His Majesty Artur Andul Ilumin Surehand requests the presence of Lord Halcyon Blithe, Squire of Lankshire, Regent of the Temple Lands, Protector of the Faithful in Lankshire, First Class Midshipwixard in His Majesty's Navy, to the Officers' Ball tonight.

A state affair, please dress as the lord you are.

Signed,

Artur Surehand

"The king signed this himself," Halcyon said in awe.

"And we haven't a moment to lose. We're going to the palace tailor to get you some new things. He might as well cut you up some officer's clothes as well." Dart was a bit too cheerful for Halcyon right at that moment, but there wasn't much that the hungover midshipwizard could do about that.

Even with a pounding head, Halcyon knew he couldn't refuse the invitation and he had to look right. With a sigh, he said, "Let's go, my friend. You steer our boat and I'll row."

Ilumin was bustling under the morning sun as merchants hawked their wares on the city streets. A royal coach took them from the admiralty over the Bridge of Tears and to the king's royal abode. The humble Halcyon was just a bit astounded at the size and grandeur of the palace. Surrounded by huge gardens, the black granite of the structure rose up as the tallest building of the city. Outer towers at the four compass points bristled with blast-tube ports. Several divisions of Arcanian troops constantly maneuvered in and around the palace. The pair noticed a squad of horse guards riding down the busy street.

Their carriage let them out several hundred yards in front of the palace, allowing the pair to walk up to the front as Dart gave his friend a verbal commentary on the palace.

"When I'm in Ilumin, I live in the west wing with all the cousins and relatives of the king and queen." Dart waved his hand toward that section of the palace as they walked up to the front portal.

Four burly guards held blast-pikes at the ready. Each was a wizard with white hair braided at the back of his helm.

"The center of the palace presents a honeycomb of chambers, the great hall, and official offices. That's where we'll find the tailor," Surehand advised.

"Dart, are you sure the royal tailor is allowed to help me?" Hal asked as they went past the guards, who obviously recognized Dart and let them in.

"Sink me, Hal, it's the least my uncle's man can do. Normally, he doesn't do much during the year but make a cloak or two for the king."

They walked through a maze of palace corridors. The guards at certain cross sections waved Dart through and gave Halcyon a bored look. There wasn't a guard less than six feet tall and the midshipwizard must have seen a hundred of them. Most of them seemed to be wizards as well, as marked by their snow white hair.

Halcyon's stomach started to growl in protest when they finally reached the chambers of the tailor.

Dart threw open the double doors and a titter of protest erupted from the tall man inside.

A high-voiced fellow, in a stunning white outfit, bowed low before the two navy officers.

"Lord Surehand, who have you brought with you today?" the man simpered.

"Chauncey, we have a tough one for you this morning. Chauncey Tailor is an amazing artist with a scissor and thread." Dart was grinning from ear to ear and Halcyon had no clue as to why.

The tailor bowed low at Dart's words.

"You are far too kind, young lord. I live to serve King and country, just as you two strapping officers do," the tailor said.

"This is Lord Blithe; he needs a new set of clothes for the king's ball tonight. He also needs uniforms and shipboard clothes for a tour of duty in the king's navy, if you please." Dart flopped himself down on a large leather chair while Chauncey circled round and round Halcyon, looking him up and down.

"Lord Blithe, please step up on the black marble stand over there," Chauncey said imperiously, pointing toward an alcove with mirrored walls. "I'm sure I've made uniforms for some of your more famous uncles. I think I can manage a few things for their gifted first-class-midshipwizard nephew."

"If you could get me something to eat and drink, I will follow you anywhere," the young Blithe pleaded, as everyone could now hear his stomach growl.

"Not a bit of it, and stop tempting me, my dear boy." Chauncey smiled. "We can't have our young heroes dying of hunger and thirst on my very doorstep." He stepped over to an alcove and pulled on a cord three times.

The room they were in displayed many different types of alcoves and doors. There was a huge pile of cloth bolts spilling over several tables on one side of the room. Halcyon knew little of cloth prices, but from the look of the silks and satins there was a king's ransom in cloth there.

Halcyon moved onto the marble, and the images in the three mirrors behind him arcanely misted into different-suited versions of himself. The first showed him in a royal blue suit with way too much lace on the neck and sleeves. The second image of Halcyon had him in a golden suit with impossibly high colors and wide lapels. The third image showed him in a perfectly tailored captain's uniform.

Halcyon much preferred the uniform.

"Is it possible that I can go to this affair of the king in my navy uniform?" Halcyon asked Dart.

A large roll filled with meat and a tankard of wine were thrust into his hands by the tailor. More trays of food and drink were packed onto a series of tables and Dart mounded a plate as he watched his nervous friend withstand the poking and prodding of Chauncey while measuring him.

"Don't be silly, my dear boy," Chauncey said, circling round and round Halcyon as he made measurements and notes in a small book. From a pouch at his side, he sprinkled a handful of blue, sparkling dust in the air atop Halcyon. The dust spread itself out into a perfect form of Halcyon's body. The dust form moved as Halcyon did, twisting this way and that as Halcyon looked at his overdressed images in the mirrors surrounding the pedestal. The midshipwizard munched on his food, taking everything in.

Halcyon noted that Chauncey's image didn't appear in the mirrors and now there were versions of the midshipwizard in green, purple, and violet suits, looking far too fancy to be functional dress.

Chauncey noted the concerned expression on Halcyon's face as the midshipwizard looked into the mirrors.

"Dear, sweet boy, don't you worry about a thing. I make clothes for all the admirals coming to the palace. I know what you sea types like and you can count on me," Chauncey minced, patting Halcyon's shoulder.

The midshipwizard didn't quite know what to think about the tailor. The man must be good or he wouldn't be working for the king, but he acted so oddly.

"Besides the normal kit of clothes, I'll need a fencing uniform. Have you made one of those before?" Halcyon asked, getting into the swing of things and sounding eager at the thought of getting into a fencing outfit again.

Chauncey snapped his fingers and all of the magical mirrors showed Halcyon in a perfect-fitting fencing uniform. There was even a fencing foil imaged at his hip.

"We fence here at the capital as well. Probably not as well as the men of Lankshire," the tailor sarcastically noted, "but well enough. I myself can often be found tilting blades with the dandies in the Royal Fencing Studio most days. I look forward to bouting with you one day, my lord."

Halcyon made a mental note to not judge people by their looks. He couldn't imagine this man with a blade in his hand. He briefly wondered how the tailor knew Halcyon was Lankshire-born.

"Oh, you probably want to practice a bit first, Hal. Chauncey here regularly beats the fencing instructors, much to their irritation." Dart had finished stuffing his face.

"That's it, that's it," Chauncey said wistfully. "I'll have the dress suit sent to Lord Surehand's chambers late this afternoon. The rest of the things, from shirts to uniforms to that natty fencing suit, will be in a magical sea chest taken to your ship in three days. Leave word on what other things you need for that chest and the staff will make sure you get what equipment you need. Now you go and do whatever you navy men do."

Chauncey turned away and ordered several aides Halcyon hadn't seen before to get various bolts of cloth.

"Hey, we've got the rest of the day, is there anything else you need for your next duty post?" Dart asked.

"There are lots of things I need. I don't know where the markets and shops are in Ilumin. I'd really appreciate your help." Halcyon felt much better now, and liked the fact that his friend Dart was available.

The music struck them long before they finally reached the ballroom. The beat of it told the pair of midshipwizards they were close to the gala event. Halcyon must have appeared nervous, because Dart felt the need to comment on his appearance.

"Stop pulling at your jacket. Don't they have grand celebrations in your castle?"

"Twenty people, tops, with a minstrel and his flute or drum. I had no sisters to teach me how to dance," Halcyon said nervously. "We were a castle of men with few women about. Come to think of it, I'd rather face a fleet of Maleen than this event tonight."

"Come on; sink me, Hal, at this affair you have lovely young women wanting to dance and old warhorses wanting to share their favorite war story. It doesn't matter how you dance, as long as you look good, and you do. You will be the man of the hour, as you know about the great victory off the coast of Drusan. It's a good chance to eat and drink the best food of the empire and enjoy yourself. It's full speed ahead, my friend." Dart said this pushing him around the corner into a huge archway.

Hal stood at the top of a ship-wide stairway. The spectacle of the grand dance, displayed in all its glory below him, took his breath away. Dancers swayed back and forth across a huge ballroom in time to the music. Clusters of women, like batches of flowers in a garden, sat or stood at the edges of the dancing area. Large tables filled with food and drink stood out on either side of the ballroom and hundreds of officers could be seen clustered about these.

"Why couldn't I wear my uniform? All of them did," Halcyon asked Dart.

"You are a lord of the realm, most of them aren't. My uncle invited the lord, not the midshipwizard," Dart answered.

"Ahem, your invitation, my lord," asked the majordomo.

Halcyon looked around to see the majordomo of the dance with his huge staff of state. Halcyon quickly handed over his invitation. To his horror, the man began shouting out all of Hal's titles.

"I present Lord Halcyon Blithe, Squire of Lankshire, Regent of the Temple Lands, and Protector of the Faithful in

Lankshire, and recently promoted First Class Midshipwizard in His Majesty's Navy."

A very dazed Halcyon started walking down the stairs, weak at the knees. How did the majordomo know of his recent promotion?

He heard his friend Surehand announced at the top of the stairs.

"I present Lord Dartolomus Surehand, Squire of the Ilumin North, Lord of the West Castle, First Nephew to Our Gracious Majesty, and recently promoted First Class Midshipwizard in His Majesty's Navy," announced the domo.

Halcyon noticed no one stopped when his name was announced. After all, he was only a minor noble of a small county in the empire. When Dart was announced, many dancers and others stopped what they were doing to look up at him.

Halcyon could almost feel the weight of the crowd's stares on his friend.

"Sink me, Hal, keep moving. When in unknown waters, don't give the enemy time to take your weather gauge. Didn't they teach you anything at the academy?" Dart quipped.

"Enemy, I see no enemy here. Do you think there are spies?" Halcyon asked in all seriousness.

"In life, especially in court life, there are enemies and there are enemies," Dart said, hurrying down the stairs now in front of Halcyon. The other midshipwizard picked up his pace in order to keep up.

"Halcyon, who's more deadly," Dart asked, "the Maleen trooper with his polearm or the ancient mother bent on getting you to marry her extremely ugly daughter?"

Halcyon didn't even need to think about that. He'd seen his share of old ladies with ugly daughters. "The old mother every time, Dart."

"Here's another one for you. Who's more dangerous, a king who really wants to command you to never sail again and wants to keep you on dry land for the rest of your life, or a murderous captain who continually puts you in the front of the battle at every opportunity because he doesn't like who your relatives are?" Dart turned and was looking at Halcyon in all seriousness as he asked the last question.

Halcyon stopped smiling, as he knew his friend wasn't joking. "You and I are destined to captain our own ships in raging battles against the enemy. Not a king or the craftiest mother with the loveliest of daughters will take that destiny from us. Did you mention something about fine food and strong drink? Just the two things for a headache, I hear."

"Sink me, I did, and it's just over the horizon from here. Full speed ahead, my friend," Dart said with a big grin on his face.

"Full speed ahead, aye, Captain," Halcyon replied.

There was all manner of finger food, making the tables groan from the weight. Dart and Halcyon filled a plate each. As they reached the end, someone bashed up against Hal, making him spill his food.

"Sorry, my lord," the man said.

Halcyon spun in anger to see a very drunk, now Lieutenant Elan Swordson. Halcyon wasn't in uniform, but he almost saluted, able to hold his hand down only with great effort.

Servants in gold rushed to clean up the mess and in seconds the spilled food was gone and so were the servants.

"Blithe, I had no idea you were a lord of the realm," Elan said, weaving back away from Dart and Halcyon. "I passed my lieutenant test this morning and was invited to this gathering as a result."

The man would not be remembering the night, both midshipwizards suspected.

"Congratulations," Halcyon said in envy. He would have to wait an entire year before he could take his test to become a lieutenant. He also knew he didn't yet have the skills to pass such an examination. Whatever unkind things he thought about Swordson, the man knew his job.

"I didn't like what you did on the *Salamander*. The crew respected your actions and I still can't understand why. You turned into a demon, for god's sake!" Elan was making a spectacle of himself.

"You need to calm yourself, Lieutenant," Dart said, trying to quiet the man.

"We could take this discussion to a quieter place," the now-grim Blithe asked Elan.

"I won't be quiet and we will be going nowhere. You need to be taken down a peg or two, Meddie, and I'm just the one to do it!" Elan was shouting now and others around them were turning to look.

Dart moved in and grabbed Swordson's arm with the obvious intent of pushing him to a side room. The drunken lieutenant pulled back out of Dart's grasp and bashed into a woman coming up to the group.

She fell to the floor and Halcyon rushed to her side and picked her up.

Even drunk, Swordson knew he'd done an unpardonable act. "I'm so sorry, my lady," he mumbled.

She didn't hear. She looked into Halcyon's eyes and found herself enchanted.

For his part, he found himself captivated by a cream-colored face framed in white curls. He was lost in her deep green eyes.

For Halcyon, the music, the people all around, even the idiot lieutenant vanished from his awareness. He drank in the beauty of the woman as he effortlessly helped her to her feet.

"My lord, you must think me a clumsy idiot," she said in a voice that was a new type of music to his ears.

"Not a bit of it, please call me Halcyon. May I have this dance?" he said in a rush, forgetting he didn't know how to dance, and just wanting to be beside her for a bit more.

"How could I refuse any request from my floor rescuer?" She canted her head and listened to the music for a bit. "This is an easy one; I shan't land on the floor again." She showed no awareness of the daze she'd put Halcyon in and the pair walked away from Dart and Elan.

Hearts beating as one, they joined the flow of the waltz, having no notion of the swirl of dancers around them.

"I'll see that one broken, I will," Swordson mumbled, more to himself than to those nearby.

"You'll find that difficult, Lieutenant," Dart remarked. "He's meeting with the king in a few moments and my uncle and I like Lord Blithe a lot, if you get my meaning."

The narrow looks Dart gave Swordson made the man back away and leave.

She felt light as a feather in Halcyon's arms. He couldn't ever remember enjoying himself more on the dance floor. "Did the lieutenant hurt you, my lady?"

"Please call me Teagan. I'm actually Lady Teagan Delesanor of the House of Et, but it would take you a week to say all that. No, he didn't hurt me at all. I've taken much worse spills on the bouting tracks here at the palace," she answered.

"They call me Halcyon Blithe, but my old and newfound friends all call me Hal," he said, looking down on her smiling face.

Teagan stood about five feet, nine inches tall, but her dress hid if she had tall shoes on or not. She was pleasantly figured, and her naturally curly white hair flowed down her back to her small waist. Her full lips held just the tint of color, but that was the only makeup touching her stunning face.

"A Blithe, why you aren't at all what I pictured from that famous family name. First, I thought Blithes never left their warships. I had heard that you were all mad battlers with two swords in your hands and deadly attack spells constantly erupting from your lips. I've never heard of a Blithe courtier before, are you unusual for your family, Hal?" The Lady Teagan said this last particularly emphasizing his name.

Halcyon quite liked the sound of his name on her lips.

"I left my swords and death spells in my chambers. I can get them if you wish. Is there an evil you need slaying?"

"No, however, there are two king's guards that I wish would fall down and die." She said this snappishly as she looked past his shoulder.

The music stopped and they found themselves near a wide entrance out of the ballroom.

"Just so you know, I would have let you kiss me tonight," she said, drawing herself out of his grasp and taking out a fan from some hidden location and quickly fanning herself with it in obvious irritation.

Halcyon turned to discover two of the king's royal guards. They both bowed low in front of him.

"Lord Blithe, the king requests your immediate presence. You must follow us." They turned to leave.

Halcyon felt a pinprick on his hand. He turned to see Teagan holding a small amulet with a drop of his blood on its pin.

"Just to remember you, I know I won't be seeing you again tonight," she said with such a sad look on her face, and he found himself not knowing what to say in response.

He turned away from her and followed the guards out of the ballroom.

They joined another pair of guards and Dart coming down the large hall.

"When my uncle the king wants to talk to someone, he makes it very hard for that someone to refuse his request. She's very pretty," Dart chided his friend.

"Talk to the king or take a lovely lady out into the garden and be kissed. It's a tough choice, but two king's guards helped me make it. She is pretty and probably won't ever talk to me again after that exit of mine," Hal remarked.

They walked quickly to a side chamber where four royal guards stood at attention. Dart's guards knocked on the door and the four guards took up positions beside the door.

"They are expecting you," one of the guards said.

The thought of the king expecting Halcyon sent chills up his spine. Halcyon had never even seen the king, let alone talked with him.

Dart led the way.

They entered a smallish chamber with several comfortable-looking chairs around a fireplace. A table off to the side showed itself filled with food and wine bottles.

"Take up a drink and come over here so that we can look at you," came a voice from the other side of a huge chair.

Dart and Halcyon did what they were told. With drinks in their hands, they came near the fireplace and saw the king and his son. There was no mistaking the fact that the two men shared the same ancestors. They looked just the same, with long noses and square chins. The same purple eyes stared back at them from each royal head. Both midshipwizards went down on one knee in respect.

"Up, up," the aged man said as he gestured them to empty chairs beside his son.

The pair stood up, but didn't want to sit down in front of the king.

The prince rose and held out his hand to Halcyon. "It's jolly good to meet the latest Blithe to join the navy."

Halcyon thought the prince had a firm grip. "Prince Viden, I'm proud to meet you and the king."

"Dartolomus, you and Halcyon sit down, my old neck doesn't want to crink up at you all night."

The two men sat down instantly.

"I've asked you here to try and convince my son of something I've known for years," the king said as he drank from his chalice. "Every year for the last five years, the Maleen have sent ambassadors to try and get Arcania to join their empire. The price for refusing their request is continued war. The prince wishes to accept their request this year. Please tell him why we can't."

"Prince Viden, you've heard my position on this topic. We can't join them in their effort to gobble up the world," Dart said. "Once the Maleen Empire has taken everything on the mainland, they will again turn their forces toward us."

"Dart, we need time to reorganize and grow strong again. Our fleets are thinly spread all over the ocean," a concerned Prince Viden replied.

"We can't ever appear to join the Maleen," a matter-of-fact Halcyon replied earnestly to the prince's remark. "I've fought their shapechangers. The Maleen can't be trusted. My father and grandfather died fighting them in this war of the enemy's making. If we join with them, the world will see us as them. Other countries will never trust us again."

"Just so, young Blithe, just so," the king said.

A petulant prince sat back in his leather chair and turned his head away from the group, clearly not happy with Halcyon's words.

"Ah, you see what happens when the prince hears anything he doesn't like." The old king smiled at his son. "He's going to have to learn to not show every thought in his head with the actions of his body. I've been working on that feature of his personality, but clearly not hard enough."

"Viden's grown up only knowing war. I can understand his desire for peace," Dart said, always the one for compromising. "He's heard of many cousins and uncles killed in a war across the sea. He battles in his own way since you won't let him fight in the armies or the navy."

"I know, I know," the king said. "I've finally allowed him to take up the air service. We've only five airships, since it requires the magic of a seventh son of a seventh son to make such vehicles. I was outmaneuvered by your uncles, Halcyon, or you would have gone right from the academy to the air force."

Halcyon had heard of the air force, but hadn't seen one of the famous airships. They were constantly fighting the large dragons and other monster types in the air. Outsiders remarked that the crafts were more trouble than they were worth. He had no idea his uncles interceded with the king on his behalf.

"We will not let this night continue on a sour note. My son, discharge your royal duty," the king ordered.

Viden leapt to his feet, all smiles now. "Midshipwizards, attention," he commanded.

Both friends stood up and came to attention.

Viden reached up on the fireplace ledge and pulled down two small cases. "By the authority of the king, I award the Golden Star of Arcania to both of you for major services to the empire."

At these words, both men's hearts beat with excitement. The Gold Star was the second-highest medal awarded in the navy. This sought-after honor was awarded only by royal decree.

Viden placed the large-ribboned medals around their necks and firmly shook their hands. He then reached over and poured them another chalice of excellent Arcanian red. The king looked on the actions of his son with fatherly pride.

The four of them talked long into the night about the naval battle of Ordune and the action where Dart took the prize ship.

The sun rose above the palace when Halcyon and Dart left the king's chamber. Neither one of the men was a bit tired, as talking with the king filled them with an enthusiasm they'd never felt before.

VII

✲ ✲ ✲

Onboard the Rage

The first-class midshipwizard stepped off the coach onto the sawdust-covered planks of the docks of Ilumin City, his sheathed sword in hand, as he couldn't wear it while sitting in the coach. His new sea chest floated off the top of the coach as Halcyon threw the coach driver a silver piece. The man acknowledged the tip with a wave of his hand, clucking his coach horses forward.

Halcyon's orders directed him to the new dragonfrigate, *Rage*, fitted and ready for sailing at the docks for its maiden voyage. The midshipwizard knew it would be the only dragonship in the harbor because dragonships didn't get along with each other and were kept apart on purpose. There were only thirty sea-dragon warships in all the numerous war fleets of Arcania. Those who served on them were considered the elite of the navy—and the craziest, as dragons were normally fond of eating humans.

Even several streets away, he could hear the nervous trumpeting of the sea-dragon ship. Plumes of water flew high in the air from the dragon's mouth. That was a sure sign the dragon wasn't happy and wanted the world to know about it.

Approaching, he could just make out the head of the dragon over the rooftops. As he turned the corner toward his new ship, he saw a number of women on the docks. He knew these women to be wives and girlfriends of ship's crew, seeing their men off, possibly for the last time.

Halcyon was amazed to see the Lady Teagan Delesanor Et walking toward him from that group of women. Meeting for the first time several days ago at the king's ball, in today's morning light, she was even more stunning than he remembered her.

He bowed low. "Lady Et, this is an unexpected pleasure."

"Unexpected for you, perhaps," she said, her frown only making her features cuter. "Do you have any idea how long it takes a lady of quality to get ready to meet anyone or anything early in the morning? No, of course you don't, you're a man, doing in minutes what it takes a lady hours to accomplish. Chance had nothing to do with this meeting, my ballroom-floor hero."

Her angry tone belied the grin on her lips and she looked at him from the side of her eyes, in a very fetching manner. "I asked my father to determine when your ship would be leaving and I got here before you to see my brave new friend off."

She said the word "friend" in an odd way to Halcyon's hearing. It seemed to be filled with a meaning that implied he could be much more than a friend.

"I'm honored in any case. Do you usually come to the docks to watch ships . . ." He suddenly realized what his question implied and shut his mouth. She was smiling at him and he found it amazingly hard to think when she did that.

"I have a present for you. Please tell me you like it," she begged.

From her white-gloved hands he took a locket. When he opened it, he discovered a rare timepiece inside.

"Lady Et, this is too princely a gift. Watches are wondrous things, I can't take this," he said in surprise.

Also inside the cover of the watch was a tiny oil painting of Teagan in the same dress she wore that morning. The pretty face in the picture smiled up at him, just as she was smiling now.

"I placed a minor air spell on the locket. I'll always know where you are, I hope you don't mind? It's a friendship gift; you do want to be my friend, don't you?" she asked.

"Of course I do, my lady; anything that helps me think of you is a welcome gift indeed." He smiled down at her. The green gown displayed her ample figure to perfection. "You really shouldn't be on the docks all alone. Should I see you to your home?" he asked, knowing he really didn't have the time to see her anywhere.

"Oh no, I have all manner of guards and a companion by my coach. I made them bide while I talked alone to you. My request quite startled Lady Alice, my guardian."

The sea dragon, his new dragon, trumpeted its nervousness not a hundred yards away. Halcyon really had to go.

"Lady Et, I would stay here forever talking to you, but my ship sails with the morning tide. It seems we're always leaving each other suddenly," Halcyon said with a heavy sigh.

"Duty, I understand. Sailing, I understand, but this time you're not leaving my side without getting a kiss goodbye," she said, rising on her tip toes and closing her eyes.

A surprised Halcyon gave her his first nonsisterly kiss. He'd kissed his female cousins a time or two, and his mother of course, but this was vastly different.

As their lips touched, she threw her arms around him and crushed her body close to his, quite taking his breath away.

She pulled back first, her smile telling him she must have been pleased with his novice effort.

"Thank you, that's a memory I'll treasure," he said.

"I have a wish to make many more memories like that, Midshipwizard Halcyon Blithe; do come back safe so that I can kiss you more than once and not fear for your life at kissing's end," she said.

For some reason, unknown to him, she burst into tears and ran from his side.

"What did I say?" he asked of the air, standing stunned on the docks. Her coach drove away and he walked glumly to his ship.

Halcyon looked over to the trumpeting sea dragon. The Arcanian frigate rested tightly on the back of the giant creature. A series of special clamps in steel caissons kept the ship on the creature's back. The creature obviously didn't like being at the docks. Vastly more maneuverable than normal ships, seadragon warships could ignore the wind in a battle, giving them a tremendous advantage in positioning themselves to fire their blast-tubes.

"*Calm down,*" Halcyon thought to the dragon.

The creature instantly stopped roaring and turned its long neck around to look down at Halcyon.

Halcyon stopped walking toward the ship for a moment, caught by surprise. Dragon speaking was a new talent to Halcyon and usually he had a coating of tannin oil on his hand to effectively communicate with the sea dragon.

"*What you?*" the sea dragon asked in his mind.

When Halcyon was on the *Sanguine*, that dragon could communicate in a sort of halting mental speech. The thoughts of the dragon coming to Halcyon's mind usually sounded like baby talk. All that changed when the midshipwizard used the tannin oil. The speech of the dragon became clear and sounded much more adult to the mind of Halcyon with the oil in use.

"*I'm your new friend. We'll get you some food soon. We'll be swimming away from this dock shortly,*" he thought to the sea dragon.

"*Good, too many bad smells here,*" the dragon answered back.

Straightening his shoulders, he stepped onto the gangplank of the *Rage*.

"*My name is Sort, not Rage,*" the sea dragon mentally told Halcyon.

Halcyon had just recently read that young sea dragons always had their own names, but quickly learned to like being called the name of the ship on their backs.

The distractions of the ship broke the communication in Halcyon's mind.

The bustle of the dragonfrigate made the midshipwizard feel at home again. Gone was the nervousness of his duty on the *Salamander*. He briefly wondered, as he was piped aboard the ship, if it was the desire to serve on a dragonship that brought the firmness to his step.

"Ahem, your orders, Midshipwizard," the huge man in front of him said, with his shovel-sized hand out.

Halcyon took the packet of orders from his breast pocket and handed them over, snapping to attention.

His captain stood about six feet tall, a massive man, almost as broad as he was tall. Not an ounce of fat on him, his arms were as muscled and almost as large as his legs.

"I'm Captain Gord-un; I've seen you've already communicated with our ship. He's a might nervous and you seem to have calmed him down considerably. That's something I've been trying to do all morning. Well done, I say, well done."

The captain wasn't smiling as he gave Halcyon praise. He had a huge red beard, very dwarflike in its cut, as the beard was at least two feet long and braided with gems in the braid as all dwarves with a bit of wealth placed in their beards. He had a shock of red unruly hair under his captain's hat that was also very dwarflike, as the hair shot out in odd angles from his head in a wild tangle. Most dwarves that Blithe had seen had the distinctive red hair Gord-un sported, but they were never six feet tall.

There was a very nonregulation war axe at his hip (nonregulation in that it was huge and Halcyon thought Arcanian captains were ordered by the admiralty to use sabers). The weapon looked too large and heavy to use effectively in combat, even considering the massive muscles the captain sported.

"I've read your file from your brief service on the *Sanguine.* Some of the things I read there do not please me. You'll find I'm a fair man, but I expect my officers to think for themselves and act in the best interests of this ship first and then their captain. If you don't toe the line and do what's needed you'll find that your proud family name and the fact that the king pinned a medal on your chest a few days ago won't save you from my wrath. Do you understand me, Midshipwizard First Class Blithe?" the captain asked.

"Aye, aye, sir," Halcyon answered, still standing at attention. A cold shiver ran down his spine. The man in front of him was fierce. Halcyon had no doubt that the sternest measures would be used against him if he made a mistake that endangered the ship and crew.

"Chief Fallow, front and center," ordered the captain.

Ashe Fallow appeared up from the ladder rising from the hold.

Halcyon couldn't believe his friend from the *Sanguine* held a commission on this dragonfrigate. It was an unusually pleasant surprise. The chief came from the same county as Halcyon. As a fellow Lankshire man, the chief had several times given Halcyon invaluable advice.

"Chief, get this midshipwizard squared away. We're sailing in an hour and I want to get my orders read to the crew as the seventh bell sounds," the captain ordered.

"Aye, aye, Captain," Ashe replied.

The captain saluted back to Halcyon and went up to the quarterdeck.

Halcyon gave the chief a warm handshake. "Chief, by the gods, how did you get here?"

The chief was smiling from ear to ear. "In this man's navy there's a special network of those in the know. I'm usually at the top of that network. Denna and I heard where you were stationed next and we thought we would come along. We like the swirl of action that seems to happen around you, Mr. Blithe."

They went down into the lower deck and Ashe showed Halcyon the wardroom and midshipmen's quarters. Hal's sea chest was there, filled with new clothes from the king's tailor.

"Attention!" came the shout, and four very nervous midshipmen stood at attention alongside their hammocks.

Ashe made the introductions. "Mr. Blithe, these are your charges on this shakedown cruise. Let me introduce you to Midshipman Fifth Class Hurchial Act-un."

The twelve-year-old stepped forward and shook Halcyon's hand in a firm grip. The young Hurchial couldn't be more than twelve, but his half-dwarven heritage brought man-sized muscles to his arms. All those of Arcania with an "-un" at the end of their names were at least half-dwarf. Hurchial stood a little over five feet tall, with broad shoulders and dark red hair cut short on his head.

"Midshipman Act-un, it's my pleasure to meet you," Halcyon said.

The young midshipman had trouble looking Halcyon in the face, from his nervousness. He quickly stepped back in line, asking, "What's a shakedown cruise?"

Halcyon smiled back at the nervous boy. "In a shakedown cruise, we put the ship through every type of sailing maneuver we can think of, all the while checking the new equipment to make sure it won't break down in the really heavy seas or in the middle of battle."

"Midshipman Fourth Class Scott Coal-un stands before you," Ashe said.

Halcyon held out his hand and noted the swordsman calluses on the midshipman's hands. "I look forward to testing your blade in practice sessions, Midshipman Coal-un." Halcyon, a fencer of many years, liked to look at people's hands and could always tell if the person fenced, watching for the special lines that formed on the hand from holding the blade.

Scott Coal-un had the ruddy red hair and short build of a dwarf.

A surprised look came on Scott's face as he stepped back into line.

Halcyon would never admit he was just as nervous as the four midshipmen in front of him. He wasn't used to commanding men at sea, but wanted to be up for the challenge.

"This is Midshipman Torance Stillwater, sir," Ashe said.

Torance had an axe to grind. He wasn't a happy man and his stance was a challenging one to Halcyon. He stood slouched and didn't step forth as the other midshipmen had done. He was a thin man, older than the other midshipmen. He looked a bit older than Halcyon. There was a long scar on his face and as he held out his hand, his small finger was missing.

"I'm glad you are with us, Midshipman Stillwater. From the look of you, you've clearly got some experience under your belt. Feel free to speak up if you see something that can be done better than we're doing it on this shakedown cruise," Halcyon ordered.

Halcyon deliberately tried to give him a bit of praise and it seemed to work. The man loosely shook Halcyon's hand, but the look of superiority left his face, as he stood a bit straighter in line.

"Midshipman Second Class Jakwater Gold-un is the last of your midshipmen, Mr. Blithe. I'll go now and let you get settled with this group. As you hear seven bells come up on the blast-tube deck. The captain is readying himself in," Ashe said.

"Mr. Fallow, when you have the time, I would like a copy of the feeding schedule for the dragon. I promised it a good feeding after we left the port," Halcyon asked.

Fallow saluted and left the area. The midshipmen all had big eyes at the thought of dealing with the dragon.

Midshipman Gold-un couldn't have been older than fourteen. He stood a head shorter than Halcyon, which made him tall for a half-dwarf. He was completely bald, but sported a huge beard.

"Midshipman Gold-un, you haven't seen combat yet, have you?" Halcyon asked.

"Why, no, sir, how did you know that, sir?" Gold-un stood there with a surprised look on his face.

"I think you will find that a beard is quite the disadvantage in a duel to the death on deck. I can assure you," Halcyon advised, "that I will be trying to grab it to pull your head down in our bouts together. Consider cutting it off, but I'm not ordering you to, mind you."

Halcyon got down on his knees and checked his two sea chests. In the one chest, he found all the clothes he would need for the voyage. The sea chest displayed many uniforms and there were several suits perfect for occasions when he would have to show himself a lord of the realm. Several of the midshipmen were crowding around him, looking at his things.

Blithe opened his other chest and took out several pairs of wrist and leg irons and a pair of manacles of Iben that had proven remarkably hard for an individual to purchase. It took the authority of Dart and his position as a lord of Ilumin to allow Halcyon to buy the magical manacles.

"Blow me down," Hurchial exclaimed. "What in the world are you doing with so many manacles?" Shocking himself at his boldness in asking the question, he added, "If you don't mind my asking, sir?"

"Not at all, Midshipman Act-un," Halcyon replied. "I'm going to teach myself how to unlock these manacles without using their keys. There have been several times in my navy career when I haven't liked being manacled. I vowed during those times that I wouldn't allow myself to be held captive again without a means to free myself."

He worked a hidden arcane lock on the chest and activated special magics allowing the sea chest to open to a different compartment filled with fifteen bottles of wine. There was an exclamation at this amount.

"Attention, officer on deck," Coal-un bellowed out.

Halcyon stood up and came to attention with the rest of them. He was disappointed to see the sneering Elan Swordson in front of him.

"Mr. Blithe, have you reported all those spirits to the ship's doctor? Why did you bring so much wine on board? Do you have a drinking problem that your officers should know about?"

Swordson's questions were swift and brutal, meant to harm Halcyon's reputation in front of the other midshipmen.

"Sir, I have only been on board for a few minutes. I'll inform the doctor of the bottles right away. I do not have a drinking problem. I wanted to be ready if the captain invited me or my midshipmen to dinner, sir." Eyes staring straight in front of him, Halcyon didn't back down from Elan's hard questions.

"Mr. Blithe, you're ordered to put these midshipmen through their paces. I myself care nothing for your dragon-speaking or rope-speaking abilities. Those qualities are useless powers when training boys to be men. I'll be standing at your back to make sure you don't coddle them in any way. Am I understood?" Lieutenant Swordson shouted.

"I'm positive these men will handle themselves in the best of navy traditions, sir," Halcyon replied, as calmly as he could considering the glaring lieutenant in front of him.

"See that they do, sir, see that they do. I don't need to tell you what happens if one of them runs afoul while under your command, do I?"

"No, you don't, sir," Halcyon replied.

The ship's bell started ringing seven bells.

"Get these ducklings up on deck. The captain wishes to speak to the crew," Swordson ordered.

"Aye, aye, sir." Halcyon saluted, not liking the unexpected surprise of seeing Swordson on his ship as well as his two friends.

All of them ran for the ladders to get on deck for the reading of the ship's orders.

The lieutenants and superior officers of the ship all arrayed themselves on the quarterdeck of the dragonfrigate and looked down at the almost four hundred men assembling on the blast-tube deck. Captain Gord-un stood at the top of the stairs to the quarterdeck with an official document in his hand. It had several ribbons and a seal on its outside that was clearly from the admiralty, since the admiralty was the only force allowed to use dark blue ribbons on important matters of service.

"I am Captain Sandal Gord-un, I now read the letters of empowerment. By the will of the Arcanian admiralty, as given to them by King Artur Andul Ilumin Surehand, Majesty, and King of Arcania, I have been named captain of the *Rage* with all the authority that title confers on me. I'm to serve as its captain until given further orders by the admiralty." He took the parchment and folded it up again as he continued to talk to the crew.

"This is to be a shakedown cruise of the dragonfrigate *Rage*. This is the first time this sea dragon has gone into harm's way. I have been with the dragon since last year and its training was a difficult one. The dragon is headstrong. I am sure that he will present some surprises for us on this cruise.

"I now introduce First Officer Townzat."

A tall man with dark hair raised his officer's hat and stood recognized.

"Second Officer Tona Dorlat has served with me on other ships of the line."

A short woman with shoulders even wider than Denna Darkwater's walked forward for the crew to see.

"Lieutenant Shard Sand-un has also served with me on past stations."

Standing less than five feet tall, the lieutenant looked more dwarf than man as he raised his red cap.

"I congratulate Lieutenant Junior Grade Elan Swordson, who has just passed his lieutenant tests. He comes from serving on the *Sanguine* and its recent success in the sea battle off of Ordune."

Elan raised his cap and stood recognized.

The captain went on with his speech. "Some of you haven't served on a dragonship before. There is no reason to fear the beast under this ship. Our dragon's training prevents it from eating its crew. In fact, such beasts think of us as pets if you can believe that." The captain laughed.

Many of the crew looked uneasy, as if they hadn't thought about the idea that the dragon could get hungry and eat them.

"I present Lieutenant Major Josiah Maxwell, commander of the ship's marines," the captain said.

Maxwell stood fourth in his green marine uniform.

"Lieutenant Jad-un and Lieutenant Macluun are his marine subordinates."

These men stood forth, raising their hands to the crew.

"Because this is a dragonfrigate, I'm sure it is one of the fastest, if not the fastest ship in the Arcanian fleet. We have a lot to be proud of in this ship. Normally, shakedown cruises are simple affairs done to the east of our island. Such is the trust that the admiralty has in my captaincy and you as the crew that we are going to take on a very important mission. The admiralty has commanded us to take Ambassador Abernathy to the Dwarven Empire to present his credentials. Many of our crew are handpicked because we came from dwarven parents. We sail for Crystal Port on the northern coast of the Dwarven Lands, far to our south. I expect everyone under my command to handle themselves as representatives of Arcania. There will be no shore leave in the Dwarven Empire. We are commanded to take on all supplies needed for the assignment and sail in two days. The crew schedules will be posted at the noon bell. That is all."

VIII

✤ ✤ ✤

Service Record Reviewed

HIS MAJESTY'S ARTICLES OF WAR: ARTICLE XXVIII

No person in the naval service shall procure stores or other articles or supplies for, and dispose thereof to, the officers or enlisted men on vessels of the navy or at navy yards or naval stations for his own account or benefit.

The quarterdeck of the *Rage* was a crowded place with all the ship's officers in attendance. The captain walked the starboard side as his officers crowded the port side.

"It was my intention to sail with the morning tide, but Ambassador Abernathy hasn't seen fit to arrive yet." There was a biting sarcasm to the captain's tone, making all of his officers uncomfortable. "We are at his pleasure and must sail as soon as possible after he arrives, whenever that is. I'm giving the ambassador my cabin," the captain said to the officers. "We will all adjust our quarters, which places our new-made lieutenant with the midshipmen. I know that's not what you expected, Lieutenant Swordson, but we all must make do." The captain said this last in an almost apologetic tone of voice.

"No worries, sir, I understand perfectly," Elan said, though the look of anguish on his face belied his words.

His face made Halcyon mentally vow to try harder not to show his feelings on his own face, because he knew there was a scowl there at the thought of Swordson sleeping with the midshipmen.

"Lieutenant Major Maxwell, I want a heavy drill schedule of your marines every morning. Let me see your plans to put your men through their paces each day." The captain stopped his own pacing to look the lieutenant major square in the face. "Also, you should know that Chief Ashe Fallow is the Arcanian bouting champion with the blast-pike. I'm told by those who know that he and Denna Darkwater, your new marine corporal, are hellers with that weapon."

"Aye, aye, sir, and that last is good to know," Maxwell replied.

"First Officer, a quarter of this crew is as green as grass. I want difficult ship maneuvers with lots of sail configurations day and night. You'll present me with a schedule for those drills this afternoon." The captain once again looked the first officer in the eye.

"Immediately, sir," Townzat replied.

"The sailing time down to the southern coasts is approximately ninety days, fair winds permitting. In that time, Second Officer Dorlat, you and the first officer will put the men through many blast-tube drills. The Arcanian navy prides itself on firing faster and more accurately than the Maleens. I personally don't think that's saying much," the captain said as he continued to walk back and forth.

Halcyon was the only one who laughed at the quip. He shut up as soon as he saw the stares of the other officers.

"I want to surprise Emert, the dwarf god of fire," Gord-un quipped, "with how quickly and how well we fire our tubes. I want to be the fastest-firing ship in the navy. Dorlat, you and Mr. Townzat will make that happen by the time we get to the Dwarven Empire. I'm sure we will be disturbing the ambassador at his high teas, but I don't much care."

Tona briefly went to attention. "Aye, aye, Captain!"

"Mr. Blithe, front and center," the captain ordered.

Halcyon came to the front of the group and saluted his captain.

"Midshipwizard First Class Halcyon Blithe comes to us, like Lieutenant Swordson, Chief Fallow, and the Marine Corporal Denna Darkwater, from the dragon first-rater *Sanguine*. Many of you might not know that the *Sanguine* took part in a huge victory over the Maleen off of Ordune. Mr. Blithe is quite new to his rank and I would urge all of you to keep a weather eye out for our first-class midshipwizard as he keeps a weather eye out for his midshipmen. Halcyon here, First Officer Peter Townzat, and I are the dragon speakers of the ship. Mr. Blithe, let me ask you, in the course of battle if all three of us were killed, what should the crew do about the dragon?" the captain asked.

"Sir, in the event all dragon speakers are cleared from a dragonship, navy regulations state that the crew is to double the food ration of the dragon and sail for the closest Arcanian port," Halcyon quickly replied.

"Correct, and while we are on the topic of rules and regulations, Mr. Blithe, what is Article Thirty-four?" the captain asked.

"Sir, Article Thirty-four states, the commander of any Arcanian vessel shall make frequent inspections into the condition of the provisions on his ship and use every precaution for their preservation," Halcyon answered instantly.

"Correct, Mr. Blithe. Our midshipwizard here is not only a dragon speaker, but a rope speaker as well. I'm ordering Mr. Blithe to inspect all of our lines. Since this is a new ship, I think there won't be many problems, but it's always good to check. Second Officer, set up a schedule of magic training with Mr. Blithe and Mr. Swordson. From Mr. Blithe's record, he needs careful instruction in tempering his spells. The records show Mr. Swordson has sound magic skills," the captain ordered.

"Aye, sir," Officer Dorlat replied.

Halcyon looked around and noticed that Swordson, Dorlat, and he were the only wizards among the officers. That was a far cry from what he lived through on the *Sanguine*.

"And you, Mr. Townzat, will drill Halcyon and the other midshipmen in navigation and the rules of order," the captain said.

"Aye, sir," Peter Townzat replied.

"I see that the barrels of salt beef and pork are arriving. First Officer, arrange for the crew to begin loading the barrels; the rest of you follow me to the dock for a lesson in Article Thirty-four," the captain said as he went from the quarterdeck to the tube deck.

Down on the docks there were six dray wagons loaded with large barrels. Each barrel had a number burnt on the side of the barrel. The twelve that Halcyon could see read 64 PORK or 70 BEEF.

A fat man jumped off the lead wagon and came up to the captain. He reeked of beef fat. He shook the captain's offered hand, then bowed to the rest of the officers on the dock.

"We captains are allowed a great deal of latitude by the admiralty on where and from whom we get our ship's provisions. Once I became captain, I started using Mr. Billy Tanner here for our beef and pork. I've never regretted it," the captain told the group.

"Ah, thank yous, sar, yous're too kind by half, yous ar," Tanner said.

"Not a bit, Mr. Tanner. I'll take barrel three from the front of the first wagon and barrel seven from the last wagon," the captain ordered. He turned to face the rest of the group while Tanner had his men pull out the mentioned barrels.

"At every port where the ship is taking on provisions, the captain or the designated officer of the ship is supposed to carefully inspect the provisions coming on board. Each of those barrels is supposed to have the number of pieces of meat that's burnt on the barrel. When each of you becomes a captain, you won't believe that number, as I don't right now. Not everyone is as honest or as careful as our Mr. Tanner here. Those barrels need checking and that's why we stand on the docks ready to count the meat from these two barrels. Feel free to check two, three, or four of the barrels. If even one of them has a wrong count, then you must check them all. Mr. Tanner, what is the penalty for misrepresenting a load of barrels?" the captain said.

Tanner got a very worried look on his face. "Why, sar, you know I would never do that. Only a fool robs the king's navy."

The captain's voice took on a hard edge and he stopped smiling. "Mr. Tanner, I asked you a question."

Tanner took a big rag from his apron and wiped his head. Clearly uncomfortable, he said, "The penalty is death by hanging, Captain."

The captain went back to smiling and turned toward his officers. "It's impossible in time and money to inspect each barrel, case, and crate coming onto the ship under normal circumstances. Ships would never be leaving the docks in that event. However, a random check of several parcels in each load does the job because the producer can never know which barrels you're picking. Some try tricks like making the end barrels in the wagons filled with special cuts of meat. Don't be fooled by those attempts at cheating our king and country."

The officers of the *Rage* spread out along the dock as two large fish-cutting tables were unloaded from the wagons. Mr. Tanner clearly knew what was going to happen and prepared for the inspection. The unloaded barrel showed 64 PORK on its side. The barrel was opened and dumped out on the table. Massive amounts of salt crystals spilled out onto the table with the meat.

A dock wizard snapped his fingers and his magic kept the flies off the spilled meat.

Captain Gord-un and the rest of the officers watched as sixty-five pieces of pork were counted out of the barrel. The captain stayed where he was, watching carefully as the meat was packed back in the barrel and the other barrel was spread out on the table. That barrel read 71 BEEF. There were seventy-two pieces of meat in the barrel. Each was as big as a man's head, and some were larger.

The captain turned to the officers while a smiling Tanner watched. "That's why I use Mr. Tanner and his service. He prides himself on selling the navy good cuts of meat and his barrels always have one more than what's stated on the side of the barrel. I appreciate a man who prides himself on his work and does more than what is expected of him. Mr. Tanner, thank you for your goods," the captain said, tossing the man a sack of gold.

Tanner bowed low and went to supervise his men in the loading of the barrels on the ship.

"Now, men, please follow me to the waterman," the captain ordered.

He continued talking as the others followed closely to hear

what he was saying. They moved through the merchant streets of the city. Sellers hawked everything from new hats to flowers overflowing wagons.

"Naval regulations for the proper filling of water tuns require the use of a clean stream or lake and clean utensils used in the filling of the two hundred and fifty-two gallons of water in a tun. Any of you on a long cruise has found water tuns filled with swimming things even as short a time as a month into the voyage. I believe this growing life isn't good for the men to drink. Because of this, I take further precautions."

They walked north into a busy commercial area of the city. Blacksmiths pounded out horseshoes alongside shops of weapon smiths working on sword blades. Coopers worked out of their barrelmaking establishments, enjoying the light breeze from the sea as they shaved the lathes used to make their barrels. There wasn't an empty shop along the mile-long street, as there was plenty of work for all in the capital.

Hurchial walked alongside Halcyon. "Mr. Blithe, I was wondering, why do they call you a rope speaker, when on a ship all the ropes are called lines?" he asked.

Halcyon laughed at the question. "I asked that very same question at the midshipwizard academy. Look around us right now; do you see ropes or lines?"

There were all manner of winches in use on the street, lifting heavy loads.

"Why, sir, there are at least four different cranes working loads on this side of the street alone. Landsmen call them ropes of course. We navy men always call them lines. Why do you ask?"

"That's the point, of course. Most rope speakers work on land and inspect ropes in the cranes and equipment in cities and towns all over the nation. Down through history, rope speakers worked on land even before sailing ships were used; the name stuck even in the navy," Halcyon replied.

"Well now, that's as plain as the nose on your face, isn't it," Midshipman Act-un said.

Halcyon laughed, "I don't know about that, but the explanation made sense to me."

The captain led them to the water drawer's establishment by Bray River. The man had several flat-bottomed barges at his dock and one of the barges was just coming back with three tuns. Other tuns of water were loaded on several large dray wagons.

A small man in a black leather apron can running up to the captain and bowed low to him.

"Officers," the captain said, "this is Mr. Alvin Dray. To my mind he's the best waterman on the docks."

The man blushed scarlet at the words of praise from the captain. "Naw, sir, there you go now. I just do my job. The job you pay good silver for."

"Not a bit of it, Alvin," the captain said as he went over to the docks with Dray in tow. "Alvin here has taught even me a thing or two about getting water for the ship. You there, bargeman, hand up your cheesecloth."

While the captain was at the barge, Halcyon noticed that the large line on the loading crane at this dock appeared bright blue to his enchanted senses. That was a sure sign of rot. He didn't know the way to mention this, so he went up to the captain and Dray.

"Mr. Dray your crane line is rotted out. It's not going to take any weight at all to snap that line and lose a barrel. You need to change it before you try to load those tuns," Halcyon said timidly.

"Better listen to him, Alvin. Our Mr. Blithe is a rope speaker and if he's half as good at that as he is at dragon speaking, he knows what he's talking about," the captain warned Alvin Dray.

Alvin ordered the rope changed out while the captain held up the white cheesecloth for everyone to see.

"This is cheesecloth. Cheesemakers take their curds and whey and fill bags of this cloth. The mesh allows the liquid to escape and keeps all the solid materials of the cheese. Alvin's water carriers row upstream above the pollution of the city and place a large swath of this cloth above the top of each barrel as they pan in water from the river. The cloth catches the algae, bugs, and sticks of the river so those things don't get into the tun. With every voyage, I have a crate of this cloth taken aboard for use when we use islands and rivers abroad to fill our water tuns."

The captain walked over to one of the empty tuns along the dock. The huge barrel was as large as the captain was. Other empty tuns took two strong men to move from place to place on the dock. The captain tipped it sideways as if it weighed nothing.

"The navy uses water wizards to coat the inside of these barrels with a special water magic keeping the barrel from leaking." He said this as he put his hand along the inside of the barrel. Wherever his hand touched the barrel, it glowed with a bright blue luminescence.

"A navy tun has a royal copper dragon branded on the side of the barrel. Sometimes unscrupulous water carriers use untreated barrels because they don't want to pay the preparation tax. You have to open a water tun or two and check for the blue glow," the captain advised.

Halcyon stopped bobbing his head up and down when he saw all of the lieutenants and the other midshipmen nodding their heads yes at their captain's words. This was all good advice and not the type of thing one learned in the midshipwizard academy.

"There's one other thing I want to show you all. Alvin, toss me your payment bar," the captain ordered.

Mr. Dray took a large bar of what looked like silver out of his apron pouch and tossed it over to the captain, who easily caught the heavy bar in one hand.

The captain held the bar up for all to see.

"This bar has fifteen mates to it, one to each of the tuns of water coming on our ship. It has my family chop on the center of the bar so that I know it's mine. Use of this silver bar is not navy regulation, but I insist there is a bar of silver at the bottom of each of the water barrels used on my ship. For generations, my family has been putting silver in their drinking water. The silver taints the water somehow, and don't ask me how because I don't know. All I know for sure is that those who drink water tainted with silver get fewer headaches and fewer of the ills commonly coming to seamen on long voyages. It's expensive to do, but to my mind, it's worth every bit of silver I spend to keep the crew off the sick list. At the emptying of each barrel, the bar is taken out. It's usually black with tarnish. I have the bars polished to mirror brightness and put back into the cleaned barrel for the next load of water.

"Navy regulations for a frigate going on a tour of duty say to have ten tuns of fresh water at the beginning of the voyage," the captain advised. "Out of my own pocket I'm paying for five more tuns to be loaded onto the ship. I do this because water and food are the most important commodities aboard. In my time at sea as a ranker, I've often needed more water. That hasn't happened to me since I became a captain."

In the distance, they all could hear the sea dragon roaring out its nervousness again. The captain looked at Blithe. "Midshipman Blithe, plan on feeding him the second you get back aboard ship. He's not going to like that we have to wait in dock for the ambassador. We'll get a few bushels of carrots on the way back. I've noticed our dragon loves the taste of carrots, for some odd reason. While I'm thinking of it, Midshipman Act-un, run back to the dock and order up a hay barge for the dragon's feeding. We'll stuff the young thing full for a change out of the port stores instead of the ship's supply."

"Aye, aye, Captain," Halcyon and Hurchial replied.

Some of the others looked on Mr. Blithe with a bit of envy at his dragon-speaking skills. Elan Swordson showed only disdain at the captain's words to Halcyon.

Perhaps noting the look on Swordson's face, the captain selected him out. "Mr. Swordson, take a navy coach to the palace and see if you can hurry our ambassador, if you please. Be as diplomatic as possible and certainly don't make it seem like we are in a rush."

"Aye, aye, sir," Elan said, saluting the captain, and ran off toward the docks to gain a coach. Several naval coaches were always in the area, ready for military use.

The rest of the group finished the day walking with the captain through the market.

IX

✤ ✤ ✤

𝕬mbassador on 𝕭oard

HIS MAJESTY'S ARTICLES OF WAR: ARTICLE XXIX

Distilled spirits shall be admitted on board of vessels of war only upon the order and under the control of the medical officers of such vessels and used only for medical purposes.

Halcyon finished feeding the sea dragon, taking several hours to get the dragon calmed down and feeling good about itself. Using tannin oil on his hand to ease the communication process, he was able to mentally deal with the dragon. As they talked, Halcyon gained a mental picture of the intelligence of the dragon and was impressed. Although the process had taken five pounds of sugar mixed in the hay and a bushel of carrots, at least the feeding caused the dragon to be pleasantly stuffed and content for the moment.

"*Here comes a very silly human,*" the dragon thought to Halcyon.

In that next instant, Scott Coal-un, the piper for the day, trilled out the piping honoring a governmental official. The notes of the pipes commanded a marine detail to present itself at the gangplank. The musical tones also alerted the officers on the quarterdeck that a person of importance was coming aboard.

Halcyon was on the forecastle and had a good view of the gangplank. He had to smile to see Elan Swordson ejected out of the coach as if a blast-tube had shot him from the coach door. The newly made lieutenant ran up the ship's gangplank and ordered a squad of sailors down to the coach to start unloading the ten huge chests piled high on the coach top. All of the clothes Halcyon owned in the world and probably his entire life could have been put in the bottom of one of those chests. He was extremely happy he wasn't hefting them down into the captain's cabin. Naturally, he could have used magic to move the chests, but no one asked him on the detail, and besides, he had his midshipman crewmen to deal with.

Out of the coach stepped the oddest man Halcyon had ever seen. He could only have been the ambassador. His outfit was blindingly white and covered in long frilly lace from head to toe. A tall man, his face was thin and when Halcyon saw his long, pointed elf ears, he was shocked. Elves weren't common in Arcania, but red-haired elves were even stranger. The ambassador had a red handlebar mustache and a shock of deep, short red hair on his head. All the elves Halcyon knew, and he only knew three by sight, had green or black hair. Halcyon didn't think that an elf could have facial hair.

As he left the coach, his white gloves turned black from the soot on the coach sides. Halcyon watched the ambassador look at his gloved hands in disgust. That look brought a smile to Halcyon's face.

Coming up the gangplank, the ambassador brushed against the rails, and black pitch creases marked his clothes. Seeing that, the man became visibly upset.

"Hideous, absolutely hideous," the ambassador exclaimed as he took the last three steps onto the dragonfrigate's tube deck.

Elan shouted out from beside the mainmast, "Lord Quantrell Abernathy, ambassador of Arcania, has arrived on deck!"

Halcyon wondered how the sea dragon could mark the ambassador as a silly man.

"Quite so, Mr. Swordson, carry on with your duties," the captain ordered. "Ambassador, I am Sandal Gord-un, captain of the *Rage*. These are my officers, First Officer Peter Townzat and Second Officer Tona Dorlat. We are all honored to have you aboard the *Rage*."

"Honored, I'm sure," the ambassador said in a nasal voice. "It can't be pleasant to be forced out of your cabin by an Arcanian ambassador. I appreciate your efforts on my behalf and I will try to stay out of the way on this hideously long voyage. I'm told there is another lord on board your craft?"

"Lord sir, I don't know what you mean. I need to see your papers from the admiralty if you please," the captain asked.

"Papers? Oh yes." The ambassador snapped his fingers and a courier pouch appeared in his hands.

Still viewing the scene from the forecastle, Halcyon marveled at the elf magic. He guessed the elf was able to keep things of importance in a special pocket dimension. Not having white hair, the ambassador's magic surprised Halcyon. For a moment, the midshipwizard thought about the magic it would take to do that same trick. He didn't think he could make it work. Elves had their own style of nature magic, special to their race. Traveling on a living ship would be just the type of thing any elf should love.

Handing over his papers, the elf asked, "Isn't Lord Blithe aboard?"

"*You're about to be in a lot of trouble, duck,*" the sea dragon advised and put its head under the water.

"Mr. Blithe, front and center!" the captain bellowed. The captain quickly read through several papers affixed with royal ribbons and seals and handed them back to the ambassador, who just as quickly made them vanish in his hands again with a snap of his magical fingers.

Halcyon rushed to the side of the captain, coming to attention and saluting.

"Ambassador Abernathy, let me present Midshipwizard First Class, and recently promoted, Halcyon Blithe. He is indeed a lord of the realm, but on my ship, and at the pleasure of the king," Captain Gord-un replied in a frosty manner, "he must put away his titles to serve at my order." The captain saluted Halcyon back, allowing the midshipwizard to let go of his salute. "At ease, Mr. Blithe," the captain ordered.

Innocent for a change, that didn't stop Halcyon from worrying that he'd gotten on the wrong side with the captain. He couldn't help his heritage. He would make it a point never to flaunt his noble birth on board any ship.

"I hope I haven't made a hideous mistake. I'm not used to things military, but I assure you I'm a damn fine ambassador," the ambassador said, seeming to know that he'd irritated the captain in asking his simple question. "Please show me where my cabin is."

"Mr. Swordson, show the ambassador to his cabin for the trip," the captain ordered. "Mr. Blithe, go about your duties."

Elan was pleased to see his captain's irritation, as he noted it directed at Blithe. The lieutenant had purposely brought up Blithe during the coach ride, imagining his captain's rage at having the ambassador think there was another lord on board who might be more in control of the ship than the captain himself.

Ashe Fallow and Denna Darkwater came up to Halcyon after the captain had left. The huge grins on their faces told Blithe they had heard what the ambassador said.

"Begging your pardon, Mr. Blithe, but we have a task that needs an officer's hand," the chief said.

"Corporal Darkwater, I'm glad you could make it aboard," Halcyon said, smiling at both of them. "We can always use your good right arm. What do you need, Chief?"

"It seems our second officer feels we'd be needing some more ordnance for all the blast-tube drills that are coming on this cruise. Could you go with us to secure the solid shot? Dorlat's already given her approval," the chief said.

"Sounds good to me," Halcyon said. "Do you know where we go?"

"I've been there a time or two," Denna said, smiling to the midshipwizard. "You'll find Tube Sergeant Eaglebone to be a mite difficult to deal with."

"After an ambassador and an irritated captain, he should be a piece of cake." Halcyon smiled. "Let's go rattle his munitions cage, shall we?"

"After you, sir, after you," Fallow said.

Halcyon summoned up the other midshipmen, as he wanted them to see a munitions factory. He had seen many of them as he went with his father on inspection trips. As he was gathering them, Swordson came up to him.

"What are you doing, Blithe?" Swordson asked with a sneer.

Halcyon came to attention. "At the order of Second Officer

Dorlat, I'm taking a squad to gather a supply of shot for the extended blast-tube drills she's planned."

"Don't dawdle on the docks, get your sorry behind back here on the double or you'll find my boot on your backside. Do I make myself perfectly clear?" the lieutenant snarled.

"I understand you perfectly, sir." Halcyon added this last a tad late and everyone around him knew exactly what he meant. The sarcasm was luckily lost on Swordson.

"Take those midshipmen with you. It'll do them good to get their hands dirty loading shot. On this voyage, I won't allow you to coddle those children. We'll turn them into men or I'll know the reason why. Dismissed," Swordson barked at them, and turned away.

Ashe had ordered a squad of ten sailors and Denna called up another batch of ten marines and all of them moved off to gather the new munitions. As they were walking down the gangplank, Ashe moved alongside Halcyon. "That wet-behind-the-ears young lieutenant sure has got it in for you," Ashe commented.

"It appears I shouldn't have beat him to a pulp a few months back when he didn't have so much rank on me," Halcyon replied. "It looks like I'm in for a bit of nasty weather where Mr. Swordson's concerned. The fact that he has to bunk with the midshipmen won't make things easier, I'm afraid."

They kept their voices down, but Denna Darkwater's half-troll ears easily followed the conversation. "I'd be happy to stave in a few of his ribs. I think that might slow him down a bit, if you know what I mean. Naturally, it would all happen by accident in the practice circle." There was a fiendish grin on her face as she thought about the deed.

Halcyon could see the looks of alarm on the faces of his junior midshipmen. They didn't know what to make of Denna.

Halcyon looked at her for a second and could well imagine what they were thinking.

Clearly female, she stood almost six feet tall. Half troll as noted by her blue hair; those locks flowed into a war braid. Her red eyes seemed to bore into anyone she studied. The massive muscles on her arms and legs weren't hidden at all by her marine uniform. Save for those troll features she was attractive by human standards. She was one of the best blast-pike wielders in the navy, second only to Ashe Fallow, and he could beat her only because of his vast experience in using the pike.

Halcyon had, by luck alone, defeated her once in a blast-pike practice session and she'd become his friend as a result. Ashe Fallow was her only other friend because he too could best her in practice duels.

Halcyon changed the subject by talking about the munitions foundry. He hadn't seen the Ilumin one before, but there was one in Lankshire that he'd visited many times and they all worked the same way. He noted the four one-hundred-and-twenty-feet-tall towers rising over the other buildings of the dock.

"Mr. Gold-un," Halcyon asked, "do you know what those towers are for?"

"Well, uh, I believe they have something to do with the making of the shot," Gold-un said, clearly having no idea what the towers did.

They turned the corner and walked up to the foundry gates. Something burning was continually dropped from each one of the four towers every minute or so.

"You are correct, sir," Halcyon replied. "When they are making thirty-pound shot, they take a slug of molten metal weighing thirty pounds and they drop it from that tower into a well of water. While falling through the air, the molten mass forms into a perfectly round ball. As it hits the water, it instantly cools and hardens. Then, all they have to do is fish the ball of metal out of the pool and they've a perfectly good blast-tube shot, ready for service in the king's artillery. Mr. Hurchial, how many blast-tubes are on the *Rage*?"

Midshipman Act-un looked very embarrassed. "I have no idea, sir," he replied.

"There are thirty twenty-four-pound blast-tubes on the tube deck; fifteen to the port-side and fifteen to the starboard side. You will find sixteen thirty-two-pound double blast-tubes on the quarterdeck at the front of the ship, six thirty-two-pound double blast-tubes on the forecastle at the rear of the ship; three forty-eight-pound stern chasers are positioned at the back of the ship, and two forty-eight-pound bow chasers are at the rear of the ship. The tubes were the first thing I looked at when I came aboard. How long have you been on the ship, Mr. Hurchial?" Halcyon asked.

"A week, sir," he answered.

"Before you go to sleep tonight, I want you to have written down the names of every tube on the *Rage* and you will read them off to me," Halcyon ordered.

"Names, sir?" Hurchial questioned, clearly having no idea what the first-class midshipwizard was asking.

"I think you'll find that the blast-tube crews wouldn't dream of firing their weapons unless they named them first. While we are at it, how long and wide is the *Rage*, Mr. Coal-un?"

"The *Rage* is two hundred feet long. Its beam is forty-four feet, sir," Scott replied. "That's the physical ship size, not counting the added length for the sea dragon."

"Excellent, you can't call yourself a sailor if you don't know your ship and its crew," Halcyon said, smiling as Ashe Fallow led the group into the foundry and the presence of Munitions Sergeant Eaglebone. Halcyon let Chief Fallow talk to the man. He continued to question his midshipmen.

"Mr. Stillwater, what is the height of the *Rage's* mainmast?"

"That mast is one-hundred-and-eighty-seven feet tall, sir," Torance answered with a smile on his face.

"Mr. Gold-un, how many men serve on the dragonfrigate?" Halcyon asked, not knowing the answer to that question.

"Sir, there are three hundred naval officers and sailors and one hundred marine officers and marines," Gold-un answered.

The shouting of the two sergeants interrupted the group.

"I don't care what your orders are!" snapped the tube sergeant. "The *Rage* has gotten its supply of munitions for its assignment and isn't getting one blast-tube shot more."

Halcyon observed that both his Chief Fallow and Eaglebone were red in the face.

"And I'm saying I have orders and by the gods you're going to obey them!" Fallow shouted back. "Or I'll know the reason why."

Somehow, Halcyon just knew that nothing was going to be accomplished on either side with them yelling at each other. He walked up to the table.

The tube sergeant was forced to stop his arguing and come to attention.

Halcyon Blithe was the lowest of officer types as a midshipwizard, but that didn't matter in the navy. A ranker, when faced with a new officer, came to attention and saluted.

Blithe saluted crisply back and ignored the tube sergeant in favor of glaring at Ashe Fallow. Halcyon deliberately turned so that Eaglebone couldn't see his face. He winked at the surprised Fallow.

"Mr. Fallow, your tone is improper for any man, let alone a Master Chief Petty Officer in the king's navy. Back off before you get stripes on that back of yours!" Halcyon snarled at the chief.

"Sir, aye, sir!" the chief answered, saluting and taking three steps backward.

"Munitions Sergeant Eaglebone, I'm Blithe of the *Rage*. Might I see your munitions yard and talk with you privately?" Halcyon said it in a way to make it seem an order and the sergeant couldn't refuse.

They walked through several doors to a large open courtyard. The area was filled with munitions of all sizes, from the mortar fifty-pound hard shot to blast-tube balls for the three-pounders. A large section of the north end of the yard spilled to overflowing with the new pointed shells.

The red-faced Eaglebone was in a mood to argue. "Sir, I can't help you no matter what your orders. You've gotten your share of munitions. There's a war on, you know, and everyone is begging for more shells. The foundry can only produce so much."

Eaglebone was a tubby little man. His red piggish face held a large mustache that couldn't hide the pinching of his lips. He was constantly wringing his hands and looking uncomfortable at the stares Halcyon was giving him.

"Those are very unusual contraptions for holding the pointed shells, aren't they, Sergeant?" Halcyon said, changing the subject to collect his thoughts. He wasn't quite sure how to get more munitions out of this sergeant; there must be a way. *What would Chief Fallow do?* Halcyon thought.

"You are looking at the worst idea the navy artillery ever had. There are five shells to each of those gods-be-damned wheeled carts. We've had to build stupid racks for the carts and no one wants those shells. They are too strange and look how much space they take up." Eaglebone wiped his forehead with a dirty rag and looked very frustrated. "This foundry doesn't make them. They come from armorer Smithy's miles away. The wheeled carts made to carry five of the shells costs almost as much as the shells do and look how much space they take up."

"Sergeant Eaglebone, I perfectly understand your pain. We all have to work with officers who don't know what they're doing," Halcyon said, trying to sound reasonable. "Since I have to bring back shells and wasn't told what type of shells, I'll take all of those pointed ones off of your hands. That way you can have room for more proper shells and I can follow my orders. How does that sound?"

"Blimy, sir, that's a wonder. Mind you, I don't have the men to load the wagons with these shells. You and your men will have to do that work. But it would be a grand thing," the now-happy Eaglebone replied.

"Well, let's get to work then," Halcyon said, patting the man on his back.

Dray wagons appeared from around the corner and a very surprised Ashe Fallow supervised the loading of the wagons with the pointed blast-tube shells. Sergeant Eaglebone showed the marines where the blast-gel could be found, and those jars, in three different colors, were loaded into special carrying cases that protected the gel from falls. Halcyon signed for the munitions and they took the loads back to the dock.

Back at the ship, they started unloading the pointed shells. The five shell loads were in a sort of wheelbarrow with a large wheel at the front and handles at the back. The shells nested in a rack between the wheels. Tona Dorlat came down the gangplank glaring at the wagons loaded with the new shells.

"What nine-goddess-cursed idiot got us those shells?" she snarled, and everyone looked to Halcyon.

He noticed that Swordson was at the top of the gangplank smiling at Dorlat's rage.

"Ma'am, we used these shells on the *Sanguine*. You'll find they double the range of your blast-tubes and still do the same damage," Halcyon said, coming to attention. He thought to himself that he was coming to attention in front of angry officers an awful lot lately.

"We've got to take these things, but I don't like it, Mr. Blithe. You load them into the lowest part of the orlop deck at the bottom of the ship. I hope that we won't need to use them any time soon. Whoever heard of such foolishness? This man's navy uses round shells. I don't want to poke the enemy's eyes out; I want to blast them to pieces," Dorlat snarled at the entire group.

"Yes, ma'am, as you say, ma'am," Halcyon answered back. He could tell she wasn't in an arguing mood. She'd find out about the effectiveness of the shells through use.

With the help of more of the crew, they quickly loaded the shells and extra gel. Elan Swordson continued to smile the entire time Halcyon and his midshipmen went down with fresh loads of shells.

The captain came up behind Elan and surprised him.

"Mr. Swordson, you were on the *Sanguine* when those pointed shells were used, weren't you?" the captain asked.

Elan whirled around and came to attention.

"Sir, I was," he replied.

"Were those stupid-looking things effective?" Gord-un asked.

"The shells were very effective, sir. We were able to put an entire broadside of those shells into a first-rater at two miles out. Our shots crippled the first-rater and they didn't get a shot in at us before we put another broadside in her at a mile and a half out," Elan said.

"Interesting, very interesting," the captain mused. "Carry on, Mr. Swordson."

"Aye, Captain," Elan replied.

X

✤ ✤ ✤

The Strain of Command

HIS MAJESTY'S ARTICLES OF WAR: ARTICLE XXX

Such punishment as a court-martial may adjudge may be inflicted on any person in the navy who is guilty of executing, attempting, or countenances any fraud against the sovereign nation of Arcania.

Halcyon had his midshipmen sleepily on deck before dawn. They were hearing the lecture Darkwater gave to her marines.

"Private Salt, what is the first Marine General Order?" Corporal Darkwater snarled the question to the marine on the deck.

"Ma'am, to take charge of the watch post and all Arcanian property in full view of the guard post!" the marine crisply replied.

"What exactly does that mean, Private?" she asked.

"Anything I see at my post is my responsibility to guard. If someone is attacking or ruining what I see, I stop them," he answered.

"Excellent answer, I know some of you might not want to do blast-pike drills in the dark," Denna said, as her glowing red eyes viewed her men.

Halcyon and his midshipmen stayed to the center of the ship, but they could still hear the marines on the forecastle. The night was crisp and clear. A cloudless sky revealed stars at their brightest. A fresh sea breeze came into the bay and forced the sawdust smells of the harbor farther inland. Halcyon knew that false dawn would brighten the horizon soon. He wanted to be up in the tops by then with his squad of midshipmen.

"The enemy can come at this ship at any time, night or day. You have to learn to find your foes and kill them as well in the dark as you do in the light and I'm here to give you those skills," Denna barked at them.

Halcyon was glad he wasn't among the marines just then. His squad climbed to the quarterdeck and Halcyon raised his hat in respect to the wheel and the ship's captain, as did the other middies.

"*Huh?*" The sleepy sea dragon communicated a questioning thought to Halcyon. The midshipwizard was surprised he could hear the thoughts of the dragon without the use of the tannin oil. "*Go back to sleep, you'll be working hard enough with the dawn,*" he mentally thought back to the ship dragon.

"The captain's orders for the day are posted on the chalk-board behind the wheel," Halcyon said, snapping his fingers to make a glow so they could all read the board by his magical light. The ship lantern was just enough to light the area for the night watch and didn't spread enough light to read the board. None of them showed surprise at Halcyon's magical ability. White-haired wizards were commonplace in Arcania. For the last two generations, more and more wizards were appearing as they reached puberty in Arcania. Many wise men speculated that the land was responding to the need of the empire.

"You'll notice we set sail at first light. Mr. Coal-un, you look the sleepiest right now. What are the first three articles of the Arcanian Code of Military Conduct?" Halcyon asked. The midshipwizard asked this question as it was constantly asked of him on his first ship, the *Sanguine*. Officers were expected to know the articles letter-perfect to be an example to the men they commanded.

The marines on the forecastle started chanting their weapon's mantra. Halcyon always liked to hear it and he cocked his head to catch every word.

Halcyon held up his hand, "A moment, Scott. Listen, all of you."

The men of the marine squad sang out in their deep voices, "This is my blast-pike." THUD! The thud was from the marines advancing and thrusting out their pikes as they chanted. There were complex blast-pike maneuvers that went with the chant. They continued, "There are many like it, but this one is mine." THUD! "It is my life. I must master it as I must master my life. Without me, my blast-pike is useless. Without my blast-pike, I am useless." THUD! The deep timbre of their voices held no trace of humor, even though there were amusing aspects to their chanting, from Halcyon's thinking.

"I must strike true with my blast-pike," they all chanted in the same cadence. "I must slice straighter than the enemy who is trying to kill me. I must stab him before he stabs me. I will." THUD! "My blast-pike and I know that what counts in war is not the swinging of the blast-pike, the yelling of the weapon user, or the show of force we make. We know that it's the hit that counts." THUD! "We will hit." THUD!

All of the midshipmen were looking over to the forecastle now. They couldn't see the marines in the darkness, but all of them could well imagine the wall of pikes moving in deadly unison.

"My blast-pike is alive, even as I am alive, because it is my life. Thus, I will learn it as a brother." THUD! "I will learn its weaknesses, its strengths, its parts, its accessories, its length, and its blade. I will keep my blast-pike clean and ready, even as I am clean and ready. We will become a part of each other." THUD!

"Before the gods, I swear this creed." THUD! THUD! "My blast-pike and I are the defenders of my country. We are the masters of our enemy. We are the saviors of my life. So be it, until victory is Arcania's and there are no more enemy to face." THUD!

Halcyon smiled at all of his midshipmen. "There is something mystical about that marine mantra you just heard. You all should learn it. I know I have. Now, Scott, what are those articles?"

"Sir, Article One states, I am an Arcanian, fighting in the armed forces which guard my country and our way of life. I am prepared and able to give my life for my country's defense. Sir, Article Two states, I will never surrender of my own free will. If in command, I will never surrender the members of my command while they still have the means to resist. Sir, Article Three states, if I am captured, I will continue to resist by all means available. I will make every effort to escape and aid others in their escape. I will accept neither parole nor special favors from the enemy, sir." Scott said each article letter-perfect and by the time he was done, all of the sleepiness was gone from his face and tone.

"Letter-perfect, we'll make sure you know what those words mean later. Notice from the board," Halcyon said to the group, "that there is fencing practice for our section at the noon bell.

You will be on deck with your weapon, at the ready before that bell rings. In an hour, the ship's bell will clang out the six bells of the morning watch. Your duty stations for the day will be up in the sticks. Act-un and Coal-un, you take the foretopsail. Stillwater, you take the maintopsail. Gold-un, you are on the mizzen topgallant. Right at this moment, we are all going up the lines to the tops of the mainmast.

"Consider this before you begin climbing. Your first-class midshipman likes to be at his duty station at least fifteen minutes before his assigned time. Why? Because he believes officers should be early to their work and stay late upon need. Get a move on!"

Halcyon watched his midshipmen begin the climb and he followed closely after them. "Mr. Stillwater, your arms are used to pull you up. Just use your feet for balance and support."

"Aye, sir!" Torance shouted, correcting his action and pulling himself up the lines instead of using his feet to push himself up.

"Mr. Gold-un, what are the remaining Articles of Conduct?" Halcyon asked as they all climbed the high rigging.

"Sir, Article Four states, if I become a prisoner of war, I will keep faith with my fellow prisoners. I will give no information nor take part in any action, which might be harmful to my comrades. If I am senior, I will take command. If not, I will obey the lawful orders of those appointed over me and will back them up in every way."

Gold-un clearly didn't like the climb. He slowed way down as he continued to detail the articles. "Sir, Article Five states, when questioned, should I become a prisoner of war, I am required to give name and rank. I will evade answering further questions to the utmost of my ability. I will make no oral or written statements disloyal to my country and its allies or harmful to their cause. Sir, Article Six, uh, Article Six . . ."

"Jakwater, it's the most important of all the articles. Come on, man," Halcyon urged.

Gold-un stopped climbing for a moment and said the article: "I will never forget that I am an Arcanian, responsible for my actions, and dedicated to the principles which made my country free. I will trust in the gods and in my king."

"Good, but we both should be in the tops by now," Halcyon said, climbing line for line beside the midshipman.

The tops of the mainmast held a platform for the crossbowmen to shoot down at the enemy. There were belts attached to the mast so that the men could lean out and get good shots at those in the enemy ships approaching the *Rage*. As Halcyon reached the tops, he saw the faces of the men he would be commanding on this voyage and suddenly he grew apprehensive with himself.

It was just a few months ago that he was a lowly fifth-class midshipwizard taking orders from almost everyone.

Now he was supposed to lead others.

Command was part of his training at the midshipwizard academy, but the thought of being responsible for others hadn't hit home until just then. While he was eager for command, he didn't want to be responsible for giving an order killing the men he commanded.

"Up here, when we are all together you have permission to speak freely. I want to hear what you're thinking," Halcyon ordered. "It's also important for me to get to know each of you so that I can tell what you do best."

Halcyon was resorting to the training methods he'd experienced himself at the academy. He had several talking sessions just as he was doing right now.

"Hurchial, you start. Where do you come from?" Halcyon asked.

"Well, sir." The slow-talking Hurchial seemed to be thinking about each word before he said them. "I, like most of the half-dwarves of the crew, come from Et Bay. My family dug in mines above the bay for years; they were hardworking folk, of course. I didn't fancy the mines myself. I saw some of my merchant friends killed by the Maleen and it riled me up. I joined the navy to make them pay a mite."

"Excellent, Mr. Act-un, and I appreciate your honesty," Halcyon replied. "Scott, you're next. Tell us a little about yourself."

"I'm an Et Bay man, no surprise there. I joined the navy because I didn't want to make a life in the mines. During training, I discovered a knack for fencing and soon I was touching my instructors with my blade." He started scratching his head as he nervously looked at the others. "I also know all of the Articles of War and others around me started saying if I knew so much I should be an officer. I don't rightly know if I have what it takes to command men, but I'm willing to give it a try. That's about all I have to say."

"That's good, Mr. Coal-un. I'm sure as we train together you will prove that you can become a fine officer," Halcyon said, wanting Coal-un and the rest to feel comfortable one hundred and fifty feet above the deck of the *Rage*. The air was crisp and clear up in the tops and the quiet was pleasant as he listened to the other midshipmen. "Torance, your turn, if you will," Halcyon said.

"My mother died when I was young. I worked the mines around Et Bay with my uncles, father, and two brothers. One day there was a cave-in that took my entire family. I lost my finger that day." He held up his hand to show them all what they had noticed already. "I could have gone back and worked the mines, but I was soured on the idea of working in the earth again. I joined the navy to get as far away from the depths of the earth as I could. I quickly advanced from junior seaman, to able seaman, to leading seaman, and thought I would like to be among the officers. I don't know that I want to captain my own ship, but I intend to become a first officer somewhere. I got this scar off Elese in a frigate action. I killed the man who gave it to me. I like dwarves and speak their two different languages, which is why I'm sure I was transferred here. I've worked frigates mainly."

"Your experience will be useful on this voyage, I'm sure, Mr. Stillwater. When we have a bit more time, I want you to teach us all a bit of the dwarven language. It could prove useful to know while we're in their empire."

Torance was scowling at what Halcyon said. That fact bothered the midshipwizard a bit, but he didn't want to call attention to it in front of the others. "Now you, Mr. Gold-un, if you would," Halcyon said.

"I'm from Alm," Midshipman Gold-un said. "My father was a merchant trading in wood from the Arcanian forests and the black marble of the Dwarven Empire. He liked the forests of Tanar so much that he settled in Alm. I can speak the dwarven trade tongue. I have enough of my human mother's traits that I can swim and not sink like a stone as most dwarves do."

The other half-dwarves smirked at this last bit. With aspects like their dwarven parents', they knew they couldn't stay afloat very long in the sea or in any body of water.

Jakwater continued, "I've served on two other frigates, but this is my first dragonfrigate and I have to admit the sea dragon scares the hell out of me. I just see that great maw coming down on the deck to feed on the hay and I can't help but think it could take me in one bite."

"I didn't notice you looking scared when we were feeding Sort yesterday," Halcyon noted.

"I'm going to do my job whether I'm afraid or not. If the dragon eats me, I can just hope it gets sick from the effort," Jakwater replied.

They had a good laugh at that.

"You all get down to the wardroom and eat your fill of the morning meal. All of you must be ready when that morning bell rings," Halcyon ordered. "Naturally, as we are in port, we won't be going to the dawn battle stations. Midshipman Stillwater, bide a moment as the others leave. I want you all to know that I'm here to guide you as well as command you. Don't be afraid to ask questions. It's the way I learned and it's a good way in this man's navy. Dismissed," he said, waving them all down the rigging.

Stillwater had a questioning look on his face as the others went down the rigging in the darkness.

The false dawn light was just creeping over the horizon. It would be a clear morning. The wind started freshening from the landside.

"Mr. Stillwater, you don't like the thought of teaching some of the others Dwarvish, do you?" Halcyon asked, knowing the answer already.

"I do what I'm ordered and it doesn't matter what I like and don't like," he replied, but the tone of his voice was challenging.

"Obeying orders is all well and good, a great many of the Articles of War deal with just that topic. I asked you to teach us Dwarvish more to have the others and myself get to know you better. From our brief encounters together, I'm seeing an anger in you that's detrimental to the good operation of this ship," Halcyon said.

"I have no idea what you are talking about, sir," Stillwater replied, maintaining his nasty tone.

"Just let me tell you one more thing and you can go," Halcyon said. "If the men like you and respect you, they will follow you into hell and back obeying your every order without question. To gain their trust you have to present an honorable aspect to the men. Several times now I've seen you scowl at things I've said. I imagine you're constantly showing a bad attitude to everyone around you. Learn to hide your true feelings or you'll never make a good officer. I myself don't especially enjoy following the orders of Mr. Swordson. I never show my dislike. From now on during this voyage, every time I catch you showing your irritation in your face or in your posture I'll let you know in no uncertain terms that you are making a mistake. Carry on, Mr. Stillwater."

"Sir." He saluted and went down the rigging.

Halcyon stayed in the tops. He'd hoped his discussion with Torance would have some positive effect. Halcyon's mood was a bit dark right then. Forced into his command position, he had thousands of doubts about his ability to command. Feeling the constant stares of Elan Swordson didn't make things any easier. Halcyon felt himself about to embark on a new adventure, but there were so many things he still didn't know about ship life and commanding men. Somehow, he strongly suspected he was in for rough seas on this voyage, and he didn't mean the bad-weather kind.

"*Leaving soon?*" the dragon questioned.

"*Right you are,*" Halcyon thought back.

"*Fish taste bad here,*" the sea dragon remarked.

"*Don't worry, we'll be sailing where the fish are big and tasty.*" Halcyon didn't know this to be true, but he wanted to reassure the dragon. As the creature's thoughts struck his mind, the creature seemed young and a little frightened.

The ship's bell rang out six clangs and everyone hit the deck running. The *Rage* was out on its first mission and woe be it on anyone or anything getting in its way.

Halcyon came below at half past the hour of eleven. He found himself pleased to see all of his midshipmen getting reading for the fencing practice of twelve bells.

"Officer on deck!" Hurchial shouted.

They all came to attention when Swordson came into the area. Elan had showed his irritation by showing his anger whenever he came down into the hammock area of the midshipmen. He didn't like not having the small area usually assigned to lieutenants on all other frigates.

"I see the little ducklings are getting ready to play with their swords. Very good, very good indeed," Elan snarled. He hadn't let them relax from their attention stance. "Mr. Blithe, present your journal for inspection and tell these others what the regulations are on a midshipman's journal."

"Sir, a midshipman will have his daily journal filled out by eleven bells of the morning watch," Halcyon replied.

"Very good, Mr. Blithe, and letter-perfect too. Hand me your journal," Elan ordered.

Halcyon opened his footlocker and handed over his journal.

Swordson inspected the middle pages of the book. "Excellent, and letter-perfect. I'd expect nothing less from the first-class midshipwizard of the *Rage*. At ease, all of you. Mr. Gold-un, your journal please."

A very worried Jakwater handed over his journal.

Elan turned the pages and a broad grin filled his face. "You haven't entered anything for three days. Administrative punishment or five demerits in the captain's log?"

"What sir, I didn't understand that," Jakwater said.

"You can have your choice between my administrative punishment or demerits in the captain's log book. Naturally, you know that such demerits will be entered into your naval record."

"I'll take administrative punishment, sir," Jakwater said.

"Strip your shirt and put your chest on the table," Elan ordered.

The room grew tense. It was a rare thing to demand administrative punishment for a minor thing like not keeping up a journal. The unfairness of the judgment wasn't lost on anyone in the room.

Jakwater leaned over the table.

Swordson took off his broad belt. "That'll be five strikes and all's done my fine duckling."

With a smile on his face, Elan lashed out with the belt strap, striking the thin back of Jakwater.

To his credit, the young half-dwarf didn't cry out and the strap slapped hard against his back. Blood welled up all along the red strip.

The rest of the group looked grimly on, not liking what they were seeing.

By the third strike, Jakwater rested fully on the table, weak from the blows. His back became bloody. At the fifth strike, he was barely able to stand.

"Who's next?" Swordson asked, flicking his belt in the air.

Stillwater presented his journal and came to attention.

Swordson paged through the middle of the book, not liking what he saw. He threw the journal in Stillwater's hammock. "Next," Elan said.

Coal-un presented his journal and stood at attention.

Swordson paged through the book, not liking the tight-filled pages of notes, and threw that book to the deck.

"And you, Midshipman Act-un?" Swordson asked with his hand out.

Hurchial, the youngest of the group, was almost sobbing as tears filled his eyes without quite falling.

Elan paged through the journal and his eyes rose as he started smiling again. "It seems from this journal that you haven't posted anything in it for weeks. Will it be demerits or administrative punishment?"

"Administrative punishment, sir," the young half-dwarf whimpered.

"Over the table with you then, and that will be ten lashes," Elan ordered.

Halcyon watched the spectacle with growing disgust. Although it was true that midshipmen were ordered to keep journals, this punishment Swordson was dealing out for this very minor offense was far too much.

The back of the youngest of the midshipmen was far different from Gold-un's back. Where Gold-un was pale and thin, Hurchial's back was broad and powerful with a dark reddish cast to his flesh. Act-un bent over the table, his chest not touching the wood. His face showed his fear of the punishment.

The first stroke flicked down on his back and made a loud slapping sound. Hurchial never moved an inch. A questioning look came to his face. The flesh on his back showed nothing of the stroke.

Elan must have noted his lack of success. He stroked down harder and faster and blows fell quickly on the midshipman's back. Faster and faster and harder and harder, the blows slapped down until all of the others were wincing as each blow fell. Hurchial's back remained unmarked no matter what Elan did, and rage showed clearly on the man's face.

His hand rose for another blow and Halcyon's open hand struck out and grabbed Swordson's wrist. The lieutenant started struggling to deliver another blow, but Blithe's firm grip didn't allow the man's arm and hand to move an inch. "Mr. Swordson, I took the liberty of counting for you, sir. I was sure you didn't want to deliver more blows than you had ordered. You have given him ten stripes."

The dazed look of rage left Swordson's face. "Carry on," he said, walking out of the wardroom.

Halcyon looked at the two midshipmen's backs. "Mr. Gold-un, you go to the ship's surgeon and get that back attended to. There will be no fencing for you today. Mr. Act-un, I can see your dwarf blood gives you a bit more toughness than our Mr. Gold-un here has. Are you up to fencing?"

"Aye, sir. The stripes didn't hurt at all," Hurchial replied with a bit of wonder in his voice.

"Carry on then, all of you. There's sword work to be done," Halcyon said with a winning smile.

XI

❧ ❧ ❧

Odd Man Out

Gord-un came to the railing and looked for Blithe among the men on the forecastle and blast-tube decks. He spotted him over on the forecastle and gave him a hail. "Mr. Blithe, summon your men to the quarterdeck!"

Halcyon moved quickly, summoning all of his midshipmen, and they raced to the quarterdeck. They came to attention in front of the captain.

"Today, you'll all deal with Boatswain Gray," the captain

said, walking back and forth in front of his midshipmen. "He's learned more about lines and rigging than I'll ever know. I regard him as the best boatswain in the navy and you should as well. Boatswain Gray, these men are yours."

Gray was a big man, with huge muscles running along his shoulders from a lifetime of pulling at the rigging. He stood a little over six feet tall, was bald, and had a graying beard. There was a youthful twinkle in his eyes, but his demeanor showed he was very serious at the moment. His hands were pitch black from handling the tar on all the lines of the ship. Those who worked with him never doubted he'd touched and knew every line on the *Rage*.

"I'm here to teach you all a bit about the lines of this ship," Gray said to them. "Let's go to the jibs first."

They walked to the prow of the *Rage* and Gray kept up a dialogue with the midshipmen. "We guard all the time against chafe and the cross-strain on the lines. Strain can pull the heart right out of any line. Lines are living things, never you doubt it. I know Mr. Blithe is a rope speaker and that's a rare talent indeed. He knows as I do that each line is a living thing. As you all know, we strip all the sail and rigging from the sticks every time we're in a friendly port. Lines need to be checked and sails need mending.

"When we put up any sail it's important to do the job right. We expect all leading seamen and officers to know every sail and line of the ship." He looked at each of the men to make sure they were listening.

Halcyon did the same and saw his midshipmen drinking in every word of Gray's lecture.

"Lines are vital and it's important to make sure they're weatherproofed. Lines can shrink so much in damp weather that they pull out the masts." The boatswain warmed to his topic. "Other times in dry weather they can go so slack that the rags hang like drapes in your mother's parlor. Captains tend to get a mite touchy when that happens." Gray grinned.

The midshipmen all smiled at the simple jest.

"Mr. Blithe, I'd like it if you didn't give away the next part," Gray asked.

Halcyon nodded, thinking he knew what was going to happen.

"The rest of you look well at the three lines I've got coiled on the deck." The boatswain waved their glances at the ropes.

The lines were the same, each coil appeared to be the same height, two were tarred, and one was obviously bare hemp. One of the lines was by the port side of the forecastle, the second was by the prow, and the third, the one with no tar, was at the starboard railing.

Halcyon stood by, knowing which of the lines was weak, as there was a blue glow coming from the line.

"Get a little dirty, my fine officers. Your lives are going to depend on these lines. Make sure you know them and tell me when you feel you know the lines." The boatswain urged them to investigate the coils. "As you all know, the mainstay is the heaviest line of the ship. Most of those lines are eleven inches wide. Shroud lines range from six to eight inches wide. These are jib lines at a little over an inch thick."

Jakwater took the time to uncoil each of the ropes and closely look at them. Halcyon was pleased with the lad's diligence.

"Now that you've checked these lines, your life is going to depend on them. Do any of you have any questions?" Gray asked.

The four midshipmen had questioning looks on their face, but none of them asked a thing.

"Well, my fine young officers, I'm glad you feel you know your lines. I would like each of you to stand by one of these three lines, stand by the one you believe to be the strongest." Gray was clearly enjoying himself.

Gold-un, Stillwater, and Coal-un stood by the first of the tarred lines. Act-un stood by the second tarred line. Halcyon started walking to a line, but Gray shot out a hand, knowing Halcyon knew the truth of the lines.

"I've set up three different hearts, block, and tackle off the tops of the foresail." Gray's gestures showed the men the pulleys. "The three of you at the first line thread that line and make it fast to the port side. Mr. Act-un and Mr. Blithe, please set up the second line and make it fast to the starboard side."

It was only a matter of minutes as the men climbed up and down the rigging of the foresail and accomplished their task.

"Mr. Stillwater, you're a likely young officer, you've seen this type of drill before, so tie yourself off with the shank of this line. Mr. Gold-un and Mr. Coal-un will then proceed to pull you up into the air. This simulates you trusting your life to the line and trusting your fine judgment," Gray ordered.

Stillwater did what he was told and tied himself off with the line. The other two grabbed the line at the block and tackle.

"Heave, officers, like you mean it!" ordered the boatswain.

The two put their weight into it and Stillwater rose with a groan ten feet into the air when the line snapped and he fell onto the deck with a thud. He landed well, but fell to his back with a groan.

"You're dead, Mr. Stillwater. That line was filled with salt rot," Gray said. "All three of you looked at the ends of the line but didn't take the time to test the core of the rope. Don't make that mistake again.

"Well, Mr. Act-un, I'm sure your choice is better." Gray was smiling, but none of the midshipmen thought any of the lesson was amusing. "Tie yourself off, my fine young gentleman. Mr.

Blithe, you will do the honors of hauling him up into the air."

Hurchial tied himself off in a manner allowing him to fall straight down if his rope broke. When he was ready he nodded to Halcyon.

Blithe pulled at the rope and Hurchial rose into the air. He rose fifteen feet in the air when his rope broke. He landed cat-like on the deck, figuring he was going to fall.

"I put extra tar on the two worn portions of the rope. I figured no one would take the rope that wasn't tarred. Let that be a lesson in appearances, my fine young gentlemen. Our rope speaker here knew the hemp rope was the only good one, didn't you now?" Gray asked.

"Yes, I could see the wrongness of both lines. It appears as a soft blue glow to my eyes," Halcyon answered.

"Such rope speakers are worth their weight in gold in the navy," Gray replied. "The rest of us have to check on the lines the old-fashioned way. We have to use our hands and eyes and check out every inch. For the rest of the afternoon we'll un-braid these bad strands of line. Nothing gets wasted on a king's ship, as you all know. Hunker down and make yourselves comfortable. We'll be at it for a while."

They did what they were told.

Hours later Halcyon had a few heartbeats to himself. He took a moment to open the pocket watch the Lady Teagan gave him. Smiling in wonder at the device, Halcyon marveled, thinking it was such a thoughtful gift from a person he barely knew. In the darkness of the hold, there was a dim glow from the inside of the watch, allowing him to see the time and the image on the other side.

The Lady Teagan was dressed in a different gown from the

one he first saw in the locket. She was dressed all in purple and sipping a cup of tea. He wondered if the image changed as the real Teagan changed. Could she see him as he was from moment to moment? With a pleasant sigh, he put the watch away, belted on his sword, took up his war helm, and went up the ladder. *There is fencing to do*, he thought.

As he grasped the ladder, he heard the captain bark an order.

"Chanter, start up 'The Bonnie *Rage*,' if you please," the captain ordered.

The ship's chanter took up the tune, and everywhere on the ship, from the orlop deck in the lowest depths to the men in the tops, everyone started singing the chantey.

> *On the bonnie Rage I serv'd my time,*
> *Hurrah for the Sea Dragon Rage!*
> *On the bonnie Rage I serv'd my time,*
> *Hurrah for the Sea Dragon Rage!*
>
> *This dragonfrigate is good and true,*
> *Hurrah for the Sea Dragon Rage!*
> *They are the ships for me and you,*
> *Hurrah for the Sea Dragon Rage!*
>
> *For once there was a sea-dragon ship,*
> *Hurrah for the Sea Dragon Rage!*
> *That fourteen knots an hour could slip,*
> *Hurrah for the Sea Dragon Rage!*
>
> *Its yards were square, its gear all new,*
> *Hurrah for the Sea Dragon Rage!*
> *It had a good and gallant crew,*
> *Hurrah for the Sea Dragon Rage!*

One day whilst sailing on the sea,
Hurrah for the Sea Dragon Rage!
We saw a vessel on our lee,
Hurrah for the Sea Dragon Rage!

We fired a shot across their bow,
Hurrah for the Sea Dragon Rage!
Which was not kind you must allow,
Hurrah for the Sea Dragon Rage!

They did not fear as you may think,
Hurrah for the Sea Dragon Rage!
And made for us as if to sink,
Hurrah for the Sea Dragon Rage!

We gave that vessel another thought,
Hurrah for the Sea Dragon Rage!
Soon they knew that they were caught,
Hurrah for the Sea Dragon Rage!

The Maleen captain became quickly seized,
Hurrah for the Sea Dragon Rage!
That made our captain very pleased,
Hurrah for the Sea Dragon Rage!

That Maleen ship and its wicked crew,
Hurrah for the Sea Dragon Rage!
We sunk beneath the waters blue,
Hurrah for the Sea Dragon Rage!

It was a plucky thing to do,
Hurrah for the Sea Dragon Rage!

To destroy that Maleen vessel through and through,
Hurrah for the Sea Dragon Rage!

Let's drink a tin to this good ship,
Hurrah for the Sea Dragon Rage!
Deep in the grog barrels we should dip,
Hurrah for the Sea Dragon Rage!

On the frigate Rage *we serve our time,*
Hurrah for the Sea Dragon Rage!
Let's find another Maleen ship 'fore dinnertime,
Hurrah for the Sea Dragon Rage!

Halcyon climbed up to the tube deck vastly pleased with the new chantey he was hearing. It was an excellent tune. His heart started racing with the chorus of "Hurrah for the Sea Dragon Rage!" He thought for a minute that the dragon wouldn't like it much, as it thought of itself as Sort, but the tune was catching.

Halcyon rushed the ladder onto the quarterdeck pleased to see his midshipmen present. He was the only one in a white fencing uniform; that unnerved him just a bit.

The ship's bell clanged out twelve noon. The captain turned from scanning the southern horizon and looked over his officers, all ready to practice the deadly art of fencing. Most of them held practice battle-axes in their hands.

"I think you will find, Mr. Blithe, that oftentimes there isn't time to put on a fancy blade-working suit like the one you have on. In the future, please wear your normal uniform for the practice sessions," the captain ordered.

"Sir, aye, sir," Halcyon replied, turning red from embarrassment at being singled out by the captain.

The sun was high in the clear blue sky.

The captain sorted out the duelists into two groups along the port and starboard side of the quarterdeck.

"I teach the use of the battle-axe on board the *Rage* alongside the use of the saber. Use whichever weapon you prefer in practice. I like the axe and am comfortable with it. I would urge you all to give the weapon a try in a few of our practice sessions."

Lord Abernathy came up on deck in a white fencing uniform, making Halcyon feel even more uncomfortable.

"Lord Abernathy, you wish to join our practice sessions?" the captain asked.

"I feel the need for a bit of sport. It's going to be a long trip and one can never tell when one needs to defend oneself, can one, what?" the ambassador replied.

"Join my group, sir, on the port side of the quarterdeck, and don't expect any of these officers to go easy on you because of your status. We practice killing arts here, what?" the captain quipped back.

Halcyon could see the expression of irritation on the ambassador's face, but the man said nothing and joined the group on the port side.

"The first and second officers will serve as referees in the matches. Each participant continues the duel to the second touch. We'll go through the group and I will comment on the actions of the officers. One member of the port side and one from the starboard, come front and center and begin. The rest of you will act as spotters and raise your hand when you see a touch scored. Let's begin," the captain ordered.

Lieutenant Sand-un showed himself a thick half-dwarf with a large axe that seemed light as a feather in his big hands. He spun the weapon nervously in a circle as he squared off against

Marine Lieutenant Macluun, who was a tall man drawing a practice saber.

The two men faced each other with First Officer Townzat in between. Townzat held his hand out between the two men, and when he said, "Ready, begin," he backed away and the two went at it.

As Halcyon watched the mock combat he earnestly wished he had worn his bracers and chest plate. The wedge of metal in the axe Sand-un was wielding was going to make a nasty bruise if it contacted, even if it was a dull weapon. The midshipwizard watched the battle with interest, as he wanted to see what an axe could do against a saber.

Time and time again the very fast marine tried to lunge his long saber into the chest of his opponent only to have it blocked time and time again by the wedge of metal the axe constantly presented.

The slower Sand-un constantly backed the marine into a corner where he couldn't dodge anymore, and the first point was scored by the axe wielder.

"Halt! Point to Sand-un," cried Townzat, as he saw the hands of many of the watchers awarding Sand-un the point. "Take your positions again."

"Marine," the captain said, "try not to get backed into the railing this time. Sand-un is as slow as grass growing."

Laughter brought a flush of red to the young marine's face.

"Begin!" shouted the first officer.

Sand-un threw his axe at the startled marine, who clearly had no idea how to stop that blow.

"Halt!" Townzat said, stopping the action. "Second point to Sand-un."

The captain glared at Sand-un. "Well thrown. Now, what do you do against the other eight enemy lunging at you?"

The question didn't require an answer.

"In our practice matches, whatever touches a fighter's chest causes a point loss. A belaying pin." The captain was stiffly walking back and forth between the groups, clearly not liking how that last point was scored. "An apple, a dagger, whatever, I don't care. The next two, up and at the ready."

Swordson from Halcyon's side and the ambassador from the captain's came to the center of the deck. Both men held practice sabers in their hands. Both were about the same height and reach. Swordson was much younger, but the handle on the ambassador's weapon showed much use. The man knew how to hold his weapon en garde.

"Begin!" ordered Second Officer Dorlat.

At first just the tips of their blades touched and retouched as each man sought weakness in the other. Swordson quickly started moving to the right and closing and drifting back and forth on the deck.

The ambassador held his ground, showing fine defensive skills.

Elan started raising his entire blade, and with each pass of the weapons the ambassador made the mistake of raising his blade at a higher angle as well to meet Elan's blade. Halcyon knew exactly what was going to happen next.

Elan feinted even higher with his blade and then angled it low for a killing point. The man was easily quick enough to deliver the blow, but slowed just before the touch. This allowed the ambassador to slash down and take the first point.

"Halt! Point to the ambassador," declared Dorlat.

The officers on the port side started stamping their feet, honoring one of their champions. The ambassador bowed toward the group.

Halcyon knew that Elan had purposely slowed his hand. The

midshipwizard wasn't sure how he felt about the obvious flattery. On one hand it would be good to have the ambassador think he did well. On the other hand, was letting the ambassador win helping the man improve his weapons skills enough to survive in a real battle? Blithe wasn't sure, but he didn't think not winning was such a good idea.

"Begin," ordered Dorlat.

The ambassador lunged quickly and Elan took the point on his chest.

"Halt! Match to the ambassador," shouted Dorlat.

The men on the port side were even louder in their stamping. The ambassador joined the group with a big smile on his face.

Match after match continued and Halcyon saw far too often that the axemen seemed to have a defensive advantage. He wondered how to counter that in his own match and a plan started forming in the back of his mind.

"Blithe and Darkwater, front and center," came the order.

Strictly speaking, Denna Darkwater wasn't an officer, but Marine Commander Maxwell could do anything he pleased and he pleased to have Denna in this mix.

She was a half troll and Halcyon saw her with an axe. He knew it wasn't a weapon she used much and he hoped that would help him. They faced each other and she gave him a huge smile, probably remembering their first match on the *Sanguine*. He weakly smiled back and put a mental plan into operation.

He began thinking to himself. *This is my saber.* Halcyon lunged when a marine would have lunged with his blast-pike. Denna backed just out of touching range. Halcyon fell back into a defensive en garde and continued chanting his own mantra to himself. *There are many like it, but this one is mine.*

While he thought those words he was all defense and Denna's twisting weapon never touched his body. Halcyon lunged again, only to be blocked again. The smile was gone from Denna's face as she started moving the battle-axe back and forth, using her vast strength. Halcyon kept his smile and kept up the mantra. *It is my life. I must master it as I must master my life. Without me, my saber is useless. Without my saber, I am useless.* He lunged again, this time purposely trying for a low touch and scoring.

"Halt!" Peter ordered, and they both backed up. "Point to Blithe," he said.

Denna was breathing hard. Anger now showed on her face as she turned away from Halcyon and whipped her weapon back and forth in vicious short strokes.

"Calm down," ordered Major Maxwell.

"Ready," Peter ordered, and both combatants faced each other. "Begin," he said.

Halcyon continued thinking; *I must strike true with my saber.* The cadence of the mantra dictated how defensive he should be and he had no problem fending off the many axe strikes Denna rained down on him. *I must slice straighter than the enemy who is trying to kill me. I must stab him before he stabs me. I will.* He lunged. Her axe shaft deflected his attack, and he quickly moved back into a defensive position. Sweat poured from him, but he was calm and pleased with his performance. Denna glared at him and began an amazing attack; her battle-axe became a wall of steel as it constantly flashed at his skull and chest. *My saber and I know that what counts in war is not the swinging of the saber, the yelling of the weapon user, or the show of force we make. We know that it's the hit that counts.* His lunge failed to push her back and she was past the tip of his weapon. Halcyon showed himself faster than the winded Darkwater as he backed up out of striking distance. *We will hit.* Even backing up, he presented a lunge, but she blocked it and closed with him. He became all defense now.

My saber is alive, even as I am alive, because it is my life. Thus, I will learn it as a brother. His lunge scored him nothing. *I will learn its weaknesses, its strengths, its parts, its accessories, its length, and its blade. I will keep my saber clean and ready, even as I am clean and ready. We will become a part of each other.* He couldn't tell how many attacks he'd stopped, but now it was necessary to duck as well as use his weapon to beat off the axe slashes.

Before the gods, I swear this creed. He never tried a double lunge before. The cadence of the marine mantra called for two attacks one after another, and that's just what he did.

"Halt! Touch and match to Blithe," the first officer said. Halcyon's side of the quarterdeck erupted in cheers. Halcyon held his hand out to Denna; she took it in a bone-crunching squeeze. He never winced as he finished the mantra in his mind.

My saber and I are the defenders of my country. We are the masters of our enemy. We are the saviors of my life. So be it, until victory is Arcania's and there's no more enemy to face.

She let go and he sheathed his practice weapon.

"It's rare I see such a good defense in a saber user," the captain noted. "If anything, I would say that Mr. Blithe should have tried attacking a bit more, but he got the job done. It's useless to tell Corporal Darkwater to try and control her temper so I won't. We'll now prepare for the melee. As those of you know who have served with me, we often board and capture ships. That means we're taking the quarterdecks of the enemy vessels. Right now we'll practice that. I'll go among you and put white armbands on those who've served the shortest time with me. Those officers will attack the quarterdeck from the tubedeck. You old hands can stand back and wait for a bit."

As he placed a white armband around Halcyon's sword arm, he said quietly, "I want you to use practice force bolts on any enemy you face, understood?" Gord-un said.

"Yes, sir," Halcyon answered. The casting of magical force bolts was an every morning drill in the academy. In a real battle, a wizard was expected to be able to launch at least three deadly bolts of energy at individual foes. Most wizards could send out five of the far-lesser-strength practice bout variety. Halcyon's record was ten.

Halcyon noticed the captain speaking quietly to Swordson as well.

The men with white armbands all gathered on the tube deck. There were nine of them with Elan as the highest-ranking navy officer.

"I'll rush the port side ladder, and Mr. Blithe, you will take the starboard side," Swordson ordered. "Ambassador, please do me the honor of attacking with my side, if you feel up to it, sir."

There was a nervous look on Abernathy's face, but he nodded assent.

First Officer Townzat stood at the railing by the port side of the quarterdeck to judge who died in the mock battle. Second Officer Dorlat stood at the railing on the starboard side. There were eleven officers ready to enter the fray on the quarterdeck as the captain came to the railing.

"You are considered victors when you've scored a point on me," the captain said. "That won't prove easy. Begin!" he roared.

Halcyon and Elan rushed the stairs and launched magical force bolts in the chests of two different targets before they knew they were under magical attack.

"Dead, dead!" shouted Dorlat.

"Dead, dead!" growled Townzat.

"Magic, they're using magic," the surprised officer shouted.

The problem of the narrow stairway up to the quarterdeck was solved as both wizards cleared the stairway, making way for more of their attacking crew members.

Halcyon saw Denna drop her axe and pick up a racked blast-pike. He tried to stop her by firing several force bolts at her, but she was too quick. The new weapon in her hand absorbed his magic with no bolts touching her.

As the fighting progressed, Halcyon's pace slowed. The effort it took to cast even weak force bolts took its toll. Finally, there was just Halcyon on his side and the captain on the other side.

"Good work, Mr. Blithe, now come and meet your end," the captain said with a bloodthirsty grin on his face. The captain had yet to strike a single blow during the melee.

Halcyon approached, thinking he didn't have the strength to enter the mantra that allowed him to win before. As he approached, the captain did something with his huge battle-axe and the weapon started to glow.

Surprised, Halcyon's eyes opened wide and he didn't know what to expect. He certainly didn't expect the captain to put his hand behind his back to reach for a throwing axe. The weapon launched straight and true at Halcyon's head and struck his helm, making it ring like a bell tolling the fight over.

The captain sheathed his axe and reached a hand down to Halcyon. "Expect the unexpected, Mr. Blithe. I know there are a couple of very surprised dead officers on this deck that didn't expect you and Mr. Swordson to use your magic against them; shame on them. Shame on you, Mr. Blithe, for allowing me to throw my axe at you. Better luck next time."

The ringing in Halcyon's ears had just about stopped as he got shakily to his feet.

✤ ✤ ✤

XII

𝕻unishment 𝕲auntlet

HIS MAJESTY'S ARTICLES OF WAR: ARTICLE XXXII

*Whenever a man enters on board, the commanding officer
shall cause an accurate entry to be made in the ship's books,
showing his name, the date, place and term of his enlistment,
the place or vessel from which he was received on board, his
rating, his descriptive list, his age, place of birth, and citizen-
ship, with such remarks as may be necessary.*

The five midshipmen were taking their ease on the forecastle
deck. They worked on various personal tasks.

Halcyon worked on his manacles of Iben. He'd lock one on
to his wrist and work the lock, trying to make it pop free. Just
then, he was using long chips of wood to work into the lock.
While his hands worked the lock, his mind went over what he
was going to have his midshipmen do during the blast-tube
drill. The ship schedule called for blast-tube practice and Hal-

cyon wanted to make sure the midshipmen worked together on their own tube. He wanted to see what they were all capable of performing under the stress of the drill.

Resting on one of the blast-tubes, Coal-un was using a file to smooth a large piece of granite. He looked like he was trying to make the chunk of stone into a round sphere. "Mr. Blithe, I would think what you're trying to do right now is illegal. Slipping out of those manacles when the captain puts them on you would be a court-martial offense, wouldn't it?" Coal-un said with a lot of doubt in his voice.

"Mr. Coal-un," Halcyon replied, "what is Article Eighteen?"

Coal-un looked up into the sky and said, "Article Eighteen says, all murders committed by . . ."

"That's Article Seventeen, you're a daft man you are," Stillwater shot back.

Halcyon smiled at both of them as he freed himself from the magical manacle. He'd managed to use wood, a piece of wire, and a shark's tooth to open the lock. Getting out of the manacles wasn't going to be a problem ever again. "You're correct about the article being seventeen, I'm not so sure about the daft part. Please, Mr. Stillwater, recite the article."

Stillwater was using a small sharpening stone to put an edge on his boot blade. Midshipmen were encouraged to constantly carry dirks somewhere on their person. Most chose their boot. He sat on the deck with his back against a blast-tube. The weapon was very similar to the two that Halcyon had in his own boots. The man looked Blithe in the eye as he continued sharpening his weapon. "Article Eighteen says, all robbery committed by any person in the fleet shall be punished with death, or otherwise, as a court martial, upon consideration of the circumstances, shall find meet."

"Excellent, Mr. Stillwater, letter-perfect. Mr. Coal-un, you will recite for me the first twenty articles after dinner tonight. To answer your question, as a wizard of Arcania, if I'm ever captured by the enemy, the first thing they'll do to me is place manacles of Iben on my wrists. I've had these things on before, and there's something about their nature that stops a wizard from casting magic," he said, raising the silvery manacles for all to see. "I didn't like them." Halcyon shuddered at the memory of the power the magical metal had over him. Wearing the things was almost like not breathing. He shook himself at the bad memories and explained, "Since it's the duty of every navy man to try and escape the enemy, a little practice in slipping these nasty things seems like a good idea to me. Should our good captain feel the need to put me in manacles, I would be bound as any officer and gentleman to stay in them until my honor was restored."

Elan Swordson could hear Blithe's words floating down onto the tube deck from above. Everything that man did irritated the junior lieutenant.

"Is something troubling you, Mr. Swordson?" the ambassador asked, noting the look of anger on Swordson's face while he strolled toward the man on the wide deck.

The startled Elan looked up. "No, not a bit, Ambassador. I'm just getting ready to inspect the blast-tubes in this section. We're a fighting ship and everything must be in constant readiness, don't you know."

The tall ambassador scanned the horizon. "Lacking enemies at present, but I certainly get your meaning. I've never had the pleasure of command. I imagine it deadly dull stuff, what?"

"Begging your pardon your grace, but not a bit of it." Elan was thrilled the politically powerful ambassador took the time to talk to him. They walked back and forth on the tube deck.

_____

"Have you seen much action against the Maleen, sir?" Act-un questioned Halcyon while he carved a large piece of ivory.

"Yes, sir, tell us about some of your experiences; I haven't seen any action and I've served for three years," Coal-un said.

Halcyon was debating telling them of his few brief encounters. He didn't want to brag about the lucky things happening to him in the recent past. He also didn't want to tell the story of his fight against the demon ship as that would detail demonic events he'd been avoiding working through in his own mind.

He was trying to unlock a pair of prison manacles and having a devil of a time getting them open. Suddenly, a wedge of metal fell into his lap. He looked up to see Ashe Fallow giving him a wink.

"Try that one, sir, and keep it. I have several others," Ashe said, starting to leave.

Halcyon knew his immediate problem was solved.

"Chief Fallow, if you have a moment please tell these midshipmen an instructional story about one of your combat actions. I'm sure they could use your wisdom." Halcyon didn't have the slightest idea if the chief could deliver on a useful story, but Blithe was sure the chief had many stories to tell.

"A quick one then." Fallow smiled. "We wouldn't want the captain to think we're all taking our ease at the king's expense."

The dark wedge of finger-thin metal Ashe gave him had the oddest V shape at one end. Halcyon inserted that in his manacles and started twisting the metal against the mechanism inside, not having the slightest idea what he was doing. A loud click opened the lock and Halcyon held up the wedge of metal, marveling at what easy work it made of the lock. He noticed his hand was marked with soot. The wedge of metal was dark and coated in the ash of something. He looked up as Fallow began his story.

"A few years ago we were off the coast of Drusan," Fallow said with a grin on his face. "Right after those bastards, the Maleen, had taken over the country. There were some Arcania military officers needing rescuing and we were just the sailors for the job. We sailed three fast little sloops over to the mainland and waited for the full moon. We were ordered to go on shore and find the hiding officers. Begging your pardon, sirs, but officers seem to hide a lot, hrmph."

All of the midshipmen laughed at the joke, even if it did impact their officer status.

"Anyway, I was leading a detail of good lads up the cliffs after we got the signal we'd been looking for. When we got to the top, there were two squads of Maleen ready to take our number. If it weren't for the night, it would have been a hard thing, let me tell you. We gave better than we got in the action and killed most of them and made the others run.

"We were lucky, I don't mind saying. If any of their spellcasters had been in the enemy fold, I wouldn't be here today. I singled out the leader, a big man using a mace, he was. I cut him some with my blast-pike and kept him at a distance until I could take out his leg. He was suffering and begged to be killed, the instant he hit the ground. I held off and asked him how he knew we were coming, promising to give him a quick end if he would tell me.

"You'll never guess what he said," Fallow exclaimed.

Spellbound, the midshipmen focused all of their attention on the chief's words. Projects fell, untouched, into their laps. All leaned in to hear what he was about to say next.

" 'You Arcanians are fools,' the Maleen said.

"I was a bit surprised by his attitude, seeing as how he was almost dead on the ground with my lads all about him," Fallow explained.

"'Arcanians shine their weapons until they're mirror-bright. I saw the moon glint off your sword hilts from a mile away. Arcanians, such fools,' he said, and died right then."

Fallow took out his sheathed dagger. Arcanian naval daggers were all made exactly the same way. Cast in an enchanted silver, the handle had a special wire wrap. The chief's weapon was black from soot.

"Many's the officer that's tried to get me to clean up the handle of this weapon until I tell him my little story. Mr. Blithe, officers, it's been a pleasure," Fallow said, leaving the group.

All of them were looking at their own mirror-bright weapon handles, the silver glinting in the noonday sun.

The carpenter's mate was putting the finishing touches on two large contraptions when the ambassador decided to take an interest in the proceedings.

"What in the world is that for?" the ambassador asked as he tripped over several poles on the deck.

Carpenter's mate Arnold Banner didn't like officers much. Ranking far below officers, in his opinion, were the lords and nobles daring to get in his way on land or the sea. "It's a target for the blast-tubes. We'll be putting it in the water now."

The ambassador looked at the two devices. Each of the contraptions had four barrels lashed together. On each barrel stood a thin pole with a white flag attached to its top.

Winches connected at the top of the mainsail started pulling them up and over the side. Each one towed a large sack on a long line.

"The sack is a sea anchor holding the raft in place." The carpenter wondered why he even bothered to explain. He moved the ambassador back so the man wouldn't be smacked with the ton of wood as it swayed up off the deck.

The ambassador tripped over the lines of the rafts. Then the ambassador barely ducked being smashed in the head by the rising winched raft.

The captain looked down at the tube deck and what the ambassador was doing to his crew. Clearly, the carpenter wasn't helping the ambassador. *If this keeps up, my ambassador will be dying at the hands of the crew, before he even gets the chance to meet the dwarves*, the captain thought. "Call Blithe up here," Gord-un ordered to Seaman Tuttle.

Tuttle climbed down the ladder of the quarterdeck and jogged to the ladder of the forecastle. "Mr. Blithe, the captain wants you to report right now," he bellowed up to the midshipwizard.

Halcyon tossed his manacles to Scott. "Put those on my bunk. You all be careful as you man your blast-tube for the exercise. It's going to happen in just a few moments. The targets are already launching."

They all nodded, but that didn't stop Halcyon from worrying. He rushed to the captain's side.

"You called for me, sir," Halcyon said, coming to attention.

"Mr. Blithe, that blasted ambassador is going to get himself and probably quite a few others killed if we don't pin him to a corner of the ship and make him stay there," Captain Gord-un said. "During this exercise, I want you to keep him at the stern, not letting him get in anyone's way, understood?"

"Aye, aye, I'll get him now," the disappointed Halcyon said. He'd really wanted to lead his crew of midshipmen at a blast-tube, but orders were orders. He went down the ladder to the tube deck.

As Halcyon approached the ambassador, the man was

watching the coast of Arcania slip by. The southernmost point of the Cloud Giant mountain range dipped under the horizon.

"Ambassador Abernathy, I would have a moment of your time, if you please," Halcyon asked.

"Lord Blithe, I was just wondering how long it would take me to swim to shore from here," the ambassador mused.

"It's further away than you might think. Please, Ambassador, call me Halcyon or Midshipwizard; my title is not the proper form of address when we are at sea," Blithe said nervously, not knowing how the ambassador would take his admonishment.

"Yes, of course, Midshipwizard. I'm just beginning to come to grips with naval regulations. When in the capital of Anatol do as the Anatols do, has the saying goes, what?" The ambassador laughed.

"If you have a moment, the ship is just about to carry out some combat drills. I think you will find them most interesting if you and I watch them from the quarterdeck. Come with me, if you please," Blithe asked.

"Of course, and thank you for asking me. It's so deadly dull in my cabin," the ambassador said, following Blithe up the stairs to the quarterdeck.

Halcyon touched the brim of his cap in respect to the captain, who stood by the binnacle. "Soon, drums will sound the beat to quarters, and the ship will transform before your eyes."

"Really." The ambassador didn't sound convinced as he was led to the stern of the ship.

Halcyon took out two wedges of beeswax. "Ambassador, I know this is going to sound odd, but you are really going to want to have this beeswax in your ears. It's that or tie rags around your face to deaden the noise of the blast-tubes. The tubes are going to be continuously firing for several minutes and a man can go deaf if he doesn't protect himself."

While Halcyon was explaining this, his fingers were squeezing the wax, making it soft and pliable. He put a piece in his own ear as an example.

"I see no one else with rags about their ears," the ambassador said, wondering if this boy was playing a joke on him.

"Everyone will have them soon, mark my words, Ambassador," Halcyon said convincingly. "It's possible to go stone-cold deaf after just one round of blasts from a frigate's tubes and we're about to hear many blasts. Please, Ambassador, I have your best interests at heart. Put in the beeswax."

"Beat to quarters, Private Salt," the captain ordered.

Marine Private Tom Salt began the ratta-tat-tat of the drum. Its beat carried all over the ship, above and belowdecks.

The sea dragon roared out a battle challenge.

"*Where is the enemy?*" it asked of the three who could communicate with it.

The dragon's head dipped into the sea and it shot a great gout of water into the air in a challenge that type of dragon issued among its kind to anything it would fight on the surface.

"*A game, we play a game,*" Halcyon thought to the dragon.

The ambassador moved toward the sound of the drum, but Halcyon reached out a hand to stop him as the dragon calmed a bit.

"They've sounded beat to quarters, our duty station will be right here for today. You are expected to not move from your duty station," Halcyon said loud enough to counter the effects of the wax in their ears.

The ambassador shook his head and moved back to the stern railing. "Did you just talk to the sea dragon?"

"I told him we were playing a game. You have to think simply when you talk to dragons," Halcyon advised.

The ambassador visibly shivered. "Imagine being able to

communicate to that great beast. It would send me stark raving mad, I'm sure."

"Belowdecks the bulkheads are being hinged up and out of the way," Halcyon explained. "All of the belowdecks furniture is being folded up and put below in the orlop deck."

Loud thuds could be heard at the back of the ship. The ambassador peered over the railing to see what the noise was.

"The stern windows are a weak point in the defense of the ship. Heavy green wood shutters are placed over them during a battle. The wood is green and springy to cause shot to bounce off their surface," Halcyon said, trying to anticipate the ambassador's questions.

Men worked the decks, placing heavy leather hatches over the open holds.

"We can't let seawater get into the ship, so the men are sealing the abovedecks hatches. Seawater striking the heart or liver of the sea dragon causes it to want to submerge, which would kill us all, of course," Halcyon said, itching to help with the work.

The dragon roared its defiance to the sky and there was definitely an amused tone to its challenge.

Me like games, the dragon thought to Halcyon.

"What are those tube things?" the ambassador asked.

"Those are the rolled-up hammocks of the men. They're stretched out in the rigging to catch falling spars when the shots rip through the sails. The enemy believes in crippling the sails of enemy ships and then closing in to melee the crew," Halcyon replied.

"Hideous, positively hideous," Abernathy remarked.

Sailors were stringing up nets along all the sides of the ship, both on the starboard and the port sides.

"The nets slow down those who would board us," Halcyon told the ambassador.

Men spread sand on the deck from buckets brought up from below. Others used bilge pumps to wet down the decks. Other hoses wet down the staysails.

"The sand and the water keep gel sparks from burning the deck or the sails. Footing can become tricky, especially when blood gets splashed on the deck," Halcyon said, warming to his topic. He didn't note the ambassador turning pale from the information and the thought of blood splashing everywhere.

"Those young men sitting on those wooden cases are called gel monkeys. They bring the blast-gel up in those cases for the blast-tubes to use. When they have gel in the tube and have brought up two more jars in those long wooden cases you see, they sit on the cases until more gel is needed. Down below," Halcyon noted, "the ship's surgeon has prepared an operating table for the wounded."

"Why in the world have they launched all the small boats from the ship? I see them all roped back there in the water," the ambassador asked.

"Splinters, Ambassador," Blithe replied. "Shot comes at such targets on a ship and smashes those boats into thousands of deadly splinters. Also, with the boats back there, men who get thrown off the ship for whatever reason can swim back to one of the boats."

Suddenly the entire ship was quiet. No one moved about the deck; the drumming had stopped.

"What's wrong?" the ambassador wondered.

"Nothing. You might want to put your hands over your ears," Halcyon said, donning his battle helm, which furthered covered his ears. He pointed toward the raft on the port side. It floated in the sea about four hundred yards off the ship.

"Fire as you bear!" the captain ordered.

"Fire as you bear!" shouted Second Officer Dorlat.

The tubes erupted from the stern of the ship on both the port and the starboard sides as each blast-tube port bore on the floating barrels.

The two men watched plumes of water shoot into the air as the shots fell around the barrels. Men cheered as two of the poles on the starboard raft blew away in the explosion. The port raft floated untouched even by a plume of water.

When the captain steered the ship to circle the rafts for new shots, the dragon spewed a jet of water onto one of the flags of the untouched barrels.

Sort looked down on the captain and Halcyon on the quarterdeck. *Me can play too,* it thought.

"Captain." Ashe Fallow's voice carried over the din of the tubes firing as they bore on the target.

Captain Gord-un came to the forward railing of the quarterdeck and looked down at the chief and the seaman struggling in the chief's grasp.

"Cease firing," the captain ordered.

"Cease firing," Dorlat shouted.

Fallow held on to the man. "This one was stealing gold coins from his mate's footlocker."

"Is that true, Seaman Denden?" the captain asked, his voice cold and harsh.

"I don't know why I did it. I'm sorry, Captain," Denden whined.

"Article Seventeen says I should hang you. You've worked well for me for three years on various ships. You'll run the gauntlet tomorrow morning. Put him in the brig," Gord-un ordered.

"What is this gauntlet?" the ambassador asked.

"The captain is being generous. In times of war, stealing is a hanging offense. The gauntlet will allow the man to live and be forgiven. All the ship's crew forms two lines along the ship. Denden runs between them all, taking whatever blows the crew wants to give him with whatever they have at hand. Usually they'll strike with their rope belts. It's harsh but it'll leave him bloody, not dead," Halcyon commented.

The ambassador could only shake his head in wonder.

XIII

❋ ❋ ❋

𝔅𝔩𝔞𝔰𝔱-𝔗𝔲𝔟𝔢 𝔄𝔠𝔱𝔦𝔬𝔫

HIS MAJESTY'S ARTICLES OF WAR: ARTICLE XXXIII

The commander of any Arcanian vessel shall in case of death of any officer, man, or passenger on said vessel take care that the paymaster secures all the property of the deceased for the benefit of that person's legal representatives.

Fog—officers and crew hated it.

Wrapped in deadly tendrils of gray, moving through the water blind was dangerous to ship and crew. The wet mist clung to the sails and sides of the dragonship, as if trying to weigh the ship down into the depths. The rigging became especially slick in the dense mist, and slipping while climbing up or down happened more often in fog than even during a driving rainstorm.

Halcyon Blithe walked as the officer-on-deck when the sun tried to force a glow to the east. For the thousandth time he looked toward the fog-shrouded prow and wasn't able to even

see the main mainsail at the middle of the frigate. In a time of
war, regulations ordered all blast-tube ports opened and the
blast-tubes manned until the light of dawn blew away the fog
and showed no enemies on the horizon. The crew always hated
this detail, as it kept those of the dogwatch up later and forced
the men of the day watch to get up sooner.

The dragon wasn't happy either, as it couldn't see its pets on
its back. The huge head constantly zoomed down out of the fog
to scan near the deck. Every time the head bobbed down, seamen or marines near its giant maw jumped away. The dragon's
training prevented it from eating its crew, but its huge teeth and
fish breath couldn't be ignored.

Halcyon walked to the forecastle, trying to calm the sea
dragon as it dipped down past the rigging for what must have
been the twentieth time.

"We're fine, is there something good to eat in the water?" Halcyon thought, trying to take Sort's mind away from looking at
the ship.

"Fish have all gone deeper, something scares them in the distance,"
the dragon thought back.

*"Try and sense what frightens them, and don't worry about your
pets,"* Halcyon chided as he walked back to the quarterdeck.

"Hal, you no pet, you good friend," the sea dragon explained
with a light tone in its thoughts.

*"Thank you, Sort, now dip your head in the water and figure out
what's around us,"* Halcyon replied.

The fog seemed to be growing thicker as one couldn't see the
tops, just eighty feet up in the air. The sails were damp and held
little breeze. The dragon's fins did most of the work of moving
the dragonfrigate through the water.

Halcyon didn't know why, but his nerves were on edge.
Maybe it was the responsibility of commanding the welfare of

the entire ship keeping him so nervous. Maybe it was his sensing the nervousness of the sea dragon Sort's thoughts of concern for its pets that kept Blithe moving on the quarterdeck as he checked the compass reading and moved to the stern of the ship to scan for the ship's wake, invisible in the dense fog.

Orders from the admiralty had them traveling due south. Sailing past the country of Elese for several days, the *Rage* would eventually sight a large mountain range on the continent, marking the edge of the Dwarven Empire. They were to drop the ambassador at Crystal City, the first of the dwarven port cities on the coast.

Elese was a mainland country as large as Arcania. Its people joined Arcania in the battle against the Maleen ten years ago. Now the country lent armies to the hard-pressed country of Dominal in the north, and Elesian fleets joined with Arcanian ones to blockade the ports taken by Maleen on the northern continent, but there was plenty of talk that Elese's folk were tired of war and even considering switching sides.

"Do you know much about the people of Elese, Chief Fallow?" Halcyon asked to take his mind off the tension.

"Damn fine fighters, with a good little navy. They're on the Arcanian side for now, but I don't know if they have the stomach for the type of war the Maleen fight," Fallow replied. "It's easy for them to send armies and fleets away from their land. I think much could change if Maleen armies landed in their homeland. Even fair-weather friends have their uses, when your back is against the wall, as Arcania's seems to be. The Maleen are working hard to isolate our island from the rest of the world."

"*Water tastes of men,*" the dragon thought to Halcyon.

"*What does that mean?*" Halcyon mentally asked Sort, not knowing what the dragon was talking about.

"*Things of men float in the water here,*" the dragon explained. "*They come with the current, from behind us.*"

"Chief, I don't want to shout, but the dragon thinks we could have company soon. You go up to the forecastle and order the doubles loaded there. I'll take care of these," Halcyon ordered. Ashe left without a word.

A breeze freshened the sails and made them billow out. Halcyon looked up and could see more of the sail now than he could before. He hoped the fog was lifting and they would be able to see the enemy in the distance.

Blithe quietly went from double-tube to double-tube, ordering the men to load the artillery without the normal shouted orders.

Marine Master Tube Sergeant Salt-un was the marine deck officer, and Halcyon went to the quarterdeck railing and got Salt-un's attention on the lower deck. Using hand signals, the midshipwizard ordered the sergeant to load all the tubes on the main deck.

Sensing the need for quiet, the work of running out the double-barreled blast-tubes went on without its usual commands from the lead member of the blast-tube squad.

Halcyon, aware of the risk of a mere midshipwizard ordering the ship into combat, briefly worried about what would happen if they didn't sight the enemy. He shook that thought off; if the dragon could sense something, Blithe knew there was a real threat of some type out in the fog.

"Two points to port, Seaman Thune," Halcyon ordered. Halcyon knew the coast of Elese was three miles away on the port side. He wanted even more distance from the coast to give them some sea room to maneuver if they were in a fight for their lives.

"Seaman Manners to the wheel," Halcyon ordered, wanting

two men on the wheel if it came to battle, in case the combat killed one.

As the ship eased to port, some more of the fog drifted away. Blithe could now see the entire length of the ship and a bit more.

Ears straining to hear anything, the lookouts and Halcyon tried to sense the unknown in the foggy mist.

Halcyon had an idea. *"Sort, roar out a challenge."*

The dragon was only too happy to oblige. Its roar growled out for miles in all directions. These were the waters for sea dragons and ones larger than most ships appeared regularly on the horizon. By habit, the creatures stayed well clear of other large creatures or ships of the line. It was only during mating season that the sea dragons challenged each other. At those times, a few blasts of the tubes kept other male dragons away from sea dragons with ships on their backs.

It roared and spewed thick columns of water into the air.

The roar surprised the men at their blast-tubes, but they knew better than to make noise themselves. Suddenly, the sound of voices rang out in the distance at the ship's stern. The word "dragon" could clearly be heard from several excited voices. Out of the mists came the blasts from boatswain horns. Some officer had just ordered a sail change and now Halcyon knew there was a ship within hailing distance of the *Rage*.

Halcyon couldn't act on his worried notion until he was sure it was an enemy they faced.

Out of the mists, confirming his suspicions, sailed a huge Maleen second-rater, not fifty yards away. Its battle flags proudly flying, the enemy vessel was twice the size of the *Rage*. Double rows of tube ports were open, evidence of its readiness to fire.

"Beat to quarters, hard to port, fire as you bear!" Halcyon roared out.

Because Halcyon had just turned the ship, the double-tubes of the forecastle sighted on the enemy.

Hot spikes drove into blast-gel jars, exploding the deadly mixture. Gouts of flame leapt from the blast-tubes, firing on the very surprised enemy only thirty yards away. The double blast-tubes carved huge chunks of wood out of the side of the enemy ship. Bullets ripped into bodies and blast-tubes all along the deck of the enemy vessel. The thirty-pound shots struck deck tubes, ripping them out of their mountings and smashing carriages and tubes into men and equipment farther down the deck of the warcraft.

Even the sea dragon got into the act as it blasted a huge column of water at the tube deck of the enemy, washing men off their feet from the massive pressure.

Half of the enemy vessel, still in the fog, couldn't see the *Rage*.

Because Halcyon ordered a turn to starboard, all the blast-tubes on that side of the ship had a chance to fire at the enemy. The dragonship and the second-rater turned away from each other as fog covered both ships. The enemy replied to the broadside with its bow chasers. One of the shots put a hole in the center of the maintopsail and the other missed entirely.

Those not reloading laughed at the bad luck of the enemy.

Captain Gord-un rushed up to the quarterdeck and relieved Halcyon of command.

The stern of the enemy ship vanished into the fog bank. There were large chunks of burning debris floated in the wake of the vessel. The sea dragon continued to roar its challenge at the fleeing enemy.

"What have you uncovered, Mr. Blithe?" the captain asked as the process of reloading the blast-tubes went on around him.

Halcyon could sense the captain ordering the dragon to be quiet, the captain obviously not wanting to give away the *Rage*'s position.

"It was a Maleen second-rater, sir," an excited Halcyon answered quickly. "We were able to fire our entire starboard broadside into her. Her only reply was with her bow chasers. Our dragon sensed the enemy, giving me enough time to load the doubles, sir."

"By the look of the sea, you gave them a nice bloody nose. Let's put on full sail and continue moving south at full speed. We are a mite small to continue tussling with a second-rater having more than twice our blast-tubes. You did exactly right, Mr. Blithe; however, in the future, seriously consider waking your captain before you take his ship into troubled waters," Gord-un quipped. "Open the weapons lockers and pass out the blades. Make sure the marines in the tops have grenades, understood, Mr. Blithe?"

The midshipwizard saluted. "Aye, aye, Captain."

As Halcyon reached the rigging for the mainmast, he saw Darkwater and Fallow conferring. "The captain's ordered the weapons lockers opened and the weapons passed out. You two take care of that. I have to get into the tops to make sure the marines have grenades."

Both of them saluted and rushed for the lockers.

Halcyon noted Midshipmen Stillwater and Coal-un manning their posts at tubes on the main deck. Coal-un smiled up at Halcyon. The midshipman worked at reloading the blast-tube and somehow managed a covering of soot from a single blast of his weapon. He waved, having a big smile on his face. A disgusted Stillwater looked into the fog with obvious irritation at not being able to see the enemy in his tube sights.

Blithe quickly climbed the rigging into the tops right above the mainsail. The tops were specially built platforms designed to hold men with crossbows. A complex series of lines and rigging attached the tops to the mainmast. There were platforms like this on all of the masts.

Seven marines were straining to see into the fog for a target. The crossbows they carried could easily fire bolts up to three hundred yards with deadly accuracy.

"Did you men come up here with grenades?" Halcyon asked.

Without taking their eyes off the foggy horizon, each said yes.

Blithe climbed down and went to the foremast, climbing the rigging to the tops where six marines were looking to the horizon.

"Grenades, do each of you have them?" he asked.

"None of us do," came the reply. "We went up here as quick as we could and didn't take any."

Halcyon didn't let the tension he was feeling fill his voice. "Half of you go to stores and get grenades for the entire group. Next time come to your duty station prepared."

As the midshipwizard moved again to the quarterdeck and its mizzenmast, he stopped in front of Marine Major Maxwell.

"Sir, the marines on the fore tops didn't have grenades. I ordered half of them to get grenades for the rest. I thought you should know." Halcyon saluted and headed for the tops on the mizzenmast.

The irritated look on the major's face spoke volumes about what would be happening to those men when ordered to stand down from the battle.

The marines had grenades on the mizzenmast, and Halcyon

climbed up above the mizzen topgallant to see if the fog was clearing. A solid wall of clinging fog swirled around him. He scanned the stern and the north fog bank. He could feel the wind picking up from the landside. He suspected the fog would clear and possibly allow them to see the enemy they briefly fought in the fog.

He smelled smoke in the damp air. He wondered if it was his imagination or if there was a glow of something burning to the north. Taking out Teagan's watch, he saw her sleeping with a tiny smile on her face. At seven in the morning, the sun should have been full on the horizon, but their entire world was filled with gray wetness. Halcyon took a moment, mentally thanking Lady Et for her gift, and then went down to the quarterdeck and his duty station.

An hour later, the fog blew away with no enemy found on any horizon. Far to the north was a plume of smoke, possibly marking the fleeing second-rater, but it was impossible to tell.

"Mr. Blithe, mark in the ship's log that you led the *Rage* into combat. I wouldn't advise making battle in the fog a lifetime career. I'd wager it would be a very short career," the captain quipped.

"Aye, sir," Halcyon replied, pleased at being able to mark the conflict in the ship's log.

At nine bells, Captain Gord-un ordered the crew to stand down and form the gauntlet for the punishment detail.

Sailors and marines formed two lines, ten feet apart on all three decks. Almost four hundred men formed two circles all the way around the ship on the port and starboard sides. Each man held a rope or some type of club. As part of the gauntlet, each sailor and marine was supposed to try and strike at Seaman Denden as he passed by.

Ambassador Abernathy looked down at the sailor from the rail of the quarterdeck. All of the midshipmen were on his right, and Lieutenant Swordson was on his left.

"You mean to tell me this sailor stole a few coins and he's now going to get beaten to a pulp for his crime, Mr. Blithe?" the ambassador asked. "That sounds perfectly hideous to me."

"Ambassador, naval regulations say theft is a hanging offense during a time of war," Halcyon tried to explain. "The captain is being lenient because of this man's past service."

"I see clubs in some of those men's hands. Your sailor could die from the blows, doesn't anyone care about that?" the amazed ambassador argued.

"Ambassador, allowing the men to strike at the criminal keeps him alive on the ship," Swordson explained. "In this way the men feel they've taken part in the punishment. They aren't as likely to throw him overboard in the night or stab him during naval combat. Believe me when I say this punishment is a tried-and-true method, rarely failing to correct the behavior of the criminal."

Halcyon heard the conviction in Elan's voice, but he wasn't as sure as the lieutenant. Blithe wasn't about to argue the issue with Swordson or the captain.

Orders were orders.

Denden stood at the center of the tube deck, before the mast. There was a hangdog expression on his face and he kept his head bowed the entire time.

"Seaman Denden!" The captain shouted so that those on the forecastle could hear him as well as those behind him on the quarterdeck. "Do you realize I have the authority to hang you at this moment?"

Denden bobbed his head up and down in assent.

"Call out, Denden, let the captain hear you understand his words," Fallow shouted at the seaman's side.

"Aye, sir," Denden replied.

"The running of the gauntlet is a time-honored tradition of the service. In ordering this, plan on changing your attitude. You've served with me for several years and performed your duty well. For that service on your record, you don't hang today. After you finish running the gauntlet, if you survive, your crime is forgiven. I will allow no man to continue to punish this sailor, unless Denden is foolish enough to try and perform a theft again. In that event, you hang on the yardarm. Run the gauntlet," the captain ordered.

Ashe had Denden take off his shirt. The man's back revealed many old scars. He'd clearly experienced the cat-o-nine-tails before. Denden was in his twenties, and appeared a big, strong man.

As officers, the midshipmen lined the rail of the quarterdeck. None of the officers of the *Rage* were to take part in the punishment and that was all right with all of the midshipmen.

The rest of the crew held their knotted ropes and spans of wood at the ready.

"Go!" shouted Fallow.

Seaman Denden ran for all he was worth.

Blows from whipping, knotted ropes rained down on him. Those with clubs were hard-pressed to swing their wood fast enough as the quick-moving sailor rushed the line.

Lengths of knotted rope whipped down, ripping at his flesh. The few lengths of wood that did strike him made loud, meaty thuds on his back and shoulders.

Arms rapidly rose and fell in their efforts to strike Denden. He rushed along the open tube deck, but had to slow down to take the ladder up to the forecastle. He took many more blows there.

The men were screaming and stamping their feet in all parts of the line now.

He must have realized running close to the port-side line kept most of the starboard-side attackers too far away to strike at him with force. He started running into the hands and arms of the port side, cutting down on the number of blows he took from those men.

Men were screaming out their rage, seeking to get their blow in to punish Denden. Each man thought of all the times they lost something and blamed Denden for those losses.

"They're wild animals," noted the ambassador in disgust. "That sailor is more like a dog than a man. Putting a man through this trial is hideous."

Elan didn't agree. "If Denden was given a choice between hanging and running, he'd take running. The captain just removed that choice." Swordson stayed calm while the other midshipmen watched, disgust clear on their faces.

Halcyon wasn't sure how he felt about this punishment. He knew that the man shouldn't hang for just stealing a few coins. However, frequent thefts could seriously undermine the confidence of the crew in each other. Some of these men spent more than a year on this ship. If they couldn't trust the men around them, they would soon grow unruly and hateful of everything from the ship to the officers ordering them.

Denden had run a quarter of the gauntlet. His head and back were all bloody from the beating as he rushed through the double lines of men. He staggered toward the stem of the ship and clearly tried to stay as far away from one side of the line as possible. He wasn't moving nearly as fast as when he started. Now he held both of his arms up to take the raining blows. Some of the men shifted their blows to strike on his lower back and stomach. Others rained blows on his arms.

Leading seamen and marine corporals kept the men from leaving the line. Otherwise, many would have cut across the deck of the ship to the part in the circle where Denden hadn't run yet to strike another blow.

By the time he climbed the ladder of the quarterdeck he was reeling from the punishment. His many cuts splashed blood onto the deck. Denden barely made it around the circle of the gauntlet on the quarterdeck and down the stairs and through the last twenty feet of the gauntlet. He fell to the deck, his punishment over. Many of the men were breathing hard, having screamed their rage. Most threw their bloody knotted ropes over the side.

The dragon honked in a questioning manner. The captain tried to calm the creature, as it smelled blood on its back.

Fallow tossed seawater on Denden's bloody back, ordering two junior seamen to carry Denden down to the ship's surgeon. "Seawater is the best thing for those cuts," Fallow remarked. "He'll be walking around this evening, mark my words. I don't think he'll try stealing from mates again."

The midshipmen were down in their wardroom quietly eating lunch and talking about the action of the morning. There was a subdued atmosphere in the area as each man thought about what he'd experienced that morning.

"How did you know to load the doubles?" Stillwater asked.

"Why did you turn to starboard instead of port?" Coal-un asked.

"The sea dragon told me there were men nearby. I thought

that must mean a ship, as we were three miles out to sea," Halcyon replied.

"Being able to talk to the sea dragon, I can't even imagine that," Hurchial said with an excited look on his face.

Junior Lieutenant Swordson came in.

Halcyon shouted, "Officer on deck!" He came to attention with the rest of the midshipmen.

"Little ducks all in a row," Elan snarled at the group. He walked back and forth between the five. "I didn't like what happened this morning, Mr. Blithe. You overreached yourself by quite a bit. You'll take ten hours of extra duty for that. Starting after the lunch bell, work those hours off."

Halcyon's face remained impassive. Jakwater and Torance couldn't help themselves; they looked shocked at the unfairness of the extra duty, and both of them gasped.

"Questioning orders is a brig offense, you two!" shouted the now enraged Elan. "You will . . ."

The entrance of Ambassador Abernathy interrupted his tirade.

Swordson whirled on the new intruder, saw who he was, and changed his demeanor instantly.

"Mr. Swordson, I'm glad I found you here," the ambassador calmly said. "Do you have time to take the noon meal with me?"

"Of course, sir, I'm finished here, to be sure. After you," Elan said, calm as you please.

They both left and the midshipmen relaxed into their hammocks.

XIV

❋ ❋ ❋

𝔅ecoming a 𝔉rigate 𝔊reencap

HIS MAJESTY'S ARTICLES OF WAR: ARTICLE XXXIV

*The commander of any Arcanian vessel shall make frequent
inspections into the condition of the provisions on his ship and
use every precaution for their preservation.*

Halcyon sat back against the double blast-tube in deep satisfaction. His efforts had taken days, and he could now quickly open all the pairs of the manacles he'd brought, using the lock pick Chief Fallow gave him or a twist of wire he kept in his boot heel. He kept the Fallow lock pick hidden in the center of his war braid. Arcanians generally allowed their hair to grow long and put it in a braid if they had time before a battle. Often they would decorate their hair with enemy ribbons and captured enemy medals. Denna placed a small ivory skull in her long blue hair for every enemy officer she'd killed. She had more than thirty in her war braid.

Red sky at night, he thought, *that will make my morning watch easier,* and he smiled at the red sky on the western horizon. Halcyon had worked a double shift at the order of Swordson. Blithe took it in stride, easily ignoring his tired muscles. As a punishment detail went, it was little effort. *If that's the worst he can do to me, I . . .*

The ambassador and Swordson came onto the upper deck. Halcyon stood up and so did all the other midshipmen.

"At ease, all of you," Elan ordered.

Both the ambassador and Swordson had nasty grins on their faces.

"Midshipwizard Blithe, I've brought you a gift." Ambassador Abernathy held out a strange little bar with an odd open ring on each end. "It's amazing what you pick up on one's travels. I saw you working on your locks and thought you might like this. Hold up your hands and let me put this on you."

Halcyon felt uneasy, but knew he didn't have much choice. He held his hands up. "Mr. Ambassador, you shouldn't have. I really can't take gifts from you."

"No, Blithe, I came along to assure you that you could take this gift," Swordson said slyly.

"I acquired this in Drusan before it was taken over by the forces of the Maleen," the ambassador told him while snapping the little rings around Halcyon's thumbs. "I've purposely left the little key in the lock at the center of the manacles. All you have to do is raise it to your mouth to turn the key and open the manacles. A clever fellow like you shouldn't have to do that, of course."

Halcyon held his hands out in front, as he stared down at an eight-inch bar of brass. A little brass key was in the lock in the middle of the device. His thumbs were trapped at the ends of the bar with metal rings. There was no way his thumbs could slip out and no amount of pressure would bend the device.

He tried picking up his piece of wire with two free fingers, but there would be no way to reach the central lock and apply any pressure at all.

He looked up at the grinning ambassador.

"This presents a difficult problem, to be sure. The gift is princely, Ambassador, and will give me many hours of entertainment as I try and figure this one out," Halcyon said politely.

"Think nothing of it, dear boy," laughed the ambassador. Showing obvious glee, he and Swordson left the deck.

Halcyon plucked the key out of the lock and spent many minutes with the pick in his mouth trying to twist it around the lock, to no avail. The rest of the midshipmen looked on in amusement.

"Well, sir, it seems to me that you shouldn't worry if you can't get the lock open on your first try. Maybe you should unlock yourself and try to work the lock without putting your thumbs in," Hurchial said, trying to be helpful.

"Begging your pardon, sir," Denna Darkwater said, approaching them on the deck. "Midshipman Act-un, that's not going to prove useful if he's ever locked up with them. I've been in a few dungeons in my time. Often they chain you up so that you can't put your hands in front of you. May I, Mr. Blithe?" the marine corporal said, holding out her hand.

Halcyon shrugged. He was getting nowhere with his efforts. He handed the key to Darkwater, who unlocked the manacles. Once the thumb device was away from his hands, Halcyon wondered to himself if there might be a magical way to open them. He went over the air and water spells he knew, with no answer there. Maybe earth magic held the solution to clicking open the brass lock. There must be some magical method to open locks or the enchanted manacles of Iben wouldn't have been invented to prevent spellcasters from working their magic.

Denna took the small manacles and sat down on the deck. She pulled off her sea boots to reveal feet with unusually long toes. The nails on those toes showed a bit more of her troll heritage, as they came to sharp points.

"Now imagine we've been captured and they have us in a dungeon where we can't use our hands to escape," she said, taking the key out of the thumb manacles and locking the manacles around her thumbs. She held up the manacles to show everyone the lock was tight. "I'm sitting in the dark with lots of time on my hands so I decide to free myself."

She whipped her long braid from her back to her front as it fell in her lap. She moved her feet and her toes pulled out a long twist of wire with a short hook in it.

"Is there some sort of navy regulation that says everyone needs a lock pick?" Torance snarled sarcastically.

"Midshipmen Stillwater." Denna smiled up at the man while her toes worked the wire into the thumb manacle lock. "There aren't regulations for a lot of things you should know and do. I notice you have shark-skin boots on. Navy regulations give you leather boots. I bet you wear those because they grasp the deck better. If you live long enough in this man's navy you'll know lots of tricks to help you survive."

Click.

The manacles popped open and she was free without ever looking at the lock her toes picked. She tossed the bar and key to Halcyon. Everyone around her clapped, showing appreciation at her effort.

Halcyon couldn't wait to try unlocking manacles with his toes, but he didn't get the chance.

Captain Gord-un called out to the lookouts at all points of

the ship. The lookout above the topgallant signaled no sails from horizon to horizon as did the port and starboard men with far lookers in their hands.

The captain moved to the binnacle and Boatswain Gray. "Boatswain, bring up the kettledrum and captain's urn. Have Purser Cor-un bring up the chest of caps. While you're down there, find out from Cookie how he's coming with the beef."

"Aye, aye, Captain," Boatswain Gray replied, and hurried down to the tubedeck.

The entire crew was all too aware of the unusual nature of the evening. Normally, at four bells the final meal came to the crew with the day's grog ration. Today, grog appeared at four, but the captain passed word down through the ranks that a special meal happened at sunset. Word had already spread that the captain ordered a steer slaughtered that morning after the foggy battle. Such an occasion was a good time for the men, because even if they didn't get the best cuts of beef, those cuts going to the officers, for the next three days there was fresh beef in their food instead of salt pork.

Setting up the large kettledrum took several minutes as two men put out the platform and lifted the heavy drum onto the support rack. The dark, well-polished wood of the drum sides appeared etched in strange runes. Drumheads on the top and bottom of the drum could only have been green dragon skin. The huge scales on the hide were more than a foot across in some places. The hides had the same runes drawn on them as appeared on the sides of the drum. A large gray stone urn, carried by four sailors, came from the captain's cabin along with a short chest.

Halcyon and the rest of the midshipmen looked down on the proceedings from the forecastle. When Stillwater saw the drum being set up, he excused himself and went belowdecks. In a few moments, he came back up wearing a green beret.

Blithe soon noted that more than half the crew was coming up from the lower decks, all wearing green berets. "Look on the quarterdeck," he said, pointing to the officers and men there who were all wearing the berets. "What's going on?" he wondered.

Gord-un came down to the tube deck and threw open the sea chest positioned behind the drum. He started tossing green berets out of the chest and toward the back of the drum. Each one of these caps hit the drum and stuck where they were flung. After taking out ten, he pulled out two large padded drumsticks.

Halcyon noted there was a single large green rune drawn on the padded head of each of the sticks.

The captain went to the front of the drum. His large hands each held one of the drumsticks. "Boatswain Gray, sound all hands on deck." With that command, the captain started slowly beating the drum.

Gray clanged the ship's bell in rapid succession, its notes flowing over the ship and down into the lower decks. There were few crew members not already on deck, but those who were below came up in answer to the deep thrums of the beat of the kettledrum as much as the ship's bell.

The boatswain went belowdecks to check to make sure all were present.

For many minutes, the drum beat out its loud booms all over the ship. Sailors' hearts actually started beating in time with the strokes of the drumsticks.

The runes on the side of the drum and on the dragon flesh began to glow with the vibration. First Officer Townzat, already in a green beret, came up to the captain, took the sticks, and continued the booming beat, never losing the cadence.

Captain Gord-un reached up to the glowing caps on the back of the drum and started tossing them to those crewmen who weren't wearing them. Even the ambassador was tossed one.

Abernathy held it in his hands as if it were a thing alive. It did glow with the green glow of the drum. Sailors around him urged him to put it on as they all wore the berets.

Halcyon was totally captivated by the scene. He could feel the magic crackle in the air all around him. "What do you think the glow of the caps means?" he asked Midshipman Coal-un beside him.

"I see no glow on the caps," Scott replied.

A surprised Blithe looked at Coal-un. "There's a glow on the drums, the drumsticks, and all the caps. There must be magic at work. Look how Second Officer Dorlat is tossing more caps on the beating drum and they're sticking on the drumhead."

The sun had set, and to Halcyon's eyes, the glowing caps easily illuminated the entire ship. To be sure, there were extra ship lanterns out as well, but their glow was muted by the magical glow all over the ship.

"*What's going on?*" the sea dragon asked.

"*I haven't the slightest idea,*" Halcyon thought back. "*Do you see any green glow?*"

"*Yes, it's coming from the heart beater. The pounding tickles,*" Sort noted.

"*It's called a kettledrum. I've never seen one quite like it,*" Halcyon told the dragon. "*It's not going to hurt you. The captain's using it, so enjoy it.*"

Suddenly, caps from one hundred feet away were sailing through the air and landing in the hands of Coal-un and Blithe. Some magic allowed the caps to travel through the air and come to all those who didn't have one. Everyone on the forecastle got their beret with impossibly long throws from the drum's side on the quarterdeck.

Filled with dozens of questions, they both instantly put them on. Many minutes later, there wasn't a person on board the ship who didn't have one of the green berets on their head.

All of the crew who owned a beret before the drum started beating had taken a turn at beating the drum to the same cadence. Once Gord-un saw that everyone had a cap, he signaled for the drumming to stop.

The silence was deafening in itself. All the men's hearts still beat together and their chests felt the pressure as if the drum was still stroking out the rhythm.

The captain held up his hand for attention. "Those of you who sailed on my last ship know when my rite of passage happens. For some captains it's when they sail above the north or south of Arcania. Some captains perform their ritual on a certain date every year. For me, it's after the first battle." There was a look of power and almost madness in the stretched lines of his hugely grinning face. "We survived a fight. It was a short one, and I wasn't on deck at the time." He glared for a moment at Halcyon and the entire crew laughed.

The captain continued, "I would make you first-timers on my ship join in common cause, becoming a band of brothers with the rest of the crew. This drum has been in my family for untold ages. We beat the drum when important occasions happen in the family to help us remember the past. We beat the drum to gather our thoughts and honor those still alive. I beat the drum now so that we all share a common memory of this day.

"This urn has been in my family for a long time as well. Ambassador Abernathy, as the highest-ranking new member of the crew, please come forward."

"What?" the ambassador squeaked in surprise. "Why, ah, yes, Captain, if you say." He stumbled forward, looking very unsure of himself. The beret canted far back on his head, showing the man didn't have the slightest idea how to wear the cap.

The gray urn tilted down, allowing the stopper to open and some type of liquid to flow out into the metal cups Gord-un had in baskets all around the jug.

To Halcyon's eyes, the runes on the jug still glowed green, as did the drum icons. He also noticed the berets had stopped glowing.

A pungent liquid poured into the cup the captain was holding. The fragrance erupted in everyone's nostrils as the liquid gushed into the tin cup. He waved his hand over the spout and it stopped delivering the clear liquid.

"I watched my grandfather pour this drink from this same urn ninety years ago. Since then, countless times drinks have come from this urn and it's never needed refilling. May the magic of this urn and drink fortify you all in the days and duty to come. I always have my new crew drink with the old from this jug in a celebration of life. Each of the rest of you new men come up and take a glass full. When all the glasses are filled, I've a toast."

For many minutes, the captain poured out drink after drink to the new and old men. There must have been many gallons poured out that evening, without a sign of the urn ever being empty.

Halcyon took his cup with the rest of the new men. He breathed in the odor of the liquid and couldn't place the smell. For some odd reason it reminded him of the family dungeons under his castle. It smelled fresh and clean with a bit of freshwater smell to it.

"*I want some,*" the dragon asked.

Halcyon instantly took hold of a large bucket and put it under the urn, thinking nothing of the action.

The captain looked at him with a questioning expression on his face.

"Sort wants a taste, sir," Halcyon replied to the unasked question.

"Really," the captain said, and turned to fill the large bucket. "You take that up to the forecastle and feed it to our dragon slowly. Warn Sort that it's powerful stuff and not to be indulged in all the time. I'll wait on my toast until you signal he's ready to drink."

The heavy bucket strained the muscles of Halcyon, as he had his own tin cup in one hand and the heavy bucket balanced in the other hand. He rushed up the ladder to the forecastle. He was careful to not spill a drop, as he suspected it might have a nasty effect on the decking.

"*Bend down and put your head on the deck,*" Halcyon thought.

The dragon complied. Its head was slightly taller than Blithe himself.

"*I had a barrel of ale once, that tasted good,*" the dragon thought to the midshipwizard.

"*This is not ale,*" Halcyon thought as he ordered the dragon to open its maw.

The captain, seeing that his midshipwizard had things well in hand, raised his cup in a toast. "I toast you new men and women, and our new dragonship. We drink to life and Arcania!" He pulled back his head and drank the entire contents of the cup.

The crew tried to do the same. Most all of the new men sputtered and gasped.

Halcyon took a careful sip and felt molten fire flow down his throat. He wasn't used to strong drink, and he was sure this was the strongest of all possible drinks.

"*Well?*" the dragon asked.

"Just be careful," Halcyon advised as he poured the contents of the bucket into the maw of the dragon.

As the last of the liquid hit the back of the dragon's throat, it roared in pain.

"Argh!"

The entire ship shuddered on the back of the dragon. The creature's head shot up and then dipped down into the sea as the dragon used the salt water to purge itself of the taste of the drink.

"*That's terrible!*" it thought to the captain and the other two.

"It would seem our good dragon didn't like the brew. Maybe when it gets a bit older, poor young thing," the captain jested.

The crew laughed. Chief Fallow was first in line for seconds.

"Mother's milk, sir, if I do say so myself. Your ancestors are to be complimented on their spirits, if I may say so," Ashe said as he held out his tin cup for a refilling.

Only a fourth of the crew stood up for more. The liquid was clearly too powerful for the taste of most.

The dragon spent the next hour roaring out a challenge into the night sky as it continued to spew out water.

"*Will this taste never leave my mouth?*" the dragon thought in pain.

Hours later, Halcyon was dreaming in his bunk when thoughts filled his sleepy mind.

"*Attack the dragon now!*"

Halcyon bolted up from his bunk. Looking all around, he wondered if he had been dreaming.

"*Rise, my leviathan, kill our enemy!*"

Someone was communicating to something in the same

manner as he talked to the sea dragon and Halcyon guessed from the strength of the mental words that they were close.

"Battle stations!" Halcyon bellowed as he raced through the lower deck to the ladders up to the open air of the blast-tube deck.

On a warship, it didn't matter who shouted the warning. When the alarm was shouted, everyone moved at their quickest pace.

Halcyon shouted one more time and the drums started beating out the call to battle stations as the marine drummers woke up and grabbed their drums.

"Argh!" screamed Sort, but its battle roar was cut short with a strangled gulp.

A great splash of water washed over the deck as the tentacles of a leviathan rose out of the ocean's depths in front of the sea dragon.

"On, my lovely, smash the ship, eat the dragon!"

Halcyon could feel the mind giving those orders. The wizard or whatever it was hid in the huge glowing shell of the monster attacking the ship.

Deck lamps dimly lit up massive tentacles taller than a man, wrapping around the prow of the ship, the heavy flesh crushed down on the crew trying to man the bow chasers on the forecastle.

The dragon fought for its life as more tentacles wrapped around its body and neck. It bit uselessly at the tough shell hiding the belly and head of the attacking leviathan.

Halcyon could hear more of the thoughts of the wizard as the enemy urged his beast to attack and kill Sort. The midship-wizard had some urging to do of his own as he rushed up to the forecastle and set an illumination spell ahead of his dash.

The death scene became clear in front of him. Man-tall tentacles coming out of the dimly glowing shell of the leviathan wrapped around the dragon. Sort bit huge chunks of the tentacles, but the terrible damage didn't seem to be doing anything to stop the monster from strangling the life out of the sea dragon. Sort still showed plenty of fight, but who knew for how long?

Other tentacles lay across the prow of the ship, stopping the *Rage* from using its front blast-tubes. It was as if the creature knew those tubes were the only ones to bear on its body.

"Unshir the port blast-tubes!" the midshipwizard shouted to Fallow as he took Fallow's blast-pike. "Elevate the tubes and fire at its shell. There's a wizard in there!"

Halcyon rushed into the rigging of the foresail, above the leviathan's tentacles.

Squads of marines used their blast-pikes to little effect on the tentacles along the prow. Darkwater stood atop one of those tentacles, chopping deep into the monster's flesh with her pike.

"*I know they sting you, my proud beauty. Ignore their pinpricks. Kill this dragon, now!*" urged the Maleen in the leviathan's shell.

Halcyon could sense more and more of the thoughts of the wizard controlling the monster. Blithe purposely didn't contact Sort for fear of revealing himself to the powerful enemy.

On the quarterdeck, gray lightning bolts leapt from Swordson's and the ambassador's weapons, striking the body of the monster. Tentacled flesh burned in great patches, but the spells didn't make the creature stop its crushing attack.

Gord-un, blazing battle-axe in hand, almost flew from the captain's cabin to the forecastle. His magical axe blasted a searing slash through a huge chunk of tentacle.

Denna, atop that same tentacle, chopped down on the other side and severed the tentacle, causing the monster to scream in pain.

"Fire!" shouted Ashe Fallow, who'd gotten the three double-barreled blast-tubes filled with chain shot and aimed properly.

The shot struck the creature's bony shell, opening man-wide holes into the interior of the beast. The twin barrels blasted back clear to the starboard side of the ship. Many frightened hands manhandled them back into position.

Halcyon was going to aim at the tentacles attacking the head of his dragon, but he feared his blast-pike shots would do little damage after seeing what the magical attacks of the two other spellcasters did to the monstrous flesh. Then he saw the Maleen wizard through the holes in the shell. Light poured out of one of the blasted holes, revealing some sort of hollowed chamber in the shell of the dragon. The wizard appeared shocked by the blast making the hole.

Halcyon aimed his blast-pike and triggered all of his magical energy through the rowan wood of the pike. He was taking another risk, as all his trainers said never to expend all your magical energy in any attack. The fear of what this controlled monster was doing to his dragon caused the midshipwizard to throw caution to the wind. In the previous months, he'd practiced using his special magics through the blast-pike. Now he was deadly accurate with the shots.

A massive bolt of blue energy shattered the blast-pike and flew through the air, striking the wizard in the shell. The charred wizard blew out of sight.

Suddenly, the tentacles of the leviathan all flew up in the air and the creature sank slowly into the ocean with the sea dragon continuing to bite at its tentacles as long as the monster was in reach.

Denna and the captain stood heaving for breath on the forecastle, their bodies covered in gore.

"Stop your nattering!" shouted Gord-un to the buzzing crew around him. "Get my ship cleaned up. Fallow, prepare those brave dead crewmen for burial. They're the real heroes today and none of you forget it."

Gord-un stood glaring at his crew as they calmed themselves and got back to work.

Halcyon thought he understood the orders of his captain. They still had a job to do.

"*Are you all right?*" asked Sort.

"*You were amazing,*" Halcyon complimented the sea dragon.

"*I've fought smaller leviathans, never one that big.*" Sort's thoughts were dazed as the sea dragon took in great gulps of air.

Thinking of the captain, Halcyon realized he would have to tell him about the controlling wizard. The midshipwizard was sure that was a Maleen wizard in the shell of the beast. This was a new menace the admiralty would have to be made aware of. He climbed down the lines to talk to the captain.

XV

❋ ❋ ❋

Fire as You Bear!

Sort gobbled the sugar-covered hay placed out for it on the middle of the forecastle. The various midshipmen looked at the sea dragon eating with differing looks of concern and horror on their faces. The dragon was given a special treat of sugar in light of the battle it just survived.

Hurchial Act-un showed his fear on his face and in his body language. He'd purposely positioned himself as far away from the dragon's head as possible.

Naturally, Halcyon ordered him to move the last hay bale closer to the dragon's tongue. "Hurchial, move that last bale closer to the dragon's mouth. Mr. Act-un, what do the regulations say about the care and feeding of a dragonship?"

"Sir, two bales of hay are to be fed twice a day to a sea dragon if the dragon feeds in the sea sometime that day. Finding no seaweed or fish in any given day changes the feeding of the dragon to three bales three times a day," replied the midshipman, forgetting some of his fear in the telling of the regulations.

"Correct," Halcyon said, while sitting himself on the head of the calmly munching dragon. The midshipwizard sat there more to show his fellow midshipmen that the dragon didn't mean them any harm than to take a comfortable resting place.

"You wouldn't want to eat any of us, would you, my young friend?" Halcyon thought to the dragon.

"Eat a pet, even if I was starving? I would eat you last, Halcyon." The dragon's thought was filled with humor.

Halcyon suddenly turned on the dragon and looked straight at Stillwater. "If our dragon's head crest and whiskers turn red, what does that mean, Torance?"

"I haven't the slightest idea, sir," Torance replied.

"Mr. Coal-un, come here for a moment," Blithe ordered.

"What's he afraid of?" the dragon thought to Halcyon.

"Mr. Coal-un, the dragon can smell your fear. You really don't want to show fear to a creature that can eat you in one bite. Try to calm down. Take a few deep breaths. Do you know what happens when its crest turns red?"

"The dragon is displaying a need for red meat. If it isn't getting enough fish in its diet the head begins turning red and the creature's body begins slowing down until it gets more meat," the nervous Scott replied. He was brave enough to stand next to the dragon's head, but he clearly didn't like it there.

"*I'm finished now*," the dragon thought to Halcyon.

"*Just a heartbeat more, then you can move your head,*" Halcyon thought back.

"Jakwater, how often does the dragonship need to return to Ilumin for refitting? Step closer so that I can hear your answer, man," Halcyon ordered just to get the midshipman to come nearer the dragon's head.

Gold-un quickly stepped up to the front of the dragon. Sort raised its eyebrows, taking the man in with both of its large eyes.

"Sir, every two years the dragon's skin turns white, signaling that within thirty days it will be shedding its skin," Jakwater correctly replied.

"Correct, Jakwater, well done," Halcyon said, hopping off the dragon's head.

The beast raised its head off the deck and around to the prow of the ship and out of sight. "*Enjoy the rest of your day,*" it thought to Halcyon.

"*You too,*" the midshipwizard thought back.

"Mr. Stillwater, what is the tactical advantage of a dragonfrigate compared to a normal sailing ship of the line?" Halcyon asked.

Torance didn't hesitate. "To my way of thinking there are two. The dragon is a fierce beast with the ability to eat men off the rigging and decks of an enemy ship. The dragon is also able to sail closer into the wind, giving the ship a maneuvering advantage."

"Midshipmen, attention on deck," shouted Elan Swordson, coming up to the forecastle.

All of the men came to attention.

"The captain wants to see you little ducklings on the orlop deck immediately. Midshipwizard Blithe, you will bide a minute before leaving. The rest of you move out," Swordson shouted.

As the rest of the men hurried off, Elan faced off against the standing-at-attention Blithe.

"Mr. Blithe, you are an idiot, and a poor excuse for an officer!" Elan shouted in Halcyon's face. "Would you like to know why you are an idiot?"

"Sir," Halcyon shouted back.

"Do you like Midshipman Gold-un and Midshipman Stillwater better than Act-un and Coal-un?" Elan asked.

"No, sir, so far they have earned my respect and done what they're told," the now-confused Blithe replied.

"When you address one man by his first name and you address another by their last name you are giving those men mixed signals. Don't ever do it again, fool, do you understand?" came the shout from Swordson.

"Sir, yes sir," Halcyon replied.

"Get yourself down to the orlop deck, you're late for the captain's muster," Elan ordered.

Halcyon rushed away, hating the fact that he agreed with every word Swordson said. He was an idiot. When commanding men, there was a need to be evenhanded to all of them. In using a person's first name and not being consistent, Halcyon was giving the signal that he liked one man over another and that just wasn't the case.

Rushing down the ladder of the decks, he quickly joined the other midshipmen, in time to hear the captain ask Act-un a question.

"Midshipman Act-un, what is the thirty-fourth Article of War?" asked the captain.

Hurchial came to attention as he recited the article. "Sir, Article Thirty-four states the commander of any Arcanian vessel shall make frequent inspections into the condition of the provisions on his ship and use every precaution for their preservation, sir."

"Letter-perfect, Midshipman, very good. I hope you know what it means as well as remembering it," said Gord-un. "It's vital for the captain of any ship to have inspected the provisions and equipment loaded on his ship. It's just as important to inspect those materials at least once a week and certainly after every bout of rough seas or combat. Mr. Blithe, you were a bit late, don't let that happen again. Why do I come down here after that battle we just had?"

"Sir, things can shift in the constant movement of the ship. Timbers could stave in water or salt-pork barrels. Lack of supplies shortens the time out to sea and impacts the successful completion of a ship's orders," Halcyon replied, having thought these things through even as a young man thinking about his father and brother's voyages.

"Good answer, Midshipwizard Blithe. Now we'll go to the heart chamber. Our Mr. Blithe here has caused some new ship regulations to apply to the heart and liver chambers on all dragonships. Midshipman Stillwater, do you know what those new regulations are?" the captain asked.

"Sir, the inside of all heart and liver chambers on dragonships of the line shall be guarded by two marines at all times. Any who enter these chambers will have their names written down in a special log for those chambers," Torance replied quickly.

As they entered the heart chamber, the two marines with blast-pikes came to attention.

"At ease, men," the captain ordered. "Midshipman Act-un, list all of our names in the log with today's date."

"Aye, aye," Hurchial replied.

"Midshipwizard Blithe, how is this heart different from the one you guarded on the *Sanguine?*" the captain asked.

Halcyon walked around the heart, inspecting it carefully before answering. This heart was about four feet long and tall. Large veins covered the outside of the organ and he could see the pumping blood moving through the ropy vessels on the outside of the heart. Walking on the dragon's flesh, he noted the large metal clamps keeping the flesh on the back of the dragon from growing over the heart as it would do normally in the wild. He also looked at the walls of the chamber and the hatches.

"The *Sanguine's* heart was about twice this one's size, no surprise in that since it is much older than *Sort*. I notice our hatches have much better seals than the hatches on the *Sanguine*. Such protection should do much better in keeping out the seawater. I notice the walls are armored in this chamber, they were just thick dragon flesh on the *Sanguine*."

"This is the first living ship I've served in. I'm glad to see they are improving as new ones are built," the captain noted.

Gord-un moved them through the corridors of the orlop deck to the liver chamber and opened its hatch. "Midshipman Gold-un, what happens when salt water gets into the liver chamber?"

Jakwater stopped his forward motion, deep in thought. "Ah, sir, I believe with salt water touching the liver the sea dragon would instinctively submerge and all hands would be lost." He turned white at the thought.

"You are correct," the captain affirmed. "That's why we work hard to make sure neither chamber gets any contact with the sea. Midshipman Act-un, when was the last time you were down among the water barrels?"

"Well, sir, I haven't been down here yet," Hurchial replied.

"You haven't . . ." The irritated captain stopped in midsentence. He cocked his head sideways. "Wait for it. . . ." he said, listening intently.

In the quiet, all of them could suddenly hear the beating of drums. It was the call to battle stations.

As one, the midshipmen ran for their wardroom and the equipment stored there. They rushed from ship deck to ship deck among the frantic movement of hundreds of men doing the exact same thing.

Hands threw open their footlockers and reached for helms, breastplates, and swords. Halcyon put on his magical bracers and slipped his sleeves over them to hide them from the first flush of battle. Magical rings came on next. He grabbed his helm and his beeswax and rushed for the ladder up to the tube deck.

His post was at the stern chasers. He found himself one of the last few manning the blast-tubes. His artillery piece was a forty-pounder at the stern of the ship. It was a long-range weapon made to blast at enemy chasing their ship. Leading seamen all around him were raising the boarding nets across the rigging of the ship. Able seamen threw buckets of seawater on all the sails within reach of the deck to keep sparks from the blast-tubes from setting the sails on fire. The bilge pumps threw many gallons of water on the decks and gel monkeys cast sand all over the deck to help with footing and hinder possible fires.

"Roll it back!" Halcyon shouted.

The six men bent their backs on the tackle and slowly moved the ponderous tube of metal away from the side of the railing.

Crew quickly lowered the ship's jolly boat and longboat, using lines to see them towed behind the ship. In the sea, trailing behind the ship, they wouldn't be turned into deadly splinters in this battle as tube shot pulped them into thousands of splinters.

Not twenty feet away, Ambassador Abernathy complained to the captain. "You can't be thinking of taking on those ships. There's three of them, sir, and we are only one." The ambassador's voice was filled with fear.

"We are a ship of war and the enemy stands between us and our goal. We have no choice," the captain answered in a firm voice.

"Open the port!" came Blithe's order. He looked at the captain and the ambassador. Abernathy was almost beside himself, hopping from foot to foot in nervousness. The captain stood like a rock, watching his ship and crew get ready for war.

"ROAR!" the dragon belched forth a huge spout of water into the air. This was the creature's standard challenge to any enemy. At least four miles to the south the creature could see three foes much like the shell on its back. It looked forward to the fight.

The loaders at the front of the stern chaser followed Halcyon's shouted orders and used wooden slats to prop open the port, opening a large window onto the sea.

While the tube crews worked, other sailors hung the crew's complement of hammocks above their heads in the rigging. Wound tightly, they would act as safety nets to catch spars and ringing falling during the battle.

"Sponge the tube," Blithe ordered. He noted the junior seaman Turlor Jorl-un sitting on the gel casing. That was a sure sign there were two jars of blue gel ready and waiting for his order to load them into the tube and fire at the enemy at long range. Big Mike was the name of this blast-tube. Naming rights were given to the first crew to use an artillery piece. Halcyon didn't have the slightest idea why this weapon had been named what was burnt into the caisson wood, but the moniker seemed to fit.

"Captain, I have to order you to turn back. I'm the civil authority on this ship. We can't fight three of them, can't you see that?" Abernathy was begging, now clearly afraid for his life.

"Ambassador, your civil authority means nothing on my ship. They have the wind at their backs. If we turn to the west, we strike the shore of Elese. If we turn to the east, those three frigates with the wind at their backs catch us and use their blast-tubes to advantage. I don't need to tell you what happens then. If we turn north, they'll follow and likely catch up with us in a day. I will engage them at long range and hope to take out one or two of them and then deal with what's left. Please go below and watch the battle from the tube ports of your cabin."

"Lieutenant Swordson." Halcyon stopped the nervous lieutenant as the man was checking all the tubes and their readiness.

"What is it, Blithe? I have a battle to prepare for," Elan growled.

"Tell the captain about our new shells. He doesn't know what they can do. It might be just the thing to even the odds," Halcyon advised.

A look of understanding came to Swordson's face. He turned and quick-stepped to the captain's side.

Halcyon went back to work. "Load the gel!"

Junior Seaman Jorl-un unlocked the wooden case he was sitting on and carefully brought out the large blue jar from the padding inside. The loader took the jar and placed it in the tube while the rammer forced it down to the back of the barrel.

Jorl-un took the empty case and ran to get another jar of blue gel for a long-range shot. Halcyon would have asked for a white jar if he planned a medium-range shot and a red jar if he planned to use a canvas bag of canister shot for close ranges of less than fifty yards.

"Sir, we can hit them at two miles out," Swordson bellowed over the din of the crew getting ready to fight.

"What are you talking about, son?" Tona Dorlat barked. "Our best weapons can only hurl a shot a mile."

"We loaded some of the new shells at the capital. I've used them before on the *Sanguine*. With the windage wheel turned for maximum range and the tubes hot, we can fire shells up to two miles away. It's worth a try, Captain," Elan suggested.

Captain Gord-un went to the railing and shouted down to the chief, "Fallow, bring up those new shells from Ilumin, fire all tubes to make 'em hot, and then load them into both sides of the ship. We'll try a bit of far-ranging today."

"Aye, aye, Captain!" Fallow replied, and sent all the gel monkeys scurrying down to the orlop deck to bring up the pointed blast-tube shot.

Halcyon cranked the windage wheel on his tube for maximum elevation. There was no nervousness in him at the moment. He knew exactly what he needed to do. His task was to command this blast-tube and fire at an enemy if it appeared in his port. If the enemy boarded his ship, he and his crew would fight. The simple focus of what he needed to do kept his mind and hands steady.

The ambassador, seeing he wasn't going to change the captain's mind, left the quarterdeck for the imagined safety of his cabin.

Blithe watched the three enemy frigates coming closer and closer. Soon they would be within two miles of their ship. Men brought up the heavier forty-pound pointed shot for his tube.

"Men, in a minute, Tube Master Dorlat will order us to dry-fire our tube. After that, we'll load in one of these pointed shells. The captain's going to broadside the enemy with his port tubes first. As he tacks around we'll get one shot at them and I mean to make it a good one. You all be ready for my orders," Halcyon said with a gleam in his eyes.

Through a speaking tube, Dorlat gave the order when she saw that all the blast-tubes had at least one of the new pointed shells. "Dry-fire the tubes, fire!"

Tubes boomed out all over the ship and the dragon roared another challenge to the vessels still more than two miles away.

"Sponge the tube," each tube aimer shouted to his band of men.

The crew member with the ramrod jammed the rag-wrapped end into a bucket filled with seawater and then rammed that into the blast-tube. Remnants of gel and jar pieces were all slammed to the back of the tube and the artillery was cooled down a bit by the water.

The loader carefully took the large blue gel jar and placed it in the opening. The opposite end of the ramrod slid the jar to the back of the piece and rags were stuffed in and rammed on top of the jar. Then the loader took the pointed shot and placed the flat end into the tube and the rammer pushed that home. The crew around the blast-tube picked up large prybars to move the heavy piece at the direction of the loader.

"Fire as you bear at the middle ship," Dorlat ordered through her speaking tube. "They're ready, sir," she informed her captain.

"Boatswain Gray, hard to starboard!" the captain ordered.

"Hard to starboard it is, Captain," the big man shouted back, turning the helm round and round.

The sea dragon helped with the motion and turned the ship far faster than a nonliving vessel could have moved.

Two miles away, the captains of the three Maleen frigates ordered full sails. They expected their prey to run, but they had the weather gauge on the enemy and would be catching her soon.

"Fire as you bear at the middle ship," Chief Fallow said repeatedly, as he ran down the line of tube crews waiting for the ship to come into their sights. "Crank that windage wheel, you damned fool!" he shouted to Seaman Manners.

Booms ranged out on the port side as tube after tube fired its shot at impossibly long range when they saw the enemy bear away in their blast port. A wall of smoke rose thicker and thicker as the shots continued. The last two blasts fired blind as the ship continued to circle around.

The crew of the three bow chasers tensed as they got their chance to fire. The turning ship allowed them to see that the center enemy had lost its jib boom. The three staysails were flying free in the wind and the boom was dragging in the water, drastically slowing down the center ship.

The crew in the sails of the *Rage* all cheered at the sight of the strike.

Halcyon watched the first of the enemy ships come into sight through his firing port. He held the spike in a pair of tongs and stood ready to slam it into the touchhole. He would be using his magic to heat the spike. Other aimers had to rely on hot spikes coming from small burning coal heaters at the side of the tubes.

As the second ship came into view, smoke was curling up from the enemy ship. Clearly more than its sails had been damaged.

"Ready to fire!" Halcyon shouted, giving his squad a chance to cover their ears. As the middle of the three ships came into view over his site, he rammed the blazing hot spike into his blast-tube. The weapon exploded and smoke obscured his view. He wanted to hit, but that wasn't his problem right then. "Sponge the tube!" he screamed.

"Sponge the tube," all of his crew shouted back at him.

"Load the jar!" he shouted, and Jorl-un ran for another jar, leaving one full box for someone else to use if he wasn't there to open it.

"Fire at the first ship to bear!" the second officer shouted down to the tube deck and the starboard crews who hadn't fired yet.

The ship was quickly turning all the way around and they would get their chance soon. The enemy was less than two miles away, but still well out of the range of their normal shot. Already the middle ship was falling far behind as their crews frantically chopped at rigging and broken booms.

Once again Chief Fallow ran up the line of the starboard artillery crews shouting, "Fire as you bear on the first ship!"

Denna Darkwater and her squads of marines stood ramrod-straight along the centerline of the frigate. Their armor gleamed in the sun. Their blast-pikes were held in one hand at their sides. It was their job to repel boarders or board another ship at need. Just the sight of them made the sailors of the ship feel calm. Those men and women were deadly fighters and looked the part. The crew liked having them on their side and battle-ready.

The tubes blasted out, their sharp shells cutting the air and reaching the enemy ship a mile and a half away. That vessel had begun to turn and made itself a larger target. Strikes hit the ship in several places and large sections of the mainsails flapped lose in the wind.

"Huzzah!" shouted the crew of the *Rage*.

"Hug the coast, Boatswain Gray. Rig for full sail. Get a man to call out the depth," the captain ordered.

"Aye, aye, Captain, down the coast it is. Stand down from battle stations, full sails aloft. Denden, call out the depth!" Gray answered back.

All three Maleen frigates moved to the west and out of range of the enemy with the unusually long reach.

"Those shells are amazing," Tona told the captain.

"They are that. I wonder how long it will be before the enemy uses them as well," Gord-un replied. The captain went over to Elan Swordson as the young lieutenant supervised the stowing of shot along the railing. "Mr. Swordson, that was an excellent idea of yours to use that shot. You saved this ship a bad beating," the captain said, offering his hand to Elan.

"Thank you, sir, all in a day's work, sir," Elan answered back.

Halcyon heard the interchange and didn't much care that Swordson hadn't told the captain whose idea it really was.

XVI

✲ ✲ ✲

Dwarven Allies?

The ship had been sailing for three months now and finally the Dwarven Mountains were far to the north of their position.

Halcyon wasn't very happy with his life at the moment.

Swordson had been more and more abusive to all the midshipmen, but especially Halcyon. Blithe had tried to lessen the sting of Swordson's words on the other men by giving them tasks they could easily accomplish. He felt he couldn't talk to his fellow countryman, Ashe Fallow, about his problems, as it was Halcyon's responsibility to learn about command. Blithe was sure that confronting Swordson again, as he did on the *Sanguine*, would only make things worse for his midshipmen.

Deep booms came to Halcyon's hearing over the sea. The noise could be nothing less than the explosion of several mortars or big blast-tubes. The horizons were empty of sail, but Halcyon could clearly hear the sound of battle carried by the wind from the south.

Halcyon hurried down the rigging. As he passed the men of the main topgallant, he gave orders. "Seaman Manners, climb the mast and report any sounds of battle or masts appearing on the southern horizon."

"Aye, aye," Manners replied.

The midshipwizard flashed down the rigging in record time. From the tube deck, he rushed up to the quarterdeck and the captain.

"Sir, sounds of battle coming from the south," he reported.

"Really," Captain Gord-un responded with a rise of his bushy eyebrows. "I was thinking about a blast-tube drill later today, now is as good as any time. Let's see what we can find down there, since we're headed that way anyway. Boatswain Gray, maximum sail, if you please. Midshipwizard Blithe, order beat to quarters."

Halcyon rushed to the railing and bellowed down to the tube deck, "Marine, beat to quarters!"

Twelve-year-old marine Ben Stone-un got up from sitting on his drum and beat out a special rat-a-tat-tat on his instrument. That rhythm was beat out every Sunday to the assembled mass of men to make them aware that whenever the drum sounded in that special beat, they were to come to their battle stations. Ben's drum sounded all over the ship. Down in the hold, another marine picked up his drum and beat out the rhythm, sounding loud and clear belowdecks. All men knew their position when the beat-to-quarters drummed out.

Halcyon rushed down to the midshipmen's wardroom. As he

got there, the bulkheads were all being taken down and placed along the ship walls to add extra support and bracing to the body of the sea dragon.

"*No enemies, why do the drums sound?*" the sea dragon Sort asked in the mind of Blithe.

"*Listen,*" Halcyon thought back as he buckled on his sword and reached into his sea chest for his two magical rings.

"Midshipwizard, what did you see up there?" Gold-un asked as he put on his breastplate.

"I didn't see anything; I heard the sounds of battle in the distance," Halcyon replied. The thought of combat made his heart race. His mind filled with not only the duties he had to perform, but the words of advice from his brothers and uncles. Climbing up and out of the hold, he checked and rechecked his equipment as he moved from the tube deck to the quarterdeck.

Halcyon's post was at the stern chasers. Once again, he watched the sea as sailors hung netting between the riggings and brought up the tied hammocks, stringing them above the heads of the crew readying the blast-tubes. He checked to see that his four midshipmen were at their posts, and they were. Each waved to him, signaling they were ready for duty.

Seventeen miles away at the horizon line, the life-and-death struggle unfolded before the far lookers in the hands of officers all over the ship.

As the ships appeared over the horizon, six sloops revealed themselves, circling three ketches.

"Those ketches fly dwarven colors," the ambassador noted.

"The sloops are pirates out for whatever gold the dwarves have on their ships," the first officer said, and the officers watched the battle.

One of the ketches was sinking and now the rest of the sloops had grappled with the other two and human pirates streamed from the sloops in waves onto the deck of the two dwarven ships.

"Boatswain Gray, everyone wears my green berets today, pass the word," the captain ordered.

"Aye, aye, Captain," Gray replied.

"Captain, we must not get into this battle. I must be at the dwarven port of Crystal. What happens if we take so much damage that we sink?" the ambassador whined.

The battle was at least twelve miles away and there were no more sounds of blast-tube fire.

Using a speaking trumpet, the boatswain shouted orders. "Men of the mizzen, come down and wear your green berets. Men of the starboard tubes, go and get your berets. Officers, exchange your helms for the captain's green caps."

Like many of the others, Halcyon didn't have the slightest idea why he was being ordered to lose the protection of his helm for the captain's green beret, but he wasn't about to question an order just before a major combat. As he was going back to his duty station, beret on his head, he heard the boatswain bellow more orders.

"Marines, wear berets only. Port tube crews, get your green caps. Forecastle and quarterdeck crews, get your berets!" Gray shouted.

The dragon roared out its challenge to the enemy in sight. Huge columns of water belched forth from its throat.

"Officer to the quarterdeck, Boatswain Gray," the captain ordered, ignoring whatever protests the ambassador might be giving him.

Once again, Gray took his speaking tube to the railing. He bellowed out, "Officers to the quarterdeck!"

In less than a minute all the marine officers, midshipmen, and other officers of the *Rage* gathered around the captain.

"We aren't going to be able to fire our tubes into that tangle. At maximum speed, I'm sailing past the top of that line and the marines are going to rappel over to the decks of the sloops and the ketch on the north side of that battle mass. The word for dwarven ally in their tongue is '*Kormac*.' Make sure the men constantly shout it out as they fight the pirates. Our dwarven friends over there don't know we're friends yet. To them, we're just more attacking humans. Let's give them a chance to learn otherwise. After our marines join the battle, I'll turn the ship to the back of that tangle and unload sailors on the other side of the combat. You all will meet in the middle. Swordson, you join the marines. I want a spellcaster on both sides of the battle. Blithe, you'll join the sailor group. Any questions?" the captain asked.

No one said anything.

"Major Maxwell, you divide up your men any way you please. Midshipwizard Blithe, have each of your midshipmen pick out twenty likely lads from among the crew. Get to work; we'll be amongst them in less than a half hour by the glass."

"Aye, Captain," the officers replied.

Two stone wheels were up on deck sharpening the axes, blast-pikes, cutlasses, and daggers of the marines and crew. Halcyon took his turn, even though his weapons were already razor-sharp.

The ships were less than five miles away now.

"Midshipwizard, why can't we wear our helms?" Coal-un asked.

"I suspect it's for the sake of the dwarves we're about to help. The pirates are dressed in black and wearing helms. I can see that all the dwarves have white berets on," Halcyon observed. "If we come boiling over their railings with green berets on just like the white ones they have, it might stop them for a moment from attacking us and give us a chance to prove we're helpers instead of enemy."

"Never thought of that. I'd still like to be wearing my helm," Scott remarked.

"So would I," Halcyon replied.

The smell of blood hit them a mile away from the struggle. Lightning exploded on the decks of the ketches, showing to everyone there was a spellcaster in the battle. The smell of fire and brimstone grew thick to their senses. An unmistakable odor of death in the air alerted any spellcaster to the certain knowledge that someone cast death magics.

The center of the frigate filled with the sailors picked for the boarding parties while the port side filled with marines ready to swing over the side of the ship. Extra lines hung from the masts. Marines in the tops fired their crossbows at any target that wasn't a dwarf.

The sloops were almost empty of men, but the ketch's decks were full of fighters. Both ketches held large bands of dwarfs at the forecastle as they tried to fight back against the overwhelming odds.

The *Rage* neared the first ketch and sloop.

The sloops were typical of the design, with a single mast and jibs, allowing it great speed and maneuverability. These has four blast-tubes on the starboard and port sides.

"Go! Go! Go!" ordered Major Maxwell as he launched himself over the side.

Sort blasted the deck of the near sloop just before the marines leapt to the decking. Archers on the sloop's tops shot down at the marines. Marines from the tops of the *Rage* shot back.

The pirates were all dressed in black, with red bandannas

tied to their left arms. In a battle with other humans, such distinctions prevented combat accidents. There was no need for this when they were fighting dwarves, who were distinctly different from humans. The Arcanian brown uniforms would ensure that the *Rage*'s crew only fought pirates.

Denna turned for a moment to give Halcyon a roguish wink, and then she and several others roped to the ketch as well.

"May the gods protect you, Denna," Halcyon whispered to himself.

"You don't have to be worrying about her," Chief Fallow said.

Halcyon turned to see the chief at his back. The man bristled with weapons, from daggers to hand axes to a huge blast-pike dripping with tannin oil.

"*Gods be damned*," Halcyon thought. He hadn't dipped his weapons in tannin oil. The chief pointed to a small barrel of the stuff by the mainmast.

As Halcyon dipped his saber and dirks into the oil, he shouted out to everyone around him, "Dip your weapons in this oil, now!"

None of the men knew why he gave that order, but they all followed his command.

Halcyon and Fallow both knew the oil could help weapons pass through any magical barriers the magicians among the enemy might have cast around their bodies.

The *Rage* tacked hard and closely circled the mass of ships grappled together.

Archers from the sloops started firing at the *Rage*.

"*Sort, blast those tops as we pass*," Blithe ordered the dragon into action.

"Furl the topsails," Boatswain Gray ordered, to slow the ship down.

Tons of water started hitting the enemy in the rigging of the sloops. Those who tied themselves to the tops didn't fall off, but their bows and crossbows were blasted out of their hands by the tons of water hitting them. They hung unconscious like puppets from their masts. They wouldn't be shooting at crew and marines any time soon.

Against the pull of its sails, the *Rage* dragon slowed the ship down, allowing the leaping crew to more easily launch themselves to the nearby ketch and sloop. Halcyon had intentionally positioned himself and his twenty men so that they would be first to land on the ketch. He and Fallow were on the same line as they kicked off, swinging through the air and onto the railing of the ketch. Its boarding netting long since cut down, they weren't slowed a bit as they came aboard.

Landing on the deck, they instantly faced a swirl of battle as well-armed and armored pirates and dwarves fought to the death.

Halcyon immediately started yelling, "Kormac!" using it as a battle cry, and he entered the swirl of battle. In front of him, three pirates showed themselves to be powerful spellcasters as they were each wrapped in some type of magical gray mist. Dwarven axes bounced off their bodies, raising white sparks with each strike but doing no damage to the spellcasters. That fact didn't stop the maces of the enchanters from reaching out and striking at the dwarves. It was a one-sided battle until Blithe and his men stepped on board.

Enemy turned to face the advancing crew of the *Rage*. Halcyon naturally rushed toward the spellcasters. One of them threw a black cloud of ink at the midshipwizard. The cloud enveloped Halcyon and he felt himself slowing down until the evil magic touched Blithe's enchanted bracers. Halcyon felt the bracers on his arms heat up and squeeze tighter and instantly he was free of the magic and lunging at the magic-user.

The man clearly expected his enchantments to stop the blade. The enemy ran afoul of the tannin oil as the saber passed through the grayness and struck at the heart of the spellcaster. The gray mist vanished to reveal a man in a pirate uniform. He didn't have the distinctive white hair of an Arcanian, so he must have been a spellcaster from the mainland. Except for the spells that surrounded him, he could have been mistaken for any of the other pirates around Halcyon.

The packed swirl of battle didn't allow Blithe to withdraw his saber as other pirates pressed him hard from both sides of the dead wizard. He abandoned his saber and drew the dirks from his boots. The weapons were perfect for close work, as the heavy blades easily blocked cutlass strokes.

For many minutes, the midshipwizard fought to stay alive as pirates struck at him and the sailors behind him. Halcyon purposely kept moving toward the gray-misted shapes, wanting to dull their power with weapons he knew would work on their enchanted shield spells.

One of the spellcasters was facing off against a large dwarf with a glowing axe. The weapon was blood-covered and having no luck penetrating the enchanted glow of the pirate wizard. A deft stroke by the wizard dropped the dwarf to the deck, with his axe flying out of his hands. As the wizard lifted his mace to make the death stroke, Halcyon, knowing he couldn't reach the two in time to save the dwarf, launched a lightning bolt of his own, at the same time tossing his dirk at the wizard.

The spell cracked out and startled everyone nearby with the loud boom of it. The tannin-covered dirk penetrated the mystical gray shield and the lightning bolt entered the shield as well, turning the spellcaster into cinders, which then fell to the deck. The press of men backed off of Halcyon, fearing more lightning. He was able to extend a hand to the dwarf.

"My leg's broke," the dwarf said in perfect Arcanian.

Halcyon's crew covered their retreat as the midshipwizard dragged the dwarf to the stern of the ketch.

Almost faint from the pain, the dwarf weakly looked back at the battle. "My axe, it's a family treasure. The pirates must not take it away with them."

Halcyon cut a strip of sail to bind the open wound. The shattered leg bone was sticking out of the flesh of the dwarf's leg. "My ship, the *Rage*, won't let any of these sloops get away. We'll get your axe back, never fear."

Torn between wanting to help the dwarf and wanting to get back in the action, Halcyon wasn't sure what to do. When the dwarf fainted from the pain, it allowed Halcyon to get up and get back into the fray. The bindings stopped the bleeding, Blithe was sure the dwarf would be all right until the battle ended.

The fighting had moved from the quarterdeck of the ketch to the middle deck. Moving across the quarterdeck, Halcyon saw piles of dead and found the pirate wizard with the midshipwizard's saber sticking out of his heart. Looking up, Halcyon saw that the final enemy magic-user was using the mizzenmast to make a stand against the crew of the *Rage*. There was still a large body of pirates pressing the dwarves and the men of the *Rage*.

All by himself his magics protected him from blast-pikes and cutlass strikes while dark tendrils of magic sucked the life out of any crew they touched. Each time a crew member died, the wizard grew a bit taller and more muscular, as if he was able to take in the life essence of the dying sailor. Halcyon had never heard of such magic.

Somehow, the wizard had been able to use his magic to make the tannin oil on the blades of some of the crew members glow.

The glowing tannin weapons bounced off the wizard's gray shield magics.

The pirate spellcaster wielded a large staff with a dwarf skull at its top. Chief Fallow led the charge against the man. The deadly magics of the enemy stopped dead on the rowan shaft of the Arcanian blast-pike. The mast protected the enchanter's back, and only the tannin-coated weapons had a chance at getting through the black mist surrounding the spellcaster. Those weapons, the pirate paid full attention to.

As Halcyon leapt to the deck from the quarterdeck, he saw the golden axe of the dwarf lying on the planking. Knowing the weapon was important to the dwarf, he picked the weapon up. The second he did, rubies covering the weapon flashed out a blinding glow. There must have been more than fifty of the red gems studding the weapon from top to bottom. The glow was almost blinding. Blithe threw it toward the unconscious dwarf. For a second he thought of using it in battle, but decided he could wield his own saber better in a fight to the death. Halcyon waded into the battle. As he neared the enemy spellcaster, the sounds of battle filled the air as dwarves, pirates, and the crew of the *Rage* shouted and used their weapons on each other. The deck was slick with blood and the smell was sickening, but there was little time to pay that attention.

"*Good eating here, you?*" came the questioning thought from the sea dragon Sort.

Halcyon had no time to even answer the dragon. He and Fallow moved their coated weapons to strike at the magic-user. A black haze covered Blithe's dirk and saber where the tannin oil coated them. The same went for Fallow's blast-pike head.

The midshipwizard didn't like the effect on his weapons and wondered if the enemy spellcaster's magic was lessening the damage done by the blades. Other crew pressed in on the sides of the wizard, but their weapons did nothing to the man. Seaman Handel Thune tried tackling the wizard, but as his large arms touched the black mist, his entire body shriveled, turning to dust while the wizard laughed and seemed to move faster.

"Arcanians, such tasty morsels," the pirate spellcaster chuckled.

"Back off, Arcanians!" Halcyon screamed. "Leave him to me!" Shocked at the death of Thune, Halcyon didn't have the slightest idea if he could defeat this wizard, but he didn't want any more of his men killed from the black magic the man was casting.

"I got your back, boy, you worry about the fool to the front of you," Fallow shouted.

Halcyon's world focused down to the evil enchanter. He ceased worrying about other attacks, sure in the knowledge that Chief Fallow would die before he let another foe sneak up on Halcyon.

Blithe had seen this spellcaster magically grow from something like six feet tall to at least nine feet tall, increasing in size as men died from the tendrils the enemy cast from the darkness all around him.

"Arcanian, what toys do you possess that stop my night touches?" the wizard hissed at Blithe.

Dark tendrils of magic constantly reached out at Halcyon. Every time the tendrils neared, they were forced to touch his forearms where his enchanted bracers lay hidden under his uniform coat. As the seven-foot-long tentacle of living darkness touched the bracer, the death tentacles turned into puffs of dust and fresh brimstone filled the air. The enemy wizard would wince as if in pain as each tendril vanished, dispelled by the magic of Blithe's bracers.

Halcyon's enemy didn't wear armor. There were amulets hanging from his arms, legs, head, and chest. The black staff weapon crackled with dark energies all its own and Halcyon dodged and ducked to keep well away from that thing. Many times the midshipwizard's luck ring squeezed his finger, a sure sign that it helped him be missed by a spell or weapon strike.

The midshipwizard's saber flashed into the body of the wizard, only to be blocked by the staff crashing toward Halcyon's head.

Both wizard and Blithe turned when the dwarves of the forecastle started singing. All the dwarves left on the ship chanted some strange song that seemed to give them strength and acted much like a chantey. Their battling became more coordinated, and during the chant, they would shout something three times that sounded like, "Tonk! Tonk! Tonk!" While they shouted that, they delivered stunning blows to the pirates facing them.

Soon, every time they began the "tonk" part of their chant, the enemies around them backed up, not wanting to face the powerful blows of the weapons they knew were coming because of the song. Backing up on the part of the pirates was their undoing. With the crew of the *Rage* on one side and the dwarves with newfound strength and determination on the other, the band of pirate attackers became smaller and smaller.

Halcyon feared using magic against the wizard, sure that his enemy could somehow absorb Halcyon's spell. They danced back and forth on the deck with the pirate shrinking in size as he tried spell after spell against Halcyon and failing to get energized by killing more of the *Rage*'s crew.

With no one to face, Fallow started using his blast-pike to block more and more of the wizard's staff strikes.

"Do something quick, Hal, this one's going to try something stupid," Ashe advised.

Halcyon kept thinking about his magics and wanting to try a

lightning strike, as that was his most damaging spell. He was just about to cast that magic when Fallow's blast-pike reached across his chest and snagged the staff of the wizard. Frozen in place for a heartbeat, Halcyon dropped his saber and grasped the shaft of the pike with both hands. Resisting Fallow's attempt to raise the weapon, Halcyon threw all his magical energies through the pike. A blue beam of energy spiraled out of the weapon, smashed through the gray magical shield of the wizard, and burned the man and his staff to dust where he stood.

Behind Blithe, Chief Fallow screamed in pain and fell to the deck. Ashe writhed, holding out his hands. The insides of them were charred flesh and the smell of cooked meat filled Halcyon's head.

"No, Ashe!" The midshipwizard bent to hold his comrade.

Agonized, Halcyon didn't know what to do for Ashe. His magic burnt his fellow Lankshire countryman. "I'll get the best doctors. You won't lose your hands, I swear by all the gods," Halcyon said, rocking the unconscious Fallow in his arms.

XVII

❊ ❊ ❊

Unexpected Enemies

HIS MAJESTY'S ARTICLES OF WAR: ARTICLE XXXVII

*All officers of the navy and marine corps who are authorized to
order either general or summary courts martial shall have the
same authority to inflict minor punishments as is conferred by
law upon the commander of a naval vessel.*

"What's the butcher's bill, ship's surgeon?" asked the captain as
he stood on the quarterdeck of the *Rage* watching the dwarves
cleaning up the sloops and their ketches in the light of the setting sun.

The battle was over and the marines and crew were back on
the *Rage*. Four bells of the afternoon saw all his men fed and
given their ration of grog. The ship stood down from battle stations and the gear set up for the battle was all taken down and
stowed.

The seas around the ship filled with predators as dead pirate bodies splashed into the water. Every once in a while the head of the sea dragon would dip into the water and pull out a large shark, munching it to bloody pieces.

The surgeon had come up to the quarterdeck after patching up the last of the men of the *Rage*. His bloodstained apron spoke volumes on the work he had to do all through the day. "We've fifty dead, with six more so badly wounded they'll be dead tomorrow. I've got four marines spell-blasted and I don't know what's going to happen to them. I can't even get their eyes shut and a black mist hovers around their heads, it's the gods-be-damnedest thing I ever saw. Another thirty have minor wounds preventing them from being fit for duty for ten days at least."

Blithe and Swordson were at the captain's side, listening to the surgeon's report as well. When Halcyon heard about the marines, he immediately took off his magical bracers. "Captain, if I may, when I was fighting those spellcasters their dark magics turned to dust as they touched these bracers of mine. I don't have the slightest idea if they will work on the marines, but I'd like the surgeon to try," he said, handing the bracers over to the surgeon.

"Capital idea, Midshipwizard. Surgeon, give those a try and report back when you have seen to the men," Gord-un ordered.

"Yes, sir," the surgeon said tiredly. He inspected the bracers as he went down to the tube deck.

Deep in thought, the captain looked at all the sloops now lined up behind the two ketches. "The *Rage* probably took on more than three hundred pirates. We'll never know for sure, but we gave a good account of ourselves, that we did." Gord-un snapped out of whatever musing he was in and looked at his pair of spellcasters. "Mr. Swordson, I'll have your report now," ordered Captain Gord-un.

"Sir, with the marines I vaulted over to the first sloop in line. We met light resistance there and killed all the pirates we found. I'd estimate there were possibly twenty dwarves left on their ketch when we arrived and they were fighting from the advantage of the quarterdeck of the ketch. As we climbed onto the ketch there were already marines fighting the pirates on the main deck. The enemy had two powerful spellcasters in their band; both were casting death magics at our marines. I naturally led my group against those men. The shafts of the blast-pikes were effective in stopping their spells, but all too often one of their dark magical tendrils moved faster than a man would wield his pike and those marines magically died from the spell's effect. The pair had dark enchantments covering their bodies, preventing even the blast-pike from touching them. Fortunately, for me, my saber has its own magical runes and I could get past their shields. I surprised one of them and the marine Darkwater surprised the other and got through his magical defenses with sheer brute strength. We killed them. . . ."

The captain held up his beefy hand for silence and shouted to the boatswain. "Gray, get Corporal Darkwater up here at once, also summon Major Maxwell. Continue, Mr. Swordson."

The boatswain went down to the tube deck to get the summoned pair.

The captain was staring up past Swordson as the lieutenant spoke.

"We began making good headway into the pirates when the dwarves started their curious singing. It was an amazing thing to watch, sir. I've never seen anything like it." Swordson stopped, noticing the captain seemed very distracted.

Both Blithe and Swordson turned to look where the captain was staring.

Major Maxwell and Corporal Darkwater joined them and everyone turned to see where the captain looked.

The major had a nasty scalp wound bandaged on his head and Denna had her arm in a sling.

"It's not right, just not right," the major remarked. "They're hanging the surviving pirates from the yardarms of the sloops."

On each of the sloops, an assemblage of dwarves roughly handled a group of the pirates. Each man had a noose placed over his neck and his hands tied behind his back. Dwarves threw the lines over the yardarms and hauled the men up into the sticks, kicking and screaming for brief moments as the noose choked them. On the six ships there were at least ten men hanging from each mast.

The crew of the *Rage* turned unruly watching the hangings. The mumbling was all about dwarves hanging humans. Many remarked that the dying men were pirates, but hanging was a tough way to go. Most of the crew showed their uneasiness at the punishment by the grim looks on their faces.

"*More food for me?*" Sort asked.

"*Don't touch any of those bodies,*" Halcyon ordered. "*If you started eating them, there's no telling what the dwarves would do.*"

"*I like shark better anyway,*" the dragon quipped back.

"Mr. Townzat, get another measure of grog into the men's bellies. Tell them it's for a job well done and keep them busy," the captain ordered.

"Aye, Captain," the first officer replied.

"Why do you say their hanging isn't right, Major?" the captain asked.

"First of all, when I saw the way the wind was blowing I made sure none of the living men were from our crew. We had two unconscious men on the decks of their ketches, the gods only know if the dwarves would have taken our men for pirates or not. It took a bit for me to make them believe those two were ours, but I persisted and they turned them over," Maxwell replied. "I also didn't like the dwarves and their attitude. If a ship like the *Rage* had just saved my sorry behind, I'd be a little more appreciative. They clearly don't like humans and I could tell that by their every thought and deed."

"Major, I want to hear your own report in my cabin. Let's let the junior lieutenant finish his report and you and I will share a bit of wine. Continue with what you were saying, Mr. Swordson," the captain ordered.

"Well, sir, like I said, after Corporal Darkwater and I finished off the spellcasters, the fight went our way. The dwarves started singing and they did a better job of fighting and killing on their side, but I don't for the life of me know why." Elan was scratching his head over the mystery of their song.

"It's a dwarven death dirge," Ambassador Abernathy noted. "They sing that song when they expect to die. I'm sure the moment our ship unloaded more fighters the dwarves thought we were pirate reinforcements, being human and all. That dirge allows them to fight their hardest for the few moments they thought they had left to live. The fact that we helped them has greatly embarrassed them. We elf and human types are not supposed to hear that dirge to their forge god. They are much more angry at themselves right now than at us, as they obviously never expected to see the sunset."

The captain looked surprised at the ambassador.

Elan tried to finish his report. "It took us a bit, but finally we chopped our way through to the dwarves and started yelling, 'Kormac.' That made the dwarves calm down a mite. When all of the pirates were on the decking, flat on their backs, the dwarves finally stopped their song and looked a bit surprised to be alive. Most of them couldn't speak Arcanian. They sort of pushed us off the ketch in an uncouth way, if you ask me. That's all I have to report."

"Very good, Mr. Swordson. Corporal, how did your blast-pike get through the magics of the enemy wizard?" asked the captain.

"I saw Chief Fallow bring up a barrel of tannin oil. On the *Sanguine*, he got through a magical shield by dipping his pike in that oil. I figured it couldn't hurt, so I dipped all my weapons in the oil. It didn't, though, at first. I punched the wizard in the face with my fist and that distracted him a bit. After that, I was pleasantly surprised when my killing blade didn't bounce off the dark magic," she said, smiling.

"Boatswain, get Chief Fallow up here on the double," the captain bellowed down to the boatswain on the tube deck.

"He'll have to be carried up, his hands are in a bad way," Boatswain Gray shouted up to the quarterdeck.

Halcyon got a grim look on his face, as it has been his fault the chief had been burned.

"That's my fault, sir," Halcyon explained. "We were fighting three spellcasters and a large group of pirates. The enemy wizards were very powerful and when they started killing our men with their spells, I ordered our sailors away from them. After two of them fell, the last magic-user proved to be the most powerful wizard of that group. Chief Fallow stayed with me to guard my back and I fenced with that enemy."

They brought Chief Fallow up on a stretcher. With every rise and fall as they went up the ladder the chief grimaced in pain. Thickly bandaged, his hands wouldn't be doing anything for a long time. As they got him up on the quarterdeck, he tried to give the group a wan smile and lifted his bandaged hand in mock salute.

"None of that, Ashe," the captain said, coming over to him.

"You've done your bit on this cruise. It's clear sailing and easy duty for you, for the rest of your stay on the *Rage*. Have Purser Cor-un bring up a bottle of my best red wine. That should help the pain a bit."

"I thank you, Captain, you're too kind," Fallow said weakly.

The officers all bent nearer in order to hear what the chief had to say. His voice was very weak.

"Don't think it's the boy's fault," Fallow said, motioning to Halcyon. "He's a Lankshire man and as steady as a rock. He sent the rest of the troops away so that none of them would lose their lives against those evil wizards. It's the bravest thing I ever saw, him being sixteen and they being in the fullness of their power. I stayed with him to make sure his back was protected," Ashe said, lying back on the cot totally exhausted from just that little speech.

"He saved me," Halcyon said in anguish at what he had done with his magics. "The wizard was using a powerful staff and I couldn't get through his defenses. At the end, Ashe's blast-pike was holding down the staff and it had gotten through the gray magical mist of the man's defenses. I grasped the pike." Halcyon choked up at the thought. Only his sense of duty and the need to report allowed him to finish the story. "I poured energy through it to kill the last wizard. In the process, my magics burnt Chief Fallow's hands, as he was still holding on to the blast-pike. I was in shock. I never meant for the accident to happen. I carried him away from the action. By the time I got back to the conflict, the men had won the day and the remaining dwarves were safe. All of the *Rage*'s sailors gave an excellent account of themselves. I'm proud of each and every one of them. That's all I have to report, Captain."

"Fallow, why did you bring up that oil and not have everyone dip their weapons in it?" asked the captain. The captain didn't even raise the question of the damage done by Halcyon to Ashe, knowing it was part of the effects of combat.

Ashe rose up a bit to speak, but his face turned deathly pale and he fell back unconscious.

"I see Ashe has had enough for today," observed the captain. "He's a good man, our chief. I've been impressed with him this entire cruise. Midshipwizard, don't worry too much about Fallow. His type are tough as nails, he'll pull through, mark my words. Men, take our senior chief petty officer below."

Suddenly horns blared out from the nearest ketch. A dwarven honor guard unfurled golden royalty flags while others used a corvus platform to breach the space between the ketch and the dragonfrigate. The corvus was a thick and long platform that angled out from the ketch on a moving hinge. Reaching over the side of the ketch it spanned the distance between that ship and the dragonship and allowed crew from the ketch to board the *Rage*.

"Oh, my," said the ambassador. "Those are flags from a royal dwarven house. A prince wants to come calling. Captain, we're expected to offer him food and drink."

"Boatswain Gray, have the stone urn from my cabin brought up as well as the kettledrum. Hurry, man," Gord-un ordered. "Midshipman Gold-un, pipe a prince aboard," he shouted down to the tube deck.

It took some doing, but by the time the squad of dwarves were going over the corvus toward the *Rage*, the things the captain ordered were brought up and Scott was ready to pipe the prince aboard.

Halcyon looked on from the quarterdeck and for the life of him couldn't remember the piping notes for a visiting prince. Then he heard them trilling out loud and clear in the darkness.

As the prince came into view, he walked on board with a crutch. Halcyon noted that it was the same dwarf he'd pulled out of the battle.

Captain Gord-un was at the kettledrum. As the prince stepped on the *Rage*, the captain rapped out a rhythmic series of beats on the drum and it began glowing. After a few moments, the entire ship glowed green, while the prince took on a white glow. There was a surprised look on the prince's face and he bowed deeply toward the captain and his drum.

The ambassador was at the edge of the corvus and spoke to the dwarf. The dwarven language sounded like rocks clacking together. Abernathy said some long sentence and then bowed low.

Halcyon couldn't hear what the prince replied, but the ambassador got a sour look on his face.

The captain walked up to the prince. Gord-un still had his drumsticks in his hand. He offered them to the prince, who clearly declined. The prince spoke a few words to the captain.

Halcyon could hear the captain turn and order a sailor to fetch Swordson, who was on the forecastle.

Ambassador Abernathy tried to tell the captain something, but the captain ignored him. Elan arrived and came to attention beside the captain. From a distance, Blithe could see the prince become visibly agitated. After a few words, the captain looked up to Halcyon and bellowed out, "Midshipwizard, to me!"

There was only one midshipwizard on the ship, and he was it. He rushed to his captain's side and came to attention.

Halcyon now got a close look at the dwarves. All of them were typical of dwarven-kind with massive shoulders and muscles layered on muscles. They all had faceted rubies in their foreheads. The leader of the group, the prince was most assuredly the dwarf Halcyon had dragged away from the battle. The prince was the only one wearing ruby-encrusted bracers on his massive arms. The gems sparkled brightly in the magical glows caused by the kettledrum.

"At ease, Midshipwizard Blithe," ordered Gord-un.

Upon seeing Halcyon, the prince bowed low. He said something in the dwarven language. Halcyon could speak a little of the dwarven language from his lessons on the ship, but the prince spoke too fast for the midshipwizard to catch anything. After bowing, the prince was handed his golden axe by a dwarf behind him. He put the axe on the deck between Halcyon and himself and folded his arms across his chest, looking grim.

The ambassador looked distressed. "The prince has come here to settle the randory between you and him. Dwarven randory is a blood debt between two individuals. The prince feels he owes you and has placed his most prized possession between the two of you. You can pick that up and be even, but the prince doesn't want to lose the axe. He wants you to ask for something, literally anything, and he will try and give it to you." The ambassador had a tension in his voice, as if the matter was a huge deal.

Halcyon thought nothing of the offer. He was impressed with the dwarf and the axe, but he didn't want a favor. He spoke directly to the prince, thinking maybe the dwarf could understand and speak Arcanian. "Prince, we were comrades in arms fighting for our lives on your ship. You would have done the same for me. You requested I get your axe and I did. You have no need to give me anything for something I would do for any brother in arms."

"No!" Ambassador Abernathy shouted. "You must watch what you say! You can't call the prince of the dwarves your brother! You have to leave us now!" There was desperation in the voice of the ambassador.

"He'll stay right where he is until the prince is finished with him," the captain ordered, putting out a hand to prevent the midshipwizard from bolting from the deck at the order of the ambassador.

While this was going on, the prince took off his enchanted bracers and placed them with the axe. In perfect Arcanian, he started speaking to Halcyon.

Halcyon's heart raced. He didn't have the slightest idea what he did wrong. Looking closely at the prince, the midshipwizard could tell the dwarf wasn't happy. The prince looked tense and seemed grim-lipped as he glared at Halcyon; then he spoke.

"I've come to show randory to you, a human from the land of Arcania. In the past your island nation and its people have traded with my people, even with our . . ." He stopped for a moment, searching for the word. Turning toward the ambassador, he spoke in Dwarvish.

Abernathy answered back, "The word doesn't translate well in Arcanian. Think of it as extreme dislike warranted by many unpleasant experiences."

"You will have to excuse my poor understanding of your language," the dwarf said. "I am Prince Theon Earthstone. You couldn't pronounce my full name, and there is no need for that between us. I would have your name?"

As he spoke, Halcyon was able to take the time to really look at all of them. The eight dwarves each had the same bushy red hair and unusually thick eyebrows. Their faces possessed odd angles at the cheeks and chin; they were almost square-cut. Each wasn't more than five feet tall, showing a massive amount of muscle, and they stood ranked by who was larger and thicker in their arms and legs. They wore tabards with a mountain-and-a-setting-sun pattern on the front of the tabard. The smallest one was still twice as thick as any normal human was. The prince was the largest dwarf by far in this collection. His uniform displayed rich appointments in amulets and badges of rank, and all of these ornaments held a ruby of some type. Easily a hundred different types of rubies covered the uniform of the prince. The largest was inset in his forehead. Halcyon couldn't imagine how he didn't spot that forehead gem during the battle.

"I am Midshipwizard First Class Halcyon Blithe, seventh son of a seventh son, Your Majesty. Please let me say that you do great honor to my ship and myself by coming aboard," Blithe said, bowing low to the prince.

"My race doesn't generally like your race. Your people try to prey on us for our gold and other riches, as these pirates you helped us kill. We appreciate your help." The prince was sounding more apologetic now. "What you did only makes us wonder at what cost that help means for all dwarfkind. We are not brothers in any manner. You are a human and I am a dwarf. Ask for something and let my spirit rest, clean of this randory life debt."

They were all looking at Halcyon. He found himself afraid to say anything. He knew he couldn't take the axe and bracers on the deck in front of him. He thought Abernathy would faint if he just refused everything. Still on his mind was his guilt at burning Chief Fallow.

"One of my men had his hands magically burned. I'm afraid he'll never use them again if they aren't cured soon. Can you help with that?" Halcyon asked.

"You don't know our ways, so let me make this perfectly clear," the dwarf said. "You can have dwarven lands, castles. I would send an army at your call. Whatever I own could be yours for the asking. Are you sure this request of yours is what you want?" The prince held out his huge hand toward the ambassador, not letting him say a word.

The pleading look in Halcyon's face was all the assurance the captain needed. "Boatswain Gray, bring Chief Fallow up here on his cot."

"Aye, Captain," Gray replied.

"So be it then," the prince replied, and issued an order to one of the dwarves. Several of them spoke quickly to the prince and he waved them off. The dwarf rushed back aboard their ketch and went below into their hold. Moments later, he came up with a chest.

"Captain, the need for this meeting has prevented me from showing you the honor you and your ship are due. For that transgression, I'm sorry. When you come to the port, I must be allowed to serve you food and drink?" It was more a question that a statement from the prince.

"Only if you'll let me give you food from my table and drink from my family urn," the captain said, walking back to the middle of the *Rage* and motioning the dwarves to come further onto the ship. Gord-un had stone cups for each of the dwarves and he personally poured drinks, giving the first one to the prince.

"Your tonga drum and tonga urn are from the Granite Clan. How did you get them?" Prince Theon asked.

"They've been passed down from father to son for seventeen generations," replied the captain. "I got them from my dwarf father when I captained my first ship. They have served me well for many years. Now I would salute you, Prince," he said, raising his stone cup and drinking deep on the white brew from the urn.

All the dwarves drank with him, smiling at the taste of the magical drink.

"I haven't sampled tonga brew in a long, long time," said the prince with a huge smile on his face. Each of his teeth was square-cut and it seemed he had several sets in his head. He didn't look happy. "I have to ask and forgive my lack of tact. You have a human mother?"

"Yes, many of the crew of this ship have one parent a dwarf and one parent a human," replied Gord-un.

The prince and the rest of his group got the oddest expression on their faces.

The chest arrived at the same time the unconscious Ashe Fallow arrived on deck. Fallow's head was shaking back and forth and the man was soaking wet from a blazing-hot fever.

Prince Earthstone took out a dark stone bracelet from the fur-lined chest. The dwarves among his group all gasped in wonder at the item. A huge ruby covered the head of the bracelet. As the dwarf put it on his wrist, the ruby glowed bright red. The dwarf spread his shovel-sized hand over the face of Fallow. Speaking in the dwarven tongue, the prince said words over the chief. A strange odor filled the area. It smelled of fresh-dug earth. When the prince lifted his hand away, a transformed Ashe Fallow sat up, completely healed.

"Chief, are you all right?" Halcyon had to ask.

The man sitting up was much changed from the Fallow they all knew. Dark wavy hair covered the formerly bald head. His tired eyes now shone with a sparkling youthfulness that Halcyon hadn't seen before.

"What in the gods' names happened to me?" Ashe asked, pulling off the bandages on his hands to see thickly corded muscle and pink flesh where charred skin presented itself before.

"Chief, stand down. I suspect our Mr. Blithe happened to you. We will talk about this healing at another time. Go below for now," Captain Gord-un ordered.

Chief Fallow came to attention, saluted, and left.

Standing like a statue, the prince spoke again. "Are you satisfied with what you asked for?"

"Of course, I'm totally satisfied," Halcyon said.

The ambassador shook his head, seeming to say by the gesture that Halcyon had again said something wrong.

"Halcyon Blithe, you shall be remembered in the stones of my clan. Captain, I hope to see you soon at Crystal Port," said the prince, bowing toward both men and leaving abruptly, along with his retinue.

"Well, that certainly could have gone better," quipped the ambassador.

"What in the world did the prince do to Fallow?" asked the captain.

"Oh, just used a magical wish," Ambassador Abernathy said in awe. "I suspect that, as with other dwarves who don't have much magical ability, that the item he used was unique to his family. Halcyon, you were just the cause of burning up a rare magical dwarven treasure. And it was used to save a human; that's not going to go down well when it's talked about in the dwarven halls."

Halcyon looked at the retreating dwarves, filled with wonder. He hadn't wanted them to use up such a treasure, but Ashe Fallow was cured, making today a good day to be alive.

XVIII

❉ ❉ ❉

𝕶idnapped!

Halcyon stood stunned, but still filled with elation, as the
dwarves left the ship and hauled up their corvus. His friend
Ashe Fallow went to the hold with healed hands and the appearance of being years younger. Blithe had been the cause of
his friend's hands burning to a crisp, and now Chief Fallow
was saved after the midshipwizard was granted a wish from the
dwarven prince. Wishes were not common magic in any land
and the use of such magic was call for much celebration, especially on Fallow's part.

"Come with me, all of you," ordered Captain Gord-un after watching the prince and his group leave.

Junior Lieutenant Swordson, Ambassador Abernathy, Major Maxwell, and Halcyon all went to the quarterdeck of the *Rage*.

"Ambassador, what just happened there?" asked the captain.

"Well, for one thing, our young firebrand here wasted a wish," Abernathy answered snidely.

Halcyon reddened at the ambassador's words.

"Hardly a waste, a good man is saved and back to duty," Maxwell interjected.

"I don't care if Blithe should have wished for an agreement between our two peoples or a ton of gold. My father never mentioned this dislike the dwarves seem to be showing to humans and half-dwarves, what's with that?" asked the irritated captain. His face looked strained and there was an angry edge to his voice.

"I'm sorry to say the dwarves you have come in contact with in Arcania are all outcasts for one reason or another from dwarven clans in their empire," answered the ambassador. "I tried to tell the admiralty and the Council of Ambassadors that a ship filled with half-caste dwarves, and please I beg your pardon for stating the obvious, but you asked, would not be appreciated by any official of the Dwarven Empire. I tried to tell them the dwarves would not appreciate half-dwarves coming to their shore.

"Someone in the admiralty thought it would be a good idea to gather up as many half-dwarves in the navy as possible and group them on a new ship to honor the dwarves we sailed toward. I think we've just seen that quite the opposite has happened. We do have one advantage we didn't have when we sailed."

"What would that be, Ambassador?" asked the captain.

"We need to fly a red flag to mark our ship's randory," answered Abernathy.

"I thought the prince settled that with Blithe," Swordson said.

"The prince settled that all right, and the young fool should have asked me before speaking. He didn't settle what those ketches and thus their entire navy owes our ship for saving them," answered the ambassador. "I think that's why he offered you food and drink at the port, Captain. He wants to get off easy. When you're invited on shore you must say you will accept his offer only after I am allowed to present my credentials."

"Ambassador, you do realize flying the red flag in the Arcanian navy means we are a plague ship," advised the captain.

"Different countries, different rules, Captain," Abernathy replied. "The dwarves fly a white flag for their version of a plague ship. The red flag shows a blood debt owed a ship. If we had those colors I'd have you fly the dwarven prince's flags to show who owed us the randory, but the prince is aware of what he owes."

"Ambassador Abernathy, I want to apologize for the recent actions of my crew and myself," Captain Gord-un said in a conciliatory tone. "My orders are clear on the matter of doing everything I can to help you get established in the dwarven port. From now on all dealings with the dwarves will be done through you and you alone. Please try to advise me on what our actions should be and I will do the utmost to make your wishes happen."

Abernathy looked surprised at the captain's tone. "Very good, Captain. I think we should follow these ships into Crystal Port. Flying the red flag, we shouldn't have to wait too long before we're met by the prince's attendants. From then on we will see."

The group turned to see the ketches and sloops sailing south. Orders had the *Rage* fly only its topsails. The ship easily kept up with the dwarven squadron.

Two days later, the dwarves of the ketches showed no sign that the *Rage* was following. The midshipmen were taking their ease on the forecastle.

Halcyon looked down at the Lady Teagan in his watch. The girl was smiling and seemed to be in a park. There were flowers all about her image. He closed the watch as Gold-un addressed him.

"Midshipwizard, if you don't mind saying," asked Jakwater, "I was wondering why the storm you caused back on the *Sanguine* couldn't be used as an attack. Why couldn't an air wizard like yourself hold storms at bay for ten or twenty days and then sail into the middle of an enemy fleet and turn it loose?"

Halcyon laughed at the question and the memory it brought. "Lieutenant Commander Daton Giantson is a half giant with amazing magical abilities. I served with him on the *Sanguine*. He's the one who taught us spellcasters how to use our magic while aboard ship. After the storm I caused, we spent two lessons on how foolish I was. I learned then that living spirits, normally invisible to our eyes, perform the magic we call on to influence the weather. I was actually forcing intelligent air spirits to hold back the normal weather we would have had in favor of the sunshine and the breeze I wanted. The commander made it very clear that anyone trying the trick you suggested would have their ship dashed in the storm while the weather spirits made sure the surrounding innocent ships took no harm at all just to spite the spellcaster."

A reborn Ashe Fallow came up to the forecastle. He looked

years younger and displayed a spring back in his step that age had slowly taken away. In the last two days, he'd showed an energy Halcyon had never seen in the man.

"Gentlemen, I suspect you're going to be ordered to put on your best kilt," Fallow said to the midshipmen. "Look yonder," he said, pointing.

Several miles away stood a promontory jutting into the sea from the mountain range they'd been sailing past for days. Most of the Dwarven Empire was nestled in and under the large range of mountains on the continent. The ketches were just sailing around it. Their huge fifty-pounders fired off a salute and several new pennants appeared on their masts. The crew of the *Rage* knew it was a salute, because of the different tone of the blast-tubes when fired without shot in the tubes. It was evident to the crew that these blasts were all from empty tubes.

"All hands on deck, parade dress," bellowed Boatswain Gray through his speaking tube from the quarterdeck. "Green caps to be worn at all times!"

Swordson looked down at the tube deck and the crew madly dashing about as they went to their stations. He'd seen Blithe go below. The young fool had stolen all of Elan's thunder days ago with the idiot prince coming aboard. Swordson had liked the way the ambassador called Blithe a fool. If there was a chance to expose Halcyon to more blame, Elan wanted to make that happen. Maybe he should get Fallow and Darkwater involved in whatever he drew Halcyon into. That pair seemed to like the midshipwizard far too much. Elan had spent many hours with the ambassador in an effort to curry the man's favor. Knowing the fool midshipwizard, there would be more chances to make him show his true colors.

———

Tall sailing ships on parade were stunning sights, and the *Rage* was no exception. Rows of crew stood tall and proud on the footlines of each sail, ten to a mast side. Normally they were bent toward the sail to work the lines, but on parade these men faced out of the sails with their hands behind their backs at parade rest. Lined up on the forecastle and quarterdeck, men stood proudly to be seen from the shore. As the *Rage* turned the promontory, Halcyon made a discovery. His far looker scanned the large hill they were sailing past.

"It's a fort," Halcyon said in surprise. He scanned the rocky sides of the promontory to see blast-tube ports opening and huge land tubes rolling out. What appeared to be a normal land feature was actually a deadly fort guarding the city.

The port city of Crystal showed itself to be amazing.

As *Rage*'s twenty-one-tube salute sounded off, the full impact of the city became clear.

Dug deep into the mountainside, Crystal City presented itself as a vast complex of stone cubes spreading itself down to the water's edge. Ships filled the huge harbor. All of the dwarven vessels seemed to have some type of stone towers where the forecastles and quarterdecks would be on Arcanian ships. The crew of the *Rage* had no idea how such weighty-looking things could sail the seas. There weren't many nondwarven ships in the harbor.

The docks at the water's edge were bustling stone platforms filled with workers loading and unloading goods.

As the far looker scanned the city, all the buildings appeared to be made out of stone and each and every one was a perfectly shaped cube with no windows in evidence.

"Captain, enemy on the starboard side," Halcyon said, focusing his far looker in that direction.

Three Maleen first-raters were at anchor, surrounded by dwarven warships.

"Beat to quarters, Boatswain Gray," ordered the captain.

There was no way in this life or any other lifetime that the *Rage* could withstand the broadsides of three enemy first-raters. The captain didn't think they would have to fight as they sailed into the harbor, but he wanted to be ready for anything they might encounter.

Halcyon noticed that the tube ports of the three ships were closed. There didn't appear to be many men working the ships and their sticks had furled sails.

Halcyon scanned the city, seeing a busy place with the streets filled with carts and dwarves going back and forth. Strange, huge bird-things pulled the carts and wagons about the city. The birds were more then ten feet tall with huge axe-shaped beaks. There wasn't a horse visible across the entire cityscape.

The city was laid out in levels going deeper and deeper into the mountain. Each level rose a little higher into the mountainside. There were scores of cube-shaped buildings rising out of the mountain floor. Most of them held the same colored stone as the mountainside, but some of them shone brightly in reds, blacks, and whites. Each of these was a solid color, seemingly made out of one piece of stone. However, they were huge buildings and many stories tall. The buildings seemed the work of giants, not dwarves.

Halcyon gasped when he looked at the top of the mountain and saw a group of dwarves mounted on huge flying birds. A group of seven of them swooped down at frightening speed and flew over the *Rage*.

"Roar!" Sort challenged. "*I bet I could knock them out of the sky*," he thought to Halcyon.

"*Calm down*," Halcyon advised. "*We're here to make friends with them, not use them for target practice.*"

The fliers circled the *Rage* for several minutes and went back to the top of the mountain.

The ketches they'd been following tied up at the piers along with the captured sloops. A large crowd of military-looking dwarves with royal flags waving came out to greet the prince. A richly appointed black coach took him away.

A sloop flying the royal golden colors of the prince sailed out of the harbor and within a bowshot of the *Rage*.

A dwarf stood at the prow of the sloop and shouted in Dwarvish at the dragonfrigate. The captain, Blithe, and the ambassador came to the prow to listen to the shouting from the other vessel. Once again, Halcyon thought the language sounded just like rocks banging together.

"They speak a dialect like none my father ever spoke. Ambassador, can you understand him?" Gord-un asked.

"Yes, I can understand him quite clearly. He's demanding we put a muzzle on the dragon's fangs," Ambassador Abernathy laughingly replied.

Everyone within hearing started laughing. The very thought of getting a muzzle large enough to cover the head of the dragon was too funny a thought for the Arcanians, who were proud of their dragonfrigate. Soon the laughter spread through the ship as the words of the dwarf echoed from deck to mast to orlop hold.

"Lower the jolly boat, bring the harbormaster on board," the captain ordered to Boatswain Gray.

Gray went to launch the jolly boat from the stern of the *Rage*.

"What can we expect from this one, Ambassador?" asked the captain.

The ambassador stared out at the sloop and the dwarf at its prow. "He's a minor harbor official. I wouldn't be a bit surprised if he ordered us away. When he does, just point to the red flag on our mast and the harbormaster will know exactly why we stay. I will tell him I have credentials to present to the prince or the king and they will eventually come around."

"Midshipwizard, you calm our young dragon down a bit. Let's have him keep his head down while this dwarf is aboard," Gord-un ordered.

"Aye, Captain," Halcyon replied.

"Water tastes funny," Sort thought.

"The captain wants you to keep your head down while the dwarves are here. What do you mean the water tastes funny?" Halcyon asked.

"Tastes like dust," Sort thought.

"Well, put up with it as long as you can and keep your head away from the dwarves and their sloop," Halcyon asked of his reptilian friend.

"I'll try. Dwarves probably taste like dust too," Sort replied.

A thoroughly disagreeable dwarf came aboard the *Rage*. Immediately, he started shouting in his own language. He stood no more than four feet tall, but could have been five feet wide. He wore a massive golden breastplate with the image of the port emblazoned on its surface. The rest of his uniform was all in black. The dwarves of his ship were uniformed in black as well. He didn't wear a weapon, but there was a huge leather holder where a warhammer must have been a short time ago.

"Ambassador, tell him to stop shouting on my ship," ordered the captain.

"Don't you want to know what he's saying?" Abernathy asked.

The harbormaster kept on shouting and gesturing with his massive arms.

The ambassador spoke several short sentences.

The harbormaster immediately shut up and left the ship.

"What did you tell him?" Gord-un asked.

"I mentioned the dwarven navy's randory and my need to see the prince. He's going to tell the king what I've said. I expect they'll feel duty-bound to see us in the morning."

"Have the men stand down from their stations," ordered the captain. "It doesn't look like we're going to be shot out of the water any time soon."

Darkness came early to the port as the setting sun fell behind the mountain ridge. Burning lights appeared on the street corners as darkness fell, throwing illumination onto the side of the buildings, whose surfaces seemed to magnify the lights somehow, making the entire city glow.

Out from the dock came a large longboat, rowed by a band of dwarves.

"Hail the ship," came a voice out of the darkness in perfect Arcanian. "The king of the dwarves under the mountain will see the ambassador and his retinue now."

"Bide a moment while we summon him," Elan shouted down to the boat.

He brought the news to the captain and ambassador at their dinner.

"Well, I didn't expect this until the morning, but the sooner it's done the better," Abernathy said. "Elan, I would like you and a few others to come with me if the captain allows."

"Of course, Ambassador, anyone you need. Mr. Swordson, pick three other likely lads to go with you," ordered the captain. "Will you need any of your sea chests, Ambassador?"

"There are three of them I'll need immediately, but the others can wait. See to them for me, Swordson. They're the red ones with the ornate locks."

"Right away, Lord Abernathy," Elan answered back.

An hour later, Denna Darkwater, Ashe Fallow, and Halcyon Blithe were dressed in their parade clothes and settling themselves in the longboat behind the ambassador.

"Could you tell me again, Ambassador, why we aren't going to this meeting with our weapons?" asked Chief Fallow for the fifth time.

"You will do what you're told and like it, crewman. We don't wear weapons to a meeting with the king because he can kill us at a whim," the ambassador said. "We're here to establish a battle pact with the Dwarven Empire. If we can get them to help us fight the Maleen, victory could come quickly for us. Why do you think there are three Maleen ships of the line in their port? Those ships are trying to do the same thing we are," Ambassador Abernathy answered curtly.

Fallow rolled his eyes and shook his head sadly.

The dwarves rowing the longboat never said a word. Soon they were at the dock and seeing a huge black coach pull up. Six of the large, strange birds pulled the vehicle. The creatures were over ten feet tall and at least that much long. Their beaks alone were larger than a man's head. Each sported a heavy leather muzzle over its beak. They stood impatiently in their harnesses, fidgeting from one talon to the other.

"Midshipwizard, you ride up above with the coachman. Darkwater and Fallow, ride behind as our coachmen. Mr. Swordson, please ride with me in the coach," ordered the ambassador.

Everyone did as ordered, the three large chests were loaded up on top of the coach, and the coach trundled off through the city streets.

In an hour, they were passing under the arch of a black stone building. They came into a large square and stopped in the darkness.

From inside the coach, Ambassador Abernathy said, "Mr. Blithe, if you please, light up the area."

Fallow and Darkwater came down and opened the coach door as Halcyon used his magical power to cast a glow about everything. His light revealed ten dark-clad humans with their weapons drawn. The coach dwarf smashed him on the head with a club and darkness took him.

"Wake up, fools!" came a shout.

Halcyon hurt from head to toe. Once again, he felt cold chains around his wrists and legs. His beret had fallen over his eyes and he shook his head to free himself from the obstruction.

He wasn't in a pleasant place.

The room was a torture chamber out of his worst nightmare. Chained to the walls with their hands over their heads, the group appeared helpless. Manacles of Iben were on everyone's hands, even the ambassador's and Fallow's. Denna's face showed signs of a terrible beating, as her eyes appeared closed shut and swollen. Her mouth dripped blood from both sides.

Racks, iron maidens, and red-hot coals in a brazier filled with branding irons occupied the center of the chamber. Two Tock demons stood guard at the only door high up a long spiral staircase. Halcyon knew enough about demons to know it took the blood sacrifice of women to draw a Tock demon to this realm. They stood seven feet tall, and demonologists said that type of demon could be harmed only by magical weapons. Their red, glowing eyes stared Halcyon down and made him look away.

"I had no idea Arcanians carried so many things in their hair," came a voice from behind an iron maiden, in perfect Arcanian.

A young man appeared from around the corner holding the two white and one blue war braids formerly worn by the prisoners. He wore the uniform of a Maleen ship captain, a demon blade was at his hip, and his badges of rank marked him as a captain for many years. He didn't look old enough for his badges. Broad-shouldered, he was as tall as Halcyon. His eyes were jet black and his hair was cut short to his head. At his shoulder was a tiny green dragon.

"Yours had a lock pick. I never imagined the Blithes to be simple thieves and rogues. What would your ancestors say?" The man walked over to Halcyon as the midshipwizard came to the realization that Halcyon's hair lay in their jailer's hand.

The little dragon on his shoulder stared into Halcyon's eyes. The creature cooed and shimmered with magical energy.

Halcyon tried to communicate with it, but had no luck.

"You have the advantage of me, sir," Halcyon quipped. "Let me assure you that if any of my ancestors were here, they would be forcing a blade into your ribs as we speak. They weren't known for their temperance." Halcyon's words were much bolder than he felt, but right then he wasn't going to let a Maleen know how afraid he was. He was remembering several stories of being captured from his brothers, uncles, and father. They all said the exact same thing. A prisoner gained much more by being bold than by being cowardly.

"Forgive me, Midshipwizard, I am Captain Duval King-maker, squadron leader of the Maleen forces in the harbor. The little friend on my shoulder is my familiar, Emer. We Maleen with magical ability often take a familiar and I was lucky enough to attract him. He's just hatched and will grow to be quite large, but for now he's happy to sit on my shoulder, aren't you, Emer?

"I have to say I find your fellow crew members amazing," Duval said. "Your half troll there struck down four of my men bare-handed and actually killed one of them with a head butt. In addition, she's lovely, displaying an amazing form and figure. I almost want to try her myself, but the demons wouldn't approve. In two days, the larvae of the Tock demons will be ready. I'll insert them into your bodies and all the information you have will be ours. I fancy you all don't know very much, but one never knows.

"Your chief petty officer actually took away the sword of the first man to face him and killed three others before he was subdued. I actually had to call for dwarf reinforcements to take him down. I noticed the troll had a dagger hidden in her braid and she seems to have killed over thirty Maleen officers. I'm looking forward to having a stern talk with her. Moreover, your chief had a lock pick in his hair as well. You Arcanians never cease to amaze me."

"When the dwarves hear about this, all your plans will be undone, Duval," Halcyon shouted.

"Well, it might be a bit early to be on a first-name basis, but if you insist," quipped Kingmaker. "These dwarves are quite foolish. Oh, I must apologize for the haircut. They are the ones who insisted. They believe cutting your hair lessens your powers. Foolish, I know, but I often give them the little things they want so that I can take major favors later."

Duval was kicking at the clothes spilling out of the three chests the ambassador had insisted on bringing. "I find this amazing, simply amazing. Did your ambassador plan on making a pact with the dwarves because he was more fashionable? It appears our new dwarven allies are interested in magic items. We brought several baubles for them and they are all agog. I expect a treaty to be signed any day now."

"I look forward to matching blades with you, Captain," Halcyon sneered. "Try not to be amazed when my stroke takes your heart."

Kingmaker walked in a leisurely manner to the stairs. "Your chances to be amazed will be over in forty-eight hours. We'll be back then. I'm sorry to say you might be a bit hungry and thirsty. It's often difficult when one is far from home to keep up the amenities. Your demon guards will be just outside if you need anything. They won't come when you call, but you should be happy to know that they are there," Duval said, chuckling.

The demons opened the door for Kingmaker, and the three of them left. The magical lights went out with their leaving.

In total darkness, Halcyon started twisting in his chains.

"I actually killed three of them," spat Denna in the darkness. "Do you need any help getting your boot up to your hand?"

"I don't think the one with two broken arms is going to make it, either," came Ashe's voice.

Click

"That one rushed me a tad," Denna said. "How many did you stop, Midshipwizard?"

Click

"I trust I put a serious dent in the club that struck the back of my head," Halcyon quipped as he snapped his fingers and made his hands glow with a dim light, as they were now free of the manacles. "Why in the world did they put three sets of manacles on you, Denna?" Halcyon was using his bit of wire on the manacles.

Click

"I lost interest after being hit a few hundred times," Denna said in the dim light. "I could have vexed them a bit."

"Be a good Lankshire man and hand me the pick from my braid before you finish her," Fallow asked.

"Oh, sure, Chief, silly of me to not think of that," Halcyon said, getting both picks and working his into Darkwater's manacles.

A series of rapid clicks freed everyone.

It took a few slaps and shakes to wake Swordson and the ambassador.

"Help me to my chests," Abernathy weakly requested.

"Lord, I don't think a change of clothes will do us much good," Elan snidely said.

The ambassador sighed heavily and reached into the turned-over chest displaying spilled cloaks and lace shirts. "I would agree, what would three magical dwarven battle-axes do to help us out?"

A secret compartment in the spilled chest opened at a touch of the ambassador's and a large golden, gem-encrusted axe fell softly to the floor in the pile of clothes.

"Tell me there are two more of those beauties in the other chests," asked Fallow.

"You're a bit ahead of me, but essentially correct," replied the ambassador as he flipped the hidden latches to the secret compartments in the chest to reveal two other wildly different axes. One of them appeared to be made out of silver and had many emeralds worked into the handle and blade. The other had a bronze sheen to the blade and was covered in jet gems. The ambassador tossed the silver axe to Halcyon. "Dear boy, I think your nature will best serve using that axe."

As Halcyon caught the handle, the weapon blazed in green light from all of the gems.

"Being a seventh son of a seventh son, your magical nature is multiplied many times by the enchantments of the axe. The other two are powerful defensive weapons, as well as having enchanted blades."

Denna Darkwater offered the bronze axe to Swordson.

"No, I'm not foolish enough to think I can use that better than you, Marine. I'll fight with these, until something better comes to hand," Elan said, picking up two red-hot pokers.

The ambassador picked up a poker as well and they moved to the stairs ready to escape or sell their lives dearly.

XIX

✦ ✦ ✦

Freedom Unlocked

HIS MAJESTY'S ARTICLES OF WAR: ARTICLE XXXIX

A summary court-martial may disrate any rated person for incompetency.

"Wait a moment," ordered the ambassador. The man was shaking in fear, realizing that his life was in deadly danger.

Rummaging in one of the spilled chests, he pulled out a small jar and opened it. Suddenly the dungeon filled with the smell of fresh flowers.

"Close your eyes, Corporal, this isn't going to hurt a bit," Abernathy said as he dipped two shaky fingers into the white cream inside the jar. Starting at her eyebrows, he rubbed the cream all over her swollen-closed eyes and across her cut cheeks and mouth. The cream vanished instantly and the swelling went down from the magical healing essences in the jar. Denna sighed in relief.

"Thank you, Lord Abernathy," Denna said, smiling from the soothing cream. She was able to use both eyes now.

"Anyone else need a spot of healing?" asked the ambassador. "There isn't much here, but it's an elfin recipe and has hideously amazing soothing properties."

For a moment no one spoke.

"Rub some on the back of my neck and our midshipwizard's bump, the one that's the size of a goose egg, if you please. He'd never complain, but I want him and me in the best shape possible when we open that door up there. Anyone ever face Tock demons before?" Ashe asked.

"Tock demons rely on their great strength and thick hides to do well in combat. I haven't fought them before, but I've read some about them," Halcyon said, taking great relief in the cream the ambassador put on his head.

"Heat and holy water are effective against the hide of the Tock demon," Elan quoted. "You aren't the only family who trains their members in demon fighting, Blithe. I haven't fought them, but I stand as ready as everyone else."

"I have holy-water vials in my chests," Abernathy sobbed, fear still filling his voice. He put the lid back on the small jar and pocketed it. Digging into all three chests, he came up with six small crystal bottles. "One never knows when one needs such things," explained the ambassador in a high-pitched voice filled with the tension he was feeling. "These are made purposely fragile and will shatter and spill against the body of any demon they strike. I have sprigs of wolfsbane and fresh garlic buds as well."

"We'll keep those in mind when we have time to eat our foes," quipped Ashe Fallow. "Ambassador, I didn't have much use for you, but I'm saying I'm sorry now. If it wasn't for you, we'd be dead. You have my thanks, Lord." He smiled, trying to ease the tension the ambassador was showing. It didn't help much.

Elan addressed the problem of the demon guards. "I'll unlock the door using magic and Blithe here will throw the hot coals from that brazier at the demons. We're hoping to blind the pair. They aren't known for their intelligence. They'll come down the stairs swinging at anyone who stands in their way. We'll line up on the stairs and those behind can hurl the holy water at the demons and that might just be enough to kill them both."

Halcyon had been holding the axe for several minutes now and the enchanted glow from it started to pulse with his quickening heartbeat. The pulsing green light of the weapon grew brighter as well. "I'll be the one in front. I don't know what this axe will do. . . ."

"Oh, you'll find them unusually useful weapons," the ambassador assured them all. "I haven't used them myself, but they are said to be ancient weapons with hideously powerful magics. Midshipwizard, the one you're holding is called Dragonsbane. The corporal is holding an axe called Headchopper. Death is the name of the chief's battle-axe. It takes a dwarf to get the most out of these weapons' magics, but I'm sure in all of your capable hands they'll do a good bit of damage. I purposely put them in secret compartments at the bottom of my clothes chests and the enemy did what I expected. They ruffled through my things thinking they were nothing but clothes. I love it when something I planned works well." Some of the terror was gone from Abernathy's voice once the axes were out and it looked like they might have a chance.

"We'll move as a group and try to escape wherever this is, making sure the ambassador makes it out," ordered Swordson. Elan thought briefly about ordering one of them to give him an axe to use, but he hated the axes. The hot pokers would do until a real weapon fell from the hands of a dead enemy. With Fallow, Darkwater, and Blithe in front of him, he had no doubt there would be fallen enemies as they moved forward.

"Gloves?" asked Halcyon of the ambassador.

"You wouldn't happen to have a few battle helms and a blast-pike in those chests?" Denna teased.

"Ambassadors don't really need battle helms, but maybe I should put them on the list for next time," he said, giving as good as he got in the teasing contest and showing a little pluck. Abernathy rummaged some more in his chests of clothes and brought out a pair of thick hide gloves with fur lining.

Putting on the gloves, Halcyon strapped the axe on his back. The second he stopped holding the axe, its magical glow vanished. He threw the branding irons on the floor, not wanting to gift his enemies with fiery weapons. Lifting the heavy brazier up, he motioned Swordson to go first up the stairs. They could move easily by the light of the burning coals.

The heat of the brazier made Halcyon's eyes blink. The metal dish full of coals was too heavy to hold out from his body. He needed his chest to help hold the thing and it was making seeing difficult in the heat and coal dust. They rushed up the stairs and Halcyon put the dish down on the landing while Swordson cast his magic.

Halcyon noticed scorch marks on his dress uniform that he knew would be a problem at the next ship's muster—if he lived to make the muster, that is.

How Swordson knew an air spell to open locks, the midship-wizard would never know, but he wanted to learn it.

Elan stood by the door and slowly moved his hands in front of the lock of the heavy portal. Swirls of air formed in front of the lock. Halcyon recognized the image of a lock's gears and tumblers forming in the air in front of the lock. As Swordson moved his hands, the image of the gears moved. Finally, the spell was ready as all the gears and tumblers were aligned in the magical image and Swordson went down the stairs to get out of Blithe's way.

"Don't screw this up, Blithe. I'll snap my fingers and the door will open. You throw the coals and be ready to fight for your life as the demons come at you," Elan ordered.

Halcyon didn't say a word. He unstrapped the axe and put it on the landing, leaning against the wall, for ready use. The heat was still intense from the brass bowl. He nodded his head, signaling everyone behind him that he was ready.

Swordson made sure holy vials were in the hands of Denna and Ashe as he went past them on the long flight of stairs. He picked up two hot pokers and held them in one hand while he motioned for the ambassador to stay behind him. Snapping his fingers, he activated his air-magic spell and the prison door at the top of the stairs flew open. If the gods gave him any luck at all, Blithe would be killed in the first rush of the demons, thought Swordson.

The Tock demons were standing to either side of the door and both turned in to look at the opening. Halcyon hurled the hot coals into their faces. He threw the dish down into the dungeon behind him and took a step back, picking up the axe. The weapon's gems burst into magical green glows and suddenly the two screaming Tock demons glowed green as well.

The first of the giant monsters rushed the stair. One talon wiped at its half-blinded eyes. The other taloned arm stretched out, reaching for the tormentor that threw coals into its eyes.

"Coming back down the stairs!" Halcyon shouted as he took two steps back and half swung at the talon reaching for his throat. The midshipwizard wasn't sure about his weapon and didn't want to commit himself to swinging as hard as he could for fear of overbalancing himself on the stairs and falling into the grip of the huge demon in front of him.

The axe surprised him by shearing through the taloned arm at the wrist. It fell to the floor with a meaty thunk and the creature roared out its pain again. The stump gushed forth a torrent of blood, covering Halcyon's face and chest with demon gore.

The battle was taken out of Blithe's hands as the axe moved of its own accord from right to left in a massively powerful stroke, guided by Halcyon's arms as if he could see. Halcyon was encouraged by the magic of the axe blade to swing as hard as he could and he did. While he was trying to blink away the blood, a talon grasped his shoulder and started ripping at him. The axe bit into something massive and the creature screeched, the volume of it filling the midshipwizard's senses as the weight of the creature went off Halcyon. The monster stopped howling halfway through its fall off the stairs. The dead Tock demon, cut in half from the action of axe, fell in two pieces to the dungeon floor below.

The midshipwizard had a heartbeat of time to wipe his eyes free of blood.

The second demon stood at the top of the stairs noting what happened to its clutchmate. It looked at its green glowing talons, clearly not liking what it saw as Halcyon's axe glowed the same green glow. The demon started casting magic, causing its body to grow even larger. Dark swirls of mist formed between its two talons as some type of deadly spell formed. Six vials of holy water hit its body, ripping the creature into six parts as giant wounds erupted from the holy-water-coated flesh. The dead demon pieces fell to the stone floor.

Spitting sulfur-tasting blood, Halcyon turned. "Good throws, you might have saved a vial or two for the next ten demons we meet." He started up the stairs, axe in hand.

"Oh, don't worry about them, my Lankshire hero," Ashe Fallow exclaimed. "With that blood all over your head, you're going to scare to death the next twenty demons we meet."

"I'm scared of him and I know he's on our side," Denna quipped with a smile on her face.

"Quiet in the ranks, you fools. We're rushing through this place and out the door. Get a move on, Blithe," Swordson ordered.

Halcyon mentally questioned the need for quiet as he moved quickly to the door. The demons had made quite a racket in their dying.

Through the dungeon door, he entered a short corridor that ended in a left turn. Halcyon could hear the echoing sound of running footsteps in the distance. Suddenly the oddest idea popped into his head. He started screaming at the top of his lungs in perfect Maleen as he lunged around the corner.

"Argh! Demons, they've gone crazy! Killing everyone, run for your lives!" Blithe shouted.

He came around the corner to see a long corridor, lit by torches. Five men were coming down the stairs in the distance at the end of the corridor, weapons drawn in their hands.

Halcyon continued running toward them, waving his glowing axe. "Run, run for your lives, the demons are eating everyone!"

Ashe held the others back as he figured out Halcyon's trick. He could just imagine what the Maleen were thinking as this crazed, bloody figure came running at them down the hall. Shouting in Maleen had been a brilliant idea and would make Halcyon one of them in their minds. None of the foe had the equipment to fight Tock demons. It was impossible to tell if it was the sight of him and his bloody body or them turning green from the effects of his axe making them act as they did. Fallow watched around the corner as the five troops turned around and ran back up the stairs.

Halcyon stopped at the stairs and waved the others forward.

The group moved past cell door after cell door. Demon talons grasped the cell bars and demonic voices from behind those doors begged for freedom.

When the group reached Halcyon's position, the ambassador said, "The enemy of my enemy is my friend. We could let these eight demons free and maybe they would fight with us to escape."

Swordson shook his head in irritation. "The demon enemy of my enemy is still a ravening fiend, hungry for the blood of friend or foe. We'll keep the cell doors shut."

Halcyon looked around the corner and up the stairs to see Duval Kingmaker, glowing saber in hand, at the top of the stairs. The man's eyes grew wide at the sight of the midshipwizard.

"Halcyon Blithe, what have you done down there?" Duval asked, knowing he wasn't likely to get an answer.

Halcyon entered the opening of the stairs and took the first step. The axe helped to give him courage. "Are you interested in dancing, Captain?"

A green glow suddenly covered Duval's body as he was recognized by the battle-axe as a potential foe. Kingmaker jumped back, fearing the magical effect. When it didn't do him damage, he visibly calmed down. He once more turned around the corner and faced Halcyon at the top of the stairs.

"I've a hundred Maleen marines up here. I don't know where you got that nasty-looking axe, but come up and we will see what we see," Duval replied.

Suddenly the entire group heard the sound of drumming and felt drumbeat vibrations running through the corridor and stairs. Even Duval cocked his head, noting the deep boom of the drumbeats. Halcyon ducked back around the corner. The drumbeats pulsed through his entire body as if the drum were right next to him. He racked his brain to think of a spell that needed a drum to do its damage, but could think of none.

Ashe was standing axe at the ready, but his head was cocked, listening to the sound of the drumbeats all around him. Suddenly, he got a huge grin on his face. He leaned against the wall and slipped to sitting on the floor. He placed his axe down on the stone floor in front of him. Taking off his beret, he started twirling it in his hand. "Mr. Blithe, could you estimate how long it would take the marines of the *Rage* to walk up here from the dock?" Fallow's tone became lighthearted, as if he didn't have a care in the world.

"Ashe, what are you talking about?" Halcyon said, growing more and more nervous with the drumbeats.

"You rode up here watching the streets," Fallow replied, almost chuckling with glee. "How long would it take our men to get here if they were on foot? Just guess for me, please."

"Two hours at the most, maybe lots less if they know exactly where they're going," Halcyon answered exasperated.

Denna leaned against the wall and sat as well, putting her axe down on the floor and smiling as Fallow was.

The drumbeats continued to sound in the corridor, causing the demons in the cells to howl in fear for some unknown reason.

Swordson and the ambassador looked at Blithe, Fallow, and Darkwater as if they were insane.

"Midshipwizard, do you still have that watch of yours?" Denna asked in the same gleeful tone as Fallow.

"No, I left it on the ship with my weapons. Why do you ask?" Blithe replied, looking back up the stairs and ducking back as two crossbow bolts fired down at him.

"My good friends," Fallow grinned. "I believe the captain has noticed we've gone missing. That would be his drum we're hearing. His tonga drum, I think he called it. It's a magical drum, don't you know. I think the last time he beat it all of our nice new berets glowed green from the beating of the drum. If it wasn't for the green glow of Mr. Blithe's new axe, I think we would see these new caps of ours glowing as well."

The ambassador ripped the beret off his head and threw it down the corridor. It went out of the aura of the axe and hit the floor. It still glowed green.

Ashe looked back at Swordson, "Mr. Swordson, I believe we have a new plan. We'll sit tight right here and wait until our marines come to join this little party."

"Fallow, we don't know this drumming we hear is the captain's doing. I know magic and I've never heard of such a spell. I don't fancy dying here and never seeing Arcania again," Swordson shouted back.

"Arcanian!" Duval shouted. "I do so hate waiting on things. What say you and I tilt on the stairs for a bit, shall we?" The pleasing tone was meant to goad Halcyon into action.

Halcyon and everyone in the corridor knew that Kingmaker wanted to kill them and get at the ambassador.

"Blithe, kill the Maleen bastard and move upward, we'll all be right behind you," ordered Elan.

"Arcanian! Are you there?" shouted Duval.

"He's coming, hold your water, you blooming sodding idjet," Fallow shouted back up the stairs as he stood up. He took a rag he had from somewhere and started wiping Halcyon's face free of gore. "You'll find fighting on stairs interesting, my Lankshire hero. Your opponent has to bend down to strike at you. You have to reach out to hit him."

Halcyon nodded his head. The pulsing green glow of his axe showed his heart rate increasing.

"Get in close, you've the advantage with this bloody great axe," Fallow advised. "Remember that little dragon of his isn't for show. It's going to be casting spells at you. I'd wager a year's pay in Arcanian gold royals, this axe is going to help with that, but don't count on it. If he kills you, I promise he won't live another minute to gloat about it."

"Why, thank you, Chief Fallow," Halcyon said with a smile on his blood-smeared face, some of the nervousness gone with the humor of his friend. "I hope to live long enough to return the favor to you someday."

"That you will, lad, that you will," Ashe said, throwing the bloody rag down on the floor. "One last thing: This isn't a gentleman's duel. It's life or death on those stairs. Figure he's faster than you are and better than you until he shows you different. Keep that axe between you and your foe at all times."

There was an unspoken offer shown in the eyes of Ashe. Blithe knew his friend would face the captain first. Fallow also knew Halcyon would refuse that offer, so he never made it.

Halcyon turned and rounded the corner to the stairs. The pulsing green glow was flashing off the axe at more than a hundred beats a minute. The midshipwizard's nervousness never showed on his grimly smiling face. His hands never shook as he tightly held the axe. For a moment he was glad he made himself practice with battle-axes aboard ship in the months of the voyage.

Looking up, the midshipwizard saw Captain Duval slowly coming down the stairs. His dragon familiar hovered above his head. Halcyon had no idea what the little creature could do magically. If there were time, he vowed to study about such creatures. Duval's saber had glowing red runes along its blade. Halcyon also thought he saw a demon head formed on its pommel. Blithe had no doubt in the world, the enchanted blade had the potential to kill him with a touch if he wasn't careful. Demon things were often deadly to the touch.

The moment Duval took the first step down the stairs his body glowed green as the midshipwizard's axe recognized Kingmaker as a potential foe. The enchanted glow made the Maleen captain hesitate and make magical passes of his own. The glow didn't go away, but Halcyon noticed the eyes of the little dragon grow brighter for a moment.

"My axe is hungry and it appears you're its next meal," Halcyon bluffed, speaking Maleen to his enemy. He had no idea why the axe caused that glow, but he was heartened by it. As he took the first step up the stairs, he found himself wishing for his own saber. He remembered his father saying, "War often forces strange weapons into one's hand."

His summoning spell! Halcyon thought to himself. He couldn't believe the stupidity of not summoning his war equipment to his hands before this battle. Using some of his reserves of magic, he summoned his luck ring and bracers to his finger and arms. He felt their comforting weight as they materialized at his enchanted summoning. He doubted he had enough strength to summon his saber and there wasn't time as Duval rushed him.

The rigid form of the flying green dragon warned him of the spell attack. Halcyon took a defensive stance with the axe flush in front of him.

Duval voiced some type of guttural spell and a wave of dark tendrils erupted from his free hand and washed past the axe.

Halcyon felt the ring on his finger squeezing him, letting him know magical luck was at work. At the same time, the tendrils slammed down hard on both of his forearms and turned to dust on his magical bracers. Remembering Ashe's advice, the midshipwizard rushed up the stairs to close with Kingmaker.

A long thrust of the dark saber stopped Halcyon's forward motion as he parried it into the wall with his axe. A huge flash of sparks erupted from the wall and a great, dark gouge in the stone marked where the magical blade melted the wall.

Halcyon couldn't help but wince as stone chips and dust blasted his face. He took a step backward to clear his vision.

"My weapon doesn't make one glow green, Blithe, but I think you'll find it effective," Duval quipped in the Arcanian language, as he thrust again trying to get past the axe's defenses.

They both fell silent as they traded blows meant to kill the other. Duval was always careful to never position his saber where the full force of Halcyon's axe could snap it like a twig. Halcyon never committed his full weight to stroke with any blow that allowed Duval to come over the top of the axe and thrust into Halcyon's exposed face and throat.

From above the stairs, in Maleen, they both heard the shouts. "Enemy at the gates, alarm, alarm! Captain Duval, you're needed at the gates!" Several men shouted that same thing down the stairs.

A look of frustration filled Duval's face. "Oh, bother, Blithe; you've proved a talented foe. I've underestimated you for the . . ." He thrust, hoping his speech would distract Halcyon; it didn't. "Yes, well, we will meet again, of that I'm sure."

The green dragon vanished in a cloud of black smoke. Suddenly a large black oval, six feet tall and as wide as the stairway, appeared between Blithe and Kingmaker. The smell of the magic was nauseating. It smelled of blood and rotting flesh as wave after wave of it took the midshipwizard's breath away.

He had to retreat several steps down the stairs, looking away from the oval, but still maintaining his guard, just to breathe freely again. When he looked up the stairs, the oval and Duval were gone.

From behind him, Elan shouted, "Charge!"

When all the rest of them got to the top of the stairs, they saw the Maleen problem just waiting for them at the other door. Ten man-tall blades pointed directly at them.

Swordson shouted, "Blithe, you and I will charge the right. Fallow and Darkwater, charge the left." They would have done exactly that, but for the thoughts of Swordson.

As Halcyon turned to face the Maleen, all of them turned green as the axe recognized them for enemies of its wielder. In that same instant so did Elan Swordson.

Fallow, seeing that, stepped between Halcyon and Elan. "I'll be taking this side. You seem a bit green to me, Lieutenant."

Denna pushed Swordson in front of her to the left of the group.

Never deviating from their orders, the Maleen in the middle of the ten turned to the sides, but didn't leave their positions, allowing the four Arcanians to attack two foes instead of more.

Axes sheared through the Maleen steel and then into breast-plates and the flesh beneath.

Blinding white spell light blinded the ones on Denna's side and Swordson acquired a long sword and helped her cut her way through those marines.

They all met in the middle as the last two Maleen fell to axe blades. The sound of fighting was clear beyond the door.

"Open it, fools!" shouted Swordson, still green from Halcyon's axe. "We'll either fight whoever's on the other side or find our saviors."

They lifted the bar of the door and threw it open to find

Gord-un ready to strike whoever opened the door. He lowered his axe, grinning from ear to ear. "Well done, men. I see the ambassador is in good health. Blithe, I trust that's mostly other people's blood?"

"Mostly, Captain." Halcyon smiled back in relief.

Marines and crew of the *Rage* were all around them now, slapping them on their backs. Everyone was just glad to be alive. The Maleen were dead all around them with Duval nowhere to be found.

As they threw open the door to the outside, they found themselves surrounded by city dwarves in full battle armor.

"By order of the King Under the Mountain, you are under arrest. Surrender your weapons or die," ordered the commander of the dwarf division with several hundred dwarves behind him, filling the streets.

"Ahem, if I may, Captain Gord-un," the ambassador whispered.

XX

✿ ✿ ✿

𝕬mbassador 𝕾tatus 𝕯enied

HIS MAJESTY'S ARTICLES OF WAR: ARTICLE XL

*No officer shall be dismissed from the naval service except by
the order of the royal head of Arcania or by sentence of a
general court martial. No officer so dropped shall be eligible
for reappointment.*

Halcyon's group stood facing the crew of the *Rage*, happy to see
their rescuers. Both groups had just finished fighting for their
lives. Many of the marines and crew were bloody and barely
able to stand.

The Maleen had died to the last man, never asking for
quarter.

"Nice axes," Gord-un laughed, leaning against the door in
exhaustion.

Suddenly a commotion erupted from the entrance and all

faces turned to see streams of dwarves in armor coming into the chambers.

The ambassador dropped his weapon first, screaming at the top of his lungs in Dwarvish and rushing to come between the dwarves and the remaining crew of the *Rage*.

Halcyon recognized the dwarven words for "King Under the Mountain." That at least got them halted enough so that Abernathy could order the crew of the *Rage* to lay down their weapons and surrender.

Looking more like a stone in armor than a living being, the captain of the king's guards argued long and hard with Abernathy. The ambassador didn't back down an inch. The city guard captain was a massive dwarf, easily five feet wide and not much over four feet tall. His gray flesh had odd rocky angles, making him look like a cut stone statue instead of a living being. His armor covered most of his body and appeared to be some type of bronze, and it too had odd square angles to it.

All of the city guards used body-covering round shields with a mountain and setting sun emblazoned on their surface.

They streamed through the crew of the *Rage* and separated them, stripping them of weapons and armor only after Gord-un gave permission for his crew to give up.

Part of what stopped the dwarves was the presentation of three magical axes the ambassador showed to the captain. A look of awe and reverence filled the angry dwarf's face at the display of the three weapons. When he lifted them up, each glowed with a fire magic, displaying their extreme power in the hands of dwarves that the axes were made for in their origin.

Abernathy was able to find out that the king had sent troops to both the *Rage* and the Maleen fortress expecting some type of scuffle between the crew of the *Rage* and the forces of

Maleen staying in the city. He just didn't expect open warfare on his streets. His orders were to bring to the palace any fighters from either location. Not given a choice, all the crew, wounded or otherwise, moved up the road at a quick march. There were no Maleen alive to take with the group.

As they marched up the hill, the ambassador and Captain Gord-un were in close conversation, whispering the entire time.

A long walk through winding streets saw the city slowly filling with dwarven carts. The troupe moved far up into the depths of the city. Coming over the final rise at the top of the cleft, the crew found the largest of all the cube-shaped stone buildings. The white stones of this palace appeared carved from the surrounding white granite of the mountain. Huge arches of the same stone rose up over the back of the city, making sure the mountain didn't fall down.

Fallow was in a rare good mood, even with a huge bump on his head from the combat. "Mr. Blithe, if we end up getting killed after all of this, let me say thank you for getting my hands healed. It was a damn fool thing to wish for when you could have had a king's treasure. From my point of view, I'm mighty pleased you did what you did."

"Think nothing of it, Chief. How's your head?" asked Halcyon.

"I'm a bit fuzzy and it hurts quite a bit. Corporal?" Fallow called.

"Yes, Chief?" Denna answered as she walked beside Halcyon and Fallow.

"What's the type of death sentence they use in this city?" asked the chief.

"How in the world am I supposed to know?" Denna answered back.

"Prisoners are fed to red dragons they keep chained in the palace," Jakwater answered from behind them. "I've studied up on this city as I have grandparents living here."

"Well, it looks like it's my lucky day." Fallow smiled back at the midshipwizard.

"Why do you say that, Chief?" asked Jakwater.

"We have a d . . . oof!" Fallow stopped talking when Halcyon placed a well-aimed elbow in his gut.

The dwarves around them moved into the column of marchers and separated Blithe, Fallow, and Darkwater.

You good? came the distant thought of Sort.

Fine, talk later, Halcyon replied. He was far from fine, but he didn't want the sea dragon to know that. Going under guard to the palace of a king who didn't like humans anyway was unsettling the midshipwizard. Smashing Fallow in the belly was the only way to keep him from revealing Halcyon's dragon-speaking abilities. Those talents might come in handy if they had to face a dragon. Halcyon was sure Fallow wouldn't have mentioned the midshipwizard's abilities if his head had been clear.

The palace of the King Under the Mountain was immense. A hundred granite stairs led to a wide road of granite. Along the road, fountains poured out blazing lava to light their way. The heat from each of the fountains radiated out from the odd structures at roasting temperatures. The dwarves didn't seem to mind it at all, but the men of the *Rage* gave each fountain a wide berth.

A set of double doors, large enough for a giant to walk through, displayed embossed images of the mountain with a setting sun behind. As the dwarves approached, the doors opened up to show a king's hall. There were well over a hundred dwarves eating and drinking in the hall with the pounding of drums booming out into the outside air. The drums were just like the captain's single kettledrum, but there were ten of them. Already the drums showed red glowing runes on their side and some type of dwarven magic was at work. More lava fountains in each of the corners of the room brightly lit this area. At the back of the hall sat the king with other important persons, including his son, who sported a leg in a cast.

The group entered the hall and immediately their skin glowed, revealing their natures from the glow.

"It's the drums; don't be frightened," Sandal whispered back to his crew.

Most of the half-dwarves took on a reddish radiance. The humans glowed with a white luminescence. There weren't many full-blooded humans in the troupe. Captain Gord-un glowed with an ash gray radiance. Denna turned a bright purple. The ambassador turned a green color and gave a little scream at the magical effect. Halcyon found himself glowing blue and it made him extremely uncomfortable. He didn't like being singled out by this strange magical glow around his body. All of the dwarves in the chamber glowed red and the rubies in their foreheads sparkled like a fire from the magic of the drums.

Denna, Gord-un, Abernathy, and Halcyon found themselves roughly culled from the troupe and put under a heavy guard. Massive crossbows were leveled at them, clearly warning they would be dead if they tried anything. Other warrior dwarves positioned themselves in the upper balconies of the hall, pointing deadly-looking crossbows with bolt tips that magically glowed red at the crew of the *Rage*. There was no doubt in anyone's mind that they all died if a misstep happened just then.

Halcyon could see the prince he saved, still on crutches. The midshipwizard had to wonder why the dwarf showed no signs of magical healing. Then he remembered that dwarves held very strong resistances to all types of magic, including healing types.

The hall displayed great wealth everywhere. Its many dwarves were richly dressed, showing amulets and gems in a wide variety on their clothes. The walls sported tapestries of dwarves at work and at war. There must have been over a hundred of them, each a wall hanging of incredible complexity. The stone tables filled to overflowing with food and drink on what appeared to be polished silver plates and bowls. The tall arches of the ceiling hung with what must have been battle prizes, as there were weapons from many different races. The giant-sized weapons were the most visible, as huge battle-axes, spears, and shields covered the arches. Giants were incredibly difficult to kill and there appeared to be at least a hundred of their oversized weapons hanging as a testimony to the skill of the dwarves in battle.

The group marched to the center of the chamber where a stage was set. The leader of the dwarven contingent knelt in front of his king and spoke in a dwarven dialect. Halcyon couldn't recognize one word of the speech.

The leader's words greatly agitated the ambassador. He moved from the group, bending down on both knees, and spoke a few sentences with his head bowed.

"Speak Arcanian, your Dwarvish is terrible," the dwarf king ordered in perfectly accented Arcanian. "Most of the people here can speak Maleen and Arcanian. We started learning your languages a hundred years ago when we saw what was happening in the north to our people. You shouldn't have been fighting in my city's streets."

The king was typical of his dwarven breed. He was a wide dwarf displaying massive muscles all over his body. His braided beard was as long as he was tall and covered in rubies tied into his hair. A large battle-axe leaned against his throne, and there was little doubt that the king was very capable of using the weapon, from the look of him.

"I've been sent by my king, His Royal Majesty Artur Andul Ilumin Surehand, ruler of all Arcania, to establish official relations with your city and the Dwarven Empire," Abernathy said very humbly. "After our ship saved the lives of your son and the other dwarves from the pirates attacking your ketches, we came here to offer gifts, those being the three powerful magical axes you see before you, and my country's offer of alliance and friendship."

Halcyon felt a great deal of admiration for the ambassador just then. The man and the rest of the crew were in a tight spot right now. The ambassador had managed to point out to the king that the people in front of him had saved the life of his son.

The prince whispered a few things into his father's ear.

"Ambassador, we will talk of gifts and countries in a moment. Where is this Blithe human and this Ashe Fallow?" asked the king.

The prince whispered a few more things and suddenly the king looked angry.

"A tonga drum! Who among you wrongfully owns one of our dwarven tonga drums?" demanded the king.

"I do," Captain Gord-un replied, standing out in front of his men. "Why do you ask?" he snarled, sounding just as angry as the king, at that moment.

"Tonga drums aren't for humans. Those are the royal drums of the dwarves and things of power. You look dwarf, but you aren't, are you?"

"My great-grandfather was Sandal Gordelic of the Stone Clan. As royal brother to the Stone King, he broke with his brother over an affair of honor. The drum was his by birthright and it passed down to me and I will fight anyone who claims differently."

The challenge was clear in his voice and many of the dwarves stood up, grasping their weapons when they heard the captain.

The ambassador almost fainted dead away.

The king motioned his people to sit.

"I knew your great-great-grandfather and great-grandfather, the best of dwarves they proved to be in thought and deed," the king said. "If you say that's your drum, I'll stand by you in its defense. If you would, I'd like to hear it sounding in this hall. We haven't had a Stone Clan drum ring out here in many generations. Now, where are these other two my son speaks about?"

Halcyon and Ashe stood out and approached the royal table.

Dwarven weapons were no longer aimed at the crew's hearts. The feast hall's tension evaporated as the king of the dwarves seemed to accept the captain of the *Rage* as a companion.

"For some odd reason, my son felt it necessary to use a wish to settle his randory with you, Halcyon Blithe. I find this amazing as there were only three wish bracelets in my entire empire and those were only supposed to be used to save royal lives," the king said, glaring down at Halcyon.

"I, for one, am glad he did," quipped Ashe Fallow, bold as brass, up to the king.

"Humans appear to be all alike. Tell me you still think that way in a hundred years, soft skin," the king grumbled.

"Your son did a great thing in saving the hands of my fellow countryman," Halcyon said, trying to pacify the king. "I think he granted my wish more because I restored his family axe to him than the fact that I saved his life."

"Yes, this was the first time he's been given the axe of his fathers. It's a precious family treasure and you did well in returning it. He shouldn't have lost it from his hand," said the king as he glared at his son.

The prince sat down on his own throne, his head bowed in obvious embarrassment.

"He was fighting in a difficult battle with enemy all around him. He led his forces bravely and well, taking the forefront of the melee and fighting against the most difficult of opponents. If it wasn't for his courage, we would have had a much harder time against the pirates," said Halcyon, exaggerating slightly.

For a change, Ambassador Abernathy was smiling at him instead of trying to shush him.

"You tell me, young human, why you and your crew were found fighting in my streets," the king ordered.

"My ship brought the ambassador to your city at the order of our king. We expected a summoning to your grand palace. When a royal-looking coach drove up and claimed to be sent by you to pick up the ambassador, naturally we went thinking it was an order from the King Under the Mountain," Halcyon explained. "The Maleen drove us to their stronghold and captured us. They were after information about what the dwarves and Arcanians were going to do in the future. We told them nothing. You should ask them why they kidnapped us."

"It seems their three ships have sailed away. I think dwarven relations will become strained with the Maleen in the future," said the king.

Halcyon looked around, noticing the drums had stopped beating. The glows from the drums vanished on everyone but him.

"Don't worry about your blue encirclement. Clearly, you are the seventh son of a seventh son. That's powerful magic and the drums reflect that magic back on you. Please go on with your story," the dwarf king ordered. "Wait a moment, set places at the tables for these warriors. Serve them food and drink, we have many things to talk about."

The crossbows vanished. More tables appeared for the crew. Halcyon, the captain, the ambassador, and Ashe supped at the king's table.

Swordson, only with a tremendous effort of will, hid the envy he felt at seeing Blithe seated in a place of honor Elan thought he deserved. After all, he was the ranking officer in that dungeon. He really needed to take sterner measures with Blithe as soon as they were back on the *Rage*. Until then, he would smile with the rest of them at their good fortune at being alive.

The king looked at Halcyon to continue.

"We were in the Maleen dungeon and their captain, Duval Kingmaker, was gloating over our capture. He planned on leaving us in the dungeon until we told him of our plans," Halcyon reported. "When we were left alone, we were able to free ourselves of our manacles and much to our surprise the ambassador . . ."

The king interrupted the midshipwizard's story. "How in the world did you free yourselves of your manacles?"

Halcyon turned beat red and naturally at that moment the blue glow of his body vanished and everyone knew he was embarrassed. "I used a wire and picked my locks. Then the chief used his lock pick and opened up most of the rest."

"Amazing," exclaimed the king. "Could you show me how?"

"Of course. The chief, Denna, and I could demonstrate how to do it if you wish, Your Grace," Halcyon answered.

Manacles were brought up to the king's table. Manacles of Iben were locked on Halcyon's wrists. Larger leg chains went on Chief Fallow. Denna sagged from the weight of manacles actually designed for trolls. Those troll chains were massive affairs weighing almost as much as a grown man.

"Begin!" shouted the king.

Halcyon sat down on the ground, took the wire out of his boot, and quickly unlocked his chains. Ashe had his lock pick in his sleeve and was free almost as quick. Denna had her lock pick hidden in the cuff of her pants and was free a few heartbeats after Fallow.

The king and his court looked on the three of them, stunned, realizing that these Arcanians would be difficult to keep in a prison.

"Let me assure you, King," said Abernathy, "that these fine young crewmen are unusually gifted, even for Arcanians."

"I think our kingdom could benefit from open relations with Arcania. After all, we've been trading with your country for years now. Ambassador, you and your people are free to take the very building where the Maleen trapped you. Let's start talking about peace and trade between our two countries," the king said.

"Your Grace, you are too kind." Ambassador Abernathy stood up and bowed low to the king.

"With your permission, Captain Gord-un, I would like my son, the prince, to sail back with you as a midshipman of the lowest class. I can tell he could learn a lot by the experience," asked the king.

"Of course, Your Grace," Gord-un replied. "We'll take good care of him, won't we, Mr. Blithe?"

"Sir, yes, sir," Halcyon said, looking forward to learning more about the dwarves through the prince, who was just then smiling back at the midshipwizard.

"Captain, I will need a contingent of ten of your marines as we discussed before," noted the ambassador. "I'd also like Elan Swordson to be stationed here as well. During the voyage he showed himself to be resourceful."

"Of course, I expected your request," the captain said. "Junior Lieutenant Swordson, that will be an automatic promotion for you to lieutenant. Get your gear and take command of the marines when we are back on the ship."

For some odd reason the look of glee on Elan Swordson's face at this unexpected promotion and assignment made Halcyon uneasy and he had no idea why.

EPILOGUE

❧ ❧ ❧

To the Naval Master of the Exchequer John Blithe
From Midshipwizard First Class Halcyon Blithe

Uncle John,

The ambassador has allowed me to send you a letter using the first Arcanian Embassy Pouch. The dwarves are going to fly it to Ilumin all the way from here in Crystal City. There're just so many exciting things to tell you, I don't know if I can get them all in one letter, but I'll try.

Please send word to the family that I'm well. We were in several major battles on the voyage to Crystal City. I'm sure one of the reports in this pouch is going to tell the admiralty about the new threat from the Maleen. A leviathan controlled by a Maleen wizard attacked us. The creature swam up from the depths and started to strangle our sea dragon. With my dragon-speaking ability, I could feel the wizard controlling the monster. It used its tentacles to stop the crew from using the blast-tube at the prow of the ship. After a fierce battle we were able to blow holes in its shell and I struck at the wizard inside. We killed the creature, but it was a close thing.

I've learned a great deal on this cruise about commanding men and being careful with my magical abilities. In an action against pirates attacking dwarven ketches, I accidentally burned a fellow crewman's hands. Ashe Fallow is a brave man from our county—you might know the Fallows for their inn down in the village by our family castle. It looked like he was going to lose his hands from the burns. Because I chanced to save the prince of the dwarves of Crystal City in that same action, the dwarf prince allowed me to use a wish to cure Fallow. It was one of the proudest days of my life when I was able to again shake the hand of my friend.

At the dwarven port a Maleen trick caused an ambassador and myself to be captured and taken to a Maleen stronghold in Crystal City. Through the bravery of Captain Gord-un and the rest of the crew we were saved and managed to force them to leave the port in fear of their lives.

I've got many more stories to tell, but the clerk is here for the parchment. I look forward to drinking some Arcanian red with you by a cozy fire.

You have my deepest respect,

                                        Nephew Halcyon Blithe